RESIDUE

RESIDUE

· · · · · · · · · · · · · · · ·

A novel

by **Jim Knipfel**

RED HEN PRESS | *Pasadena, CA*

Book design and layout by Nicholas Smith

Knipfel, Jim.
  Residue : a novel / by Jim Knipfel—First edition.
    pages ; cm
  ISBN 978-1-59709-302-6 (softcover : acid-free paper)
  I. Title.
  PS3611.N574R47 2015
  813'.6—dc23
                    2014037131

The Los Angeles County Arts Commission, the National Endowment for the Arts, the Pasadena Arts & Culture Commission and the City of Pasadena Cultural Affairs Division, Sony Pictures Entertainment, the Dwight Stuart Youth Fund, the Los Angeles Department of Cultural Affairs, and the Ahmanson Foundation partially support Red Hen Press.

First Edition
Published by Red Hen Press
www.redhen.org

ACKNOWLEDGMENTS

I would like to thank the following people for their continued patience, perseverance, support, and, well, all those other things they do.

My agent Melanie Jackson, who somehow continues to pull off the impossible; Samantha Haney and the rest of the staff at Red Hen Press; my friend and copyeditor, the great and remarkable Donald Kennison; Philip Harris of ElectronPress.com; Derek Davis; Ken Swezey and Laura Lindgren; Erik Horn; David Read; the editors at Den of Geek; the staff at Chiseler.org; Tony Sokol; Ryan Knighton; Daniel Riccuito and Marilyn Palmeri; William Bryk and Mimi Kramer; Homer Flynn; Leif Solem; Linda Hunsaker; Kate Crane; Roland Sheehan; John Engstrom at Smashpipe.com; TRP; John Strausbaugh; David E. Williams; Mark Dennison; Mom; Mary; Jordan Adrians; McKenzie Adrians; Marcellus Dawson; and Harper Dawson.

As ever, my endless gratitude goes to my wife, Morgan Intrieri, who's put up with me this long with a razor sharp intelligence, humor, and understanding that is nothing short of inspirational. I love her very much.

I would also like to offer my special thanks to my father, George J. Knipfel (1933–2013), my one true hero and a man quite unlike any other (as well as the man who first pointed the story out to me). If I could ever be half of what he was, I'd be a much better person.

This time around Richard Wagner provided the soundtrack.

For my sister, Mary Adrians,
though she'd probably rather forget why

"We belong dead."
—Karloff, *The Bride of Frankenstein*

RESIDUE

prologue

A tangle of three wide, dust-gray leather straps drooped in a loose knot from a chain hoist attached to the ceiling. On those rare occasions when he looked up, it struck him as almost humorous, maybe even intentional, that the straps were the color of dead flesh. For the moment the straps and the chain had been hooked off to the side away from the light to avoid any spiderweb shadows. He wouldn't need it until later, and by then shadows would no longer matter.

From the compact portable stereo in the corner came the strains of the glorious third act of *Parsifal*. It was loud. He insisted it be loud. At least loud enough to cover the droning white hum of the ventilation system and the drainage pump, the assorted clanks and belches and echoes that filled the low, wide room whenever he was working. At that volume there was no avoiding distortion, but he knew the music and could hear the perfection beneath the warp and rattle.

On the stainless steel table before him lay a nude woman, her loose, chalky skin still drying beneath the intense, warm, and shadowless light from the two rectangular concave surgical lamps fixed above her. Her mouth hung open, revealing the brown and yellow teeth and dark tongue. Her eyes were closed. The futile vanity of her sparse dyed hair repulsed him, but still she remained beautiful, not for what she was but for what she would become. It was only a matter of moments. One black rubber tube held firmly in place with a silver clamp led from her sagging throat just beneath her chin and another from her left ankle.

Sie wartet nur darauf, he thought. *Dass ein neues Leben beginnt.*

The room was stark, save for the shelves running the length of the far wall, overloaded with collections of squat, arcane jars and bottles, their labels tattered and long since smeared illegible. The counter beneath them was scattered with a plunder of glassware, coils of more rubber tubing, and an incoherent jumble of unrecognizable alien tools. To the lost and ignorant, they might look like the instruments of inconceivable torture.

The air was still and cool, but even with the ventilation system it left an aftertaste of chemicals and decay at the back of the throat. After all these years, all these times, there was no escaping it. Those few visitors who felt compelled to disturb him (they never stayed long) found the room uncomfortably frigid, but again like the music it had to be that way. The cold had never bothered him, which helped explain, in part at least, why he'd chosen this place. The room's only real warmth radiated from the two lamps over the table. In order to feel it, however, you had to be on the table, and by then it was too late for trifles like warmth to matter.

From behind the plastic faceplate he glanced to the black and white wall clock, glaring almost accusingly at the second hand. He squinted to follow it as it twitched, too quickly for his taste, toward the seven. His eyes moved to the small dark glass bottle and the empty syringe on the square metal tray beside the woman's head. He looked to the clock again impatiently.

Keeping an eye on the woman's face, he reached into an open drawer of curved and sharpened instruments. Without looking, he plucked free a long, hollow, gleaming silver tube. At one end was a valve and connection, while the other had been filed to a razor point.

Narren. He placed the deadly point against the sagging, resistant skin of the woman's belly, pressing on it slightly, testing. The woman did not react. Her eyes remained closed. He would attach the tube later, if at all. It wasn't his fault, his failure, but hers. And theirs. She didn't deserve it anyway. He grimaced beneath two surgical masks.

Bitch.

He waited as the music rose in waves of voices and brass. He closed his eyes and listened and felt his heart swell as it always did during the Mittag interlude.

As the crescendo peaked and crashed, he plunged the metal tool into her body, puncturing the thin gray flesh and driving it deep into the stomach cavity, smiling slightly at the sensation of resistance giving way. No blood spurted from the wound. He reached for the flexible hose he would soon attach to the exposed end of the hollow instrument. Her own fault for not waking up.

As the once trapped, putrid gas began puffing from the stomach through the tube, he flipped back the faceplate, pulled down the two masks, and inhaled deeply. To him, these bloating gases were the true breath of life. As he continued to breathe them in, feeling them spread throughout his system like morphine, there was a knock on the door.

"Kirby, *ja*," he said, without turning. Standing upright again, he straightened the surgical masks and lowered the faceplate, then attached the hose. He twisted the metal tube, digging deeper into the hidden cavities of the woman's body, probing for the hollow organs. The door never opened. "Kirby! *Ja!*" he shouted to be heard over the music. He shook his head.

At last he heard the latch slip as the handle was turned. The light in the room shifted slightly as the door opened. Still he continued working without any acknowledgment, angling the tip of the device as he began probing for the kidneys. "Vat?" he asked.

The sharp metallic snap and click and ratchet were unmistakable, but it had been so many years ago.

I

The woman's eyes were tightly closed. She wore a flowing, gold-trimmed white robe with a green and gold sunburst pattern sequined across the breast and was rocking back and forth. As she rocked, she clapped her hands and stomped her left foot to the beat of an ungainly, faltering tune only she could hear. The twenty-two others seated in the industrial gray folding chairs in front of her tried to follow her lead as best they could, as did the elderly woman seated off to the side, banging futilely away at a small Casio keyboard whose rhythm track had been stuck on "samba" ever since she'd dropped it eight months ago. She had been given no sheet music so was forced to improvise, casting pitiful, nervous glances at the woman in the robe for guidance. The small, humid, green-carpeted room quickly filled with a cacophonous splattering of noise. Any passersby on the sidewalk peering casually through the unshielded plate glass window might have surmised it was the weekly meeting of a support group for spastics.

The woman in the white robe began to sing.

✠

The glass door opened with a hush and a slight, pinch-faced man in a dark overcoat and fur cap stepped inside. He stomped his feet on the rubber mat to dislodge as much snow as he could, turned the corner into the dim reception area, and looked around. Kirby wasn't at the front desk. It wasn't unusual but it meant he'd have to go looking.

There was no muffled canned music coming through the speakers mounted in the lobby, which was a comfort. It meant there weren't any customers around. He preferred not to meet them, as his presence tended to make everyone more uneasy than they already were. "Klaus?" he called to the empty space. It was foolish, he knew. Klaus would never answer. He headed down the thickly carpeted hallway through the subdued pink-golden light, past the antique armchairs and end tables, pausing at the set of double oak doors that opened onto the visitation room. The doors, like the heavy, dark wood trimming along the walls, had been decorated with carved Germanic runes. He never asked Klaus why this was. It seemed an odd design choice. Maybe they were original to the building, but he didn't think so. The runes seemed to appear after Klaus's remodeling.

He knocked, considered his hands, removed the thick right glove, and knocked again. "Kirby?" He opened the door to find the room empty and dark. The gauze curtains over the windows allowed in enough light for him to see the folding chairs stacked and leaning against the wall beside the couch.

He closed the door quietly and considered heading upstairs to the office. Kirby was probably up there taking care of the paperwork Klaus wouldn't touch, or cleaning the showroom. No. That would be useless, too. It was Klaus he needed to see, because it was Klaus's signature that was required on the vital statistics forms.

He stepped across the hall and opened one of the doors into the tiny chapel. It was empty, the air still and grim. Closing that door, he returned down the hallway, through the lobby, and through an unmarked door. He paused and unbuttoned his coat. It was warm in there. He didn't hear any of the usual music drifting up from the basement. At least that meant if Klaus was down there he wasn't working. He'd learned almost immediately never, ever to interrupt Klaus when he was working.

"Klaus?" he called as a warning before heading down the stairs. Always best not to startle Klaus down there, music or no music.

He clomped his boots heavily on the steps as he descended. It was an exaggeration but still, the more warning the better. He was in no mood for Klaus's temper.

The steel doors of the prep room were closed. He listened but heard nothing. If Klaus was working, he would've heard something. He knocked. "Klaus, you in there? It's Vern."

More silence. If he wasn't here he'd check the delivery bay out back. Maybe they were out on a removal, but it didn't seem likely. He stood on his tiptoes and peeked through the porthole window. At least one set of lights was on, that much he could tell, but he saw no signs of life. Klaus had to be around someplace. He sure didn't want to make a second trip out here.

He knocked again, then turned the handle and pushed one of the heavy doors inward with his shoulder. He could hear the ventilation system whirring smoothly.

Apart from one small bank of lights glowing weakly in the far corner, the prep room was lost in deep shadow. This was making no sense. Where the hell was everyone? It was too early for lunch. And what if they got some customers? Maybe they really were both out on a call. He reached for the bank of light switches and flipped three of them. "Klaus, jeepers, you takin' a snooze?"

The brain does funny things when confronted with images and information that cannot find a way to slip neatly into our expectations. The first move is to try to piece the given details together in a way that makes at least a little sense. Take the blood Vern Cameron was seeing at that moment. Given where he was, blood was not at all uncommon. That much was certainly true—it was all a perfectly natural and expected part of the business. The problem was it wasn't supposed to be splattered on the walls that way, or pooled on the floor in such quantities.

"In the dream, see . . ."

"Wait now. Just stop before you say another word, there. Lemme ask. Am I—do I—let me ask you—do I look like a headshrinker, here? No, I surely do not. An' so I am not real interested in your dream. You wanna talk about your dreams, go see that Doctor Landin over on Gilman, in that medical arts building. Yah, I hear he's real good."

"But it's important."

"Yah, uh-huh." Sheriff Koznowski excused himself for a moment and headed to the other side of the office. He walked with a rocking, shuffling gait, like a mildly retarded child or the grossly obese (which the sheriff was not). He stopped beside another desk, where Deputy Keller was typing up the previous weekend's accident reports.

"Heya, sorry to interrupt you there, Deke, but I'm wondering if you'd take Mr. Truttman's statement." He pointed back toward the desk where Eddie Truttman was looking lonely and unloved.

Keller stopped typing. On the wall behind him, next to a personally annotated Packers schedule and a calendar from Ingersoll's Tractor Supply, was a framed portrait of a smiling Ronald Reagan, looking for all the world like a man who had no idea what he was smiling about. "Oh, you betcha, Chief. What's the problem today?"

"Someone stole his turkey."

"Oh that sucks for sure—wait." He glanced quickly to Mr. Truttman. "He don't live on a farm, I don't think, right? Taken enough statements I should know by now."

"No . . . no, it was just the frozen kind. Picked it up at the W. C. Jones store last week. He thinks they mighta taken a pie too."

"What kind of pie?"

Koznowski paused to think a moment, then his mouth tightened. "I'm sure I don't know what the hell kinda pie. Just go do it, why don'cha?"

Keller's face drooped. "Yah . . . I mean, with Thanksgiving comin' an' all, that's still gotta suck, but why give it to me? Don't Ziegler usually handle him these days?"

"Ziegler drew patrol duty. An' besides, Mr. Truttman there had a dream about you last night. Ask him about it. It might be an important clue."

The deputy looked to Mr. Truttman, then back to Sheriff Koznowski. Something sour and sickly passed through his eyes. "Jeeze," he said.

"Oh lookatim there," Koznowski said. "He's gettin' all curious and bothered."

"Jeeze," Deputy Keller repeated as he pushed his chair away from his cluttered desk and the half-finished accident report. He snatched up a pen and legal pad and reluctantly moved toward Mr. Truttman.

"Sheriff?" a woman called from a desk near the front of the office. "Call for you."

Koznowski paused and looked at Leona, the station's receptionist and dispatcher. She was a broad woman with straight red hair who'd been with the Kausheenah County Sheriff's Department for about ten years now. It was a small sheriff's department and a small switchboard, which meant her job involved a lot of yelling. For being such a small department on a late Tuesday morning it sure was jumping. It made Koznowski feel useful, somehow.

"Who is it?" he called back.

"Coroner." Leona was smiling. She loved being able to shout things like "coroner" across the room now and again.

"Coroner? Aw, crap." Those were the only calls he really dreaded. Well, those and calls from the mayor, but the mayor he could usually duck. "Okay, I'll take it over here." He pointed toward his desk and shuffled in that direction. The phone rang a moment before he was fully seated. He dropped himself heavily into his chair and grabbed the receiver on the second ring. "Doctor Cameron? Heya, how goes it?" He was always tempted to ask him who'd croaked straight out to save them both time and discomfort, all the usual pussyfooting around, but he figured that might sound rude.

After listening for a moment, Koznowski's face stiffened. He said nothing more. He looked confused. "What, now?" he said eventually. "Holy shit . . . Well, who called you?" He began to look around the desk for a pen and paper. He gave up. "Jesus, Vern. So where are you now?" He nodded. "We'll be right there . . . Oh, you betcha, yah. Bye." He hung up but could not move. He stared silently at the phone.

"What is it, Chief?" Deputy Deliah Vandenberg had half been watching him since the call came through.

"That was Vern Cameron. He just found a mortician shot to death at the Unterhumm Funeral Home over in Beaver Rapids."

In the course of his eighteen years as sheriff of Kausheenah County, he never once had to deal with a murder before. An actual honest-to-God murder. Hunting accidents, sure, drunk driving fatalities, farm accidents, and two suicides. But no deliberate murders. Even with guns in nearly every house he could think of around those parts, no one ever saw fit to turn them on each other with criminal intent. In fact, according to the records, the last murder case in the county happened in 1967 over in Neubauer, when nineteen-year-old Jackie Johnson beat his seventeen-year-old brother Scott to death with a shovel in a drunken spat over whose turn it was to clear the driveway. Nothing at all since. Until now, apparently. Jesus.

"A mortician in a funeral home?" Deputy Vandenberg said by way of being helpful. "Well, if nothing else it's at least convenient."

Koznowski tried to ignore her. "Leona! Get on the horn, tell every last man jack out there who's not occupied fightin' crime to get the hell over to Beaver Rapids. The Unterhumm Funeral Home. Those who get there first, secure the crime scene and search the premises. I'll talk to the coroner when I get there."

"But Sheriff," Leona reminded him, "the only one out there now is Ziegler."

Pausing for a moment he closed his eyes and breathed an obscenity.

"You still want me to tell him?"

Koznowski slowly reopened his eyes in defeat. "Might as well, I s'pose." He turned to the rest of the office. "That goes for all youse here. You ain't in the middle a somethin', get over there. We got a murder on our hands, so no screwing around." Having never found himself in this position before, the only dialogue available to the sheriff came directly from television and the movies.

The office erupted with the squeaks of half a dozen chairs pushed back from desks and footsteps pounding toward the parking lot. Deputy Keller looked at the sheriff hopelessly. Beside him Mr. Truttman was still talking, and gesturing theatrically as he did so.

"I'll be right behind you," Koznowski shouted after the retreating officers. "I . . . gotta take a leak first."

11

Outside the windows of the screaming Sheriff's Department truck, the west central Wisconsin November stretched out flat, bleak, and frozen, interrupted only rarely by stark black trees and abandoned farmhouses, half collapsed and gray in the distance. Winter is never a surprise in Wisconsin, but that year it had slammed in early and hard. The season's first snowstorm had arrived the last week of October, leaving everyone quietly (and sometimes not so quietly) anxious about what lay ahead in January, when things really got bad.

Back at the academy he'd read all the textbooks and listened to all the teachers. Since then, and earlier too for that matter, back when he was a kid, he'd seen all the movies and the TV shows. And all he knew was this: murder just ain't like what they say. It's a lot dirtier than that. Uglier than that, that's for damn sure. And it ain't always wrapped up neat by the end of the hour.

To his left he roared past the twenty-foot-tall fiberglass cow standing just a few feet off the highway to call attention to Humboldt's Discount Dairy Outlet. Koznowski glanced at Humboldt's parking lot and saw it was packed as usual. Damn cow really worked. He snapped his eyes back to the road.

They didn't get murders around there. They just didn't. Not since that one in '67, three years before he became sheriff, and even that one was plain stone asinine. Mostly he just tried to sober up the drunk drivers and chase the kids out from under the 118 overpass. See, that's where they went every weekend to drink their beer and do whatever. Either there or out in the old train yard. Same things the sheriff had to deal with when Koznowski was a kid. Hell, he used to get chased away from that same train yard himself. But murder? That's different. And he was just being honest with himself when he admitted he wasn't one hundred percent sure what the fuck he was doing. Sometimes he half wished he still owned a TV so he could take a glance now and again to see how the television cops did it these days.

Jack Webb never broke a sweat out in L.A., but here in Wisconsin, fifteen degrees outside, Leonard Koznowski was already sweating pretty bad. He couldn't afford to screw up something like this.

The radio mounted below the dashboard was spitting a blur of half a dozen staccato voices, some giggling, some whooping outright in excitement, thrilled at the prospect of having a real live crime scene to investigate. Koznowski snapped off the radio. He began passing the car dealerships and warehouses that let him know he was getting closer to downtown. He'd be there soon enough and see for himself.

Beaver Rapids, about forty-five miles to the northwest of Oshkosh, was another paper mill town. Not huge, but there was certainly more going on there than in those "three bars and a church" towns you hit along the highway heading north. It might not've been L.A. or Chicago or nothing like that, but it was still plenty big for his purposes, with a population of almost ten thousand. The people who lived there were proud and happy with what they had. They had a movie house, three bowling alleys, a softball stadium, a nice park over by the river, a weekly newspaper, a town band, and now a murder rate, even. Just like the big cities.

It sure wasn't the town it used to be when he was growing up there, no sir, Koznowski thought as he sped down the main commercial strip, sirens blaring. All those signs in foreign languages now. He couldn't read them. Even old Wilcox's Hardware had foreign signs out front.

Folks around there (the ones who'd been there awhile anyway) said things started to get iffy when the Vietnamese and the Mexicans started moving in. He didn't much cater to that notion, and he tried to make sure his officers didn't either. It didn't matter that it sometimes made him just as uncomfortable as it made most everyone else. The whole damn world was changing around them, is all, and as unchangeable as this small wedge of west central Wisconsin might've seemed, it was changing too. It was getting bigger, anyway, that's for damn sure. And as the county got bigger, the headaches were bound to get bigger with it.

On the bright side, at least the town was big enough now to support two undertakers. Well, before all this, anyway. At least they still had one left.

As he passed them, shoppers and business owners alike paused to stare. They weren't much accustomed to hearing sirens shrieking down Main like that. In a town that small, everyone who saw him stopped a moment to wonder if someone they knew was in some kind of trouble. Those who were at home when he passed immediately got on the phone to find out.

He turned the wheel hard to the right on LaFoote Drive, then took another potentially deadly turn onto the much narrower Sampson Street, and up ahead saw three county cruisers parked outside the Unterhumm Funeral Home. There was a fourth car there, too, a dark sedan he recognized as Vern Cameron's. KAUSHEENAH COUNTY MEDICAL EXAMINER'S OFFICE was stenciled in small white letters on both doors. He was glad he'd opted to hit the bathroom before he left the station. Better to puke with as few witnesses as possible. Having the sheriff puking at a major crime scene wouldn't do much for morale, and he sure didn't want to risk contaminating any vital bits of evidence.

There was nothing imposing or ominous about the building. Unterhumm's was a solid, square, two-story beige brick building with a maroon awning that stretched across the sidewalk from the double glass doors of the entrance to the curb. UNTERHUMM had been painted in austere letters above the door with FUNERAL HOME in much smaller letters beneath, as if the painters had tried to sneak it in quietly without anyone noticing. To either side of the name were little squiggly designs, just to make things cheerier, Koznowski guessed.

There was a small parking lot in back with a driveway letting out onto Marston, he recalled. That might've been more convenient, come to think of it, but out front here it was easier to control the traffic and the neighborhood busybodies. Didn't need anyone stomping in to see what's what and messing up the crime scene. The sheriff pulled in behind the three brown and white county patrols and killed the engine, leaving the blue lights flashing. He took a deep breath in a vain effort to settle his stomach one last time, pocketed the keys, and headed for the funeral home entrance.

Up ahead standing guard he saw Anthony Ramirez, fresh from the academy, smiling broadly beside the three strips of yellow caution tape blocking the doorway. Even from a distance you could see his breath. "Hey, Chief. Hey, pretty brisk day, huh? My feet're goin' all numb." He stomped them for effect.

Koznowski nodded at him absently as he considered the strips of tape across the doorway.

"Ramirez," he began, not certain he wanted to know. "Why didn't you use the, y'know, crime scene tape instead of caution? Makes it look like a renovation or something's goin' on here."

"Didn't have none," Ramirez explained. "Couldn't find none in the closet, anyways."

"Yah, uh-huh. And, ah, why exactly did you use three strips?"

Ramirez was undaunted. "Well, Chief, you said we was supposed to secure the place when we got here, and so three of 'em here just seemed . . . well, more secure, I guess."

Koznowski realized he couldn't much fault either the rookie's reasoning or his enthusiasm. "Uh-huh. But tell me this. How in the hell, exactly, am I supposed to get in there now?"

"Oh, no sweat," Ramirez offered with a quick gesture. "You can squeeze in there, Chief."

After a beat, the sheriff decided to let it go. "Super, yah. So things under control here?"

"I guess. I been up here the whole time, makin' sure no one comes in. Ain't even seen the victim yet."

"Yah, I'll see what I can arrange, there. Get you a relief or something." He plucked two strips of the caution tape far enough apart to allow himself to clumsily half lunge, half roll through.

"See? There you go, Chief. You got it."

He stumbled to the other side of the tape barrier but kept his footing. Straightening himself he began heading farther inside, but then stopped again and turned back. "Ah, Ramirez? Ah, yah, where exactly is the crime scene?"

"Oh, no sweat there either, Chief. Just get through those inner doors there and listen. You'll hear 'em fine. Something, ain't it, though? A real murder an' everything?"

The sheriff nodded and took another deep breath. "Y'know, Ramirez, I never can get used to these things."

"What, murder scenes? When've you ever had to get used to them before?"

"Just shut up, Ramirez," he said as he turned and pushed through the inner doors to Unterhumm's lobby.

Well, Ramirez was right about one thing. At least he wouldn't have any trouble finding the crime scene, though he still wasn't sure if he was going to bother with arranging any relief at the front door.

It might've been a kegger down there in the basement, or it might've been a bar fight or halftime at a Packers game. Whatever it was, he wasn't sure he wanted to know what he was about to find down there.

As he slowly made his way down the stairs on suddenly aching legs, a thick spool of plastic caution tape tottered toward him from the unseen end of the dimly lit hallway, bounced against the bottom step, wobbled uncertainly for a moment, then toppled on its side. Over and above the shouts and laughter of the other stout-hearted members of his law enforcement team he heard an unmistakable whoop of joyous victory from that same hidden end of the hall.

Koznowski reached the bottom step, carefully stepped over the roll of tape, and considered the scene. Following the fifty-foot trail of plastic yellow tape back down the corridor, Koznowski's eyes met the sheepish eyes of Sgt. Ziegler, who was clutching the free end.

"Oh. Hi. Sorry, Chief," Ziegler began. "They ... there wasn't, like ... They said if I didn't stop crying I had to go stand in the hall. That's what ... it's what they said." His thumb jerked to the open double doors leading into what was presumably the crime scene, from the sound of it.

"Uh-huh," Koznowski said, scooping up the spool of tape and walking it back to Ziegler. He'd leave it to Ziegler to roll it all back up. "Has the rest of the building been, y'know, searched thoroughly and secured?" For the moment he was trying to ignore the noise coming out of the prep room, which had been quashed to a murmur of *shhh*s and stifled giggles the moment he walked past the open doors.

The twenty-one-year-old shook his head. "No? I mean, not exactly? When we all showed up, everybody just, like, came down here, an' well ... Deliah said someone should search the place, but nobody ... nobody wanted to leave. Then they were arguing about who'd be in charge until you showed up and then I . . . I guess that's when I looked at the body an' started crying or something, an'—"

Koznowski raised a hand. "Yah, there, Sergeant Ziegler? Please stop babbling,, an' go search the damn building, there, okay? You'll have a few others to help you in a sec. Secure the premises, do all that stuff from training. Then when you're all done, relieve Ramirez at the front door."

"Oh, but c'mon, Chief, it's real cold out there . . ."

Realizing if he were to continue this conversation much longer he might well end up smothering the young officer, Koznowski handed Ziegler the tape, turned around, and stepped into the prep room, almost reaching for his sidearm as he did so.

The four grinning officers in the room fell silent as he entered. The only one of the four who seemed to be doing anything at all was Deputy Vandenberg, who was dusting a counter full of equipment of some kind for fingerprints. Dr. Cameron sat in a chair off to the side, hands knotted tightly in his lap, looking both stunned and agitated.

Koznowski's eyes went from the blood-soaked body on the floor to the nude elderly woman with the metal pipe sticking out of her stomach, then back to the body on the floor.

"Jeremy H. Christmas," he whispered. "Two?" He turned to the coroner. "Doc, you didn't mention the other one on the phone. What the hell happened here?"

"Doc says the old lady ain't a vic, that she was just here. Y'know . . . dead."

"It's Hattie Dankowski," Cameron offered wearily from his chair. "She passed away at home three days ago."

"That's Mrs. Dankowski?" He took a wary step forward, not much wanting to ever think about ole Mrs. Dankowski naked, and took a closer look at her face, now nearly unrecognizable. He fought the urge to whistle slowly through his teeth. "Jeeze, I guess it is. But why would someone do that to her? I mean, y'know, mutilate her like that? She was just a nice old lady. What kinda sick son of a bitch are we dealing with here?"

"It's not mutilation, Chief," Vandenberg said. "It's a trocar, right, Doc?"

Everyone looked to Cameron for confirmation. He nodded weakly, and Vandenberg continued. "It's part of the whole embalming thing. It breaks up organs and lets gas outa the body, there, and . . . well, it does other stuff. So, you ask me, it looks like the mortician here was killed while he was working on her." She pointed to Unterhumm's crumpled body beside the examination table. "He's our real problem."

Koznowski, noticing nobody else seemed to be wearing them, made a minor show of pulling on a pair of rubber gloves before he approached the body. "You others," he said, nodding to his officers. "Check for prints, get Orville in here to take some pictures, anything, got it? Like this bloody footprint here. Get a picture, take measurements. It probably belongs to our suspect."

"Uh, no, Chief . . . um, that's just me."

Koznowski looked to Sgt. Jerry Knudson with hopeless eyes. "All right then, ignore the footprint. And Knudson, bein' as you're such a whizbang around crime scenes, you go upstairs and help nimrod search and secure the rest of the premises."

"Aw, but Chief, he's such a retard."

"Hey, Chief," Deputy Ellsworth added from the other side of the room. "You think this thing's gonna interfere at all with deer season? I mean, I got them days off comin' up."

"Yah, me too."

Koznowski, his back to all of them, raised a hand, effectively putting an end to any more whining. He was once again very glad he'd emptied his guts before leaving the station. He wouldn't very well be able to exude that sense of authority if he threw up here. Still, he could feel and taste the bile rising. The thick, rank stench in the room certainly wasn't helping. He coughed twice, then paused, breathing through his mouth. Nothing happened.

He bent down over Unterhumm, taking care not to step in the blood (like some people).

The mortician was wearing a hood with a clear plastic face shield. Beneath it, two surgical masks had been pulled away from his mouth and drooped beneath his chin. His eyes were open and glassy in a look that told the sheriff that, you betcha, Unterhumm was pretty well dead all right.

For all the years they'd both been working in the area, Koznowski had never met Unterhumm personally. He'd been to a few viewings and such at Unterhumm's—neighbors and distant relatives and retired colleagues who'd passed on—but the mortician himself never made an appearance. Unterhumm looked to be in his mid- to late seventies, but it was hard to tell much with all that gear on.

The sheriff peered more closely through the faceplate, trying to see beyond and around the reflection of the overhead lights. Unterhumm's mouth seemed to be filled with something white. It was bloody around the edges, but bleached white toward the center. It didn't seem to be foam or spittle. It wasn't his teeth or dentures, either, but seemed definitely solid.

"What the heck's that in his mouth?" he asked himself aloud.

"Packing," answered Dr. Cameron, who'd been watching him. Koznowski looked up.

"What, now?" The remaining officers were scurrying about the room, trying to look busy.

"Packing material. It's used in prepping the body. Someone had cancer or dentures, something like that, it fills out the cheeks. Looks more natural."

"Oh. Thank you." He'd been in the room for only ten minutes, but Koznowski was already learning more about embalming than he'd really care to know. "So what's it doing in there?"

"I'm afraid I can't answer that. You're the damned sheriff in the room here."

Yah, don't go reminding me.

After a cursory examination of the body it appeared to Koznowski that Unterhumm had taken two shotgun blasts to the back at close range. Given the way things were positioned, he guessed Vandenberg was right—that he was working on Hattie here (he tried not to think of that thing sticking out of her belly) when someone came through the doors and shot him before he even had a chance to turn around. He looked at the blood around the body and sprayed on the wall, the table, and Hattie. Didn't look like the body'd been moved, either. He was about to ask the doc if he'd gone ahead and determined a rough time of death. Some of the blood was still wet, so it couldn't've been that long ago.

From the look on the coroner's face, though, Koznowski decided it might be a good idea to get him out of here and upstairs before he went much further. Poor bastard'd been sitting there with two corpses for the last hour or more. That sort of thing was part of his job and all, but still. It seemed it would be a little easier to ask him a few questions up there instead.

As Koznowski painfully pushed himself to his feet, there was a knock on the prep room's metal door. He turned and saw Ramirez staring wide-eyed around the scene. For the moment he seemed speechless.

"Yah, Ramirez, you got some trouble?"

Ramirez snapped back into the moment, though as he spoke his eyes kept straying to the old woman on the table. "Chief? Ah, no. No trouble, really. The ambulance guys is here."

"Thanks, there, Sergeant. Tell 'em to cool their jets for a minute. We still got some crap to do here. Besides, I got the coroner with me so . . . y'know. They can leave together."

"Will do, Chief. Ah . . . but what do I tell the priest?"

Koznowski stopped. "What priest is that? Father Molloy? Mallory? What the hell's his name? The old one. What the hell's he want?"

"No," Ramirez said, still snatching glances at Hattie Dankowski. "Father Avalone? From Saint Tim's?"

Koznowski had never met Avalone but had heard of him. Father Tim from St. Tim's, the junior priest in charge of the youth ministry. "Yah, he's probably got business . . . Well, you better just tell him the funeral home's closed for the time being. But that's all. Nothin' about none a this." He nodded toward Unterhumm's body as he peeled off his rubber gloves.

"Oh." Ramirez's eyes met Koznowski's briefly, then dropped to his shoes.

The sheriff didn't like the sound of that, or the expression that accompanied it. "Whaddya mean, 'oh'?"

"Well," Ramirez began uncertainly, "I kinda told him what happened?"

"Oh, for Pete's sake, Ramirez. Ya don't go blabbin' to civilians."

"Naw, Chief, he saw the ambulance and all the police cars out front and stopped. He just wants to know if there's anything he can do to help. He says Mr. Unterhumm was a good friend of his."

Koznowski looked down at the corpse. "Well he's a little late for last rites, that's what he means."

"He was asking about that."

Koznowski closed his eyes. "Look, just please tell the padre thanks, but the best thing he can do is go back to Saint Tim's and pray or light some candles or whatever the hell they do. But be nice about it. We got our hands full here."

"Gotcha."

As the rookie turned to head back upstairs, Koznowski called after him. "And get a number where's I can reach him. I might wanna be talking to him. But don't be tellin' him anything more'n that, okay? Jeeze."

After Ramirez bounded upstairs, Koznowski turned to Dr. Cameron, hoping to share a moment of silent, frustrated empathy. Instead he found the coroner looking pretty close to death himself. "Heya, Doc? Why don'cha come with me, there? We'll get you outa here, so's I can ask you a few questions about all this, eh?"

Dr. Cameron nodded and stood, and the two men left the room. Koznowski was feeling like Cameron was looking. From the moment he first saw a naked Hattie Dankowski with that thing sticking out of her and Unterhumm curled up and bloody on the floor, a kind of numbness had soaked through him. It was as if he'd stepped outside for something but his body had stayed behind, moving like it was underwater. He knew he couldn't let anybody see, so he collected what strength he had left to carry on as normally as possible. This wasn't the sort of thing that happened in Kausheenah. It felt to him like he'd been dropped into some kind of nightmare world where he didn't belong and didn't know any of the rules. He wanted to take the doc out of the room as much for himself as for the doc.

"I just can't never get used to this," Koznowski said as they headed toward the stairs.

"When have you ever had to before?"

The sheriff ignored him, pausing at the bottom of the short flight of stairs and looking up. Staircases, no matter how short, always gave him pause.

"Legs still bothering you?" Cameron asked.

"Oh, yah."

"You taking anything for it?"

"Oh, yah. Doc Peters gave me something. But in the cold like this, y'know . . . All the screws an' what have you. All that squatting didn't help neither." He shook his head and glanced at the coroner. "Ah, listen to me. Got a man dead in there an' I'm complaining about my aches an' pains here. Sorry." They both headed up the stairs.

Once in the lobby Koznowski began looking around for a place to sit.

"Why not the chapel?" Cameron suggested. "Quiet in there." Stepping out of the prep room and away from Klaus's body had helped. Dealing with the dead was something he did on a daily basis, but only rarely was it someone he knew, let alone considered a friend, and almost never was it someone who'd been murdered with a shotgun. Up here he was beginning to feel better.

He felt even better a few minutes later after they'd walked down the carpeted hallway and into the small chapel, closing the door behind them. It was silent in there, and still. A single muted spotlight shone on the back wall of the altar. There were no immediately identifiable religious icons in the room, no crucifixes, nothing that would indicate a leaning toward one denomination or another. Given the makeup of the community it seemed silly to maintain a nondenominational chapel, but that was the way Klaus wanted it. The only decorations in the chapel were the same runes carved into the dark wood of the hallways and in the viewing room. In here the pattern continued along the walls and across the backs of the small pews where Koznowski and Cameron had just seated themselves.

"I was trying to tell your men down there, Leonard," Cameron began before Koznowski had a chance to speak, "but they were too preoccupied. I think your first order of business should be finding Kirby Mudge."

"Who's this, now?" Koznowski asked as he pulled a notebook and pen out of his jacket pocket. He sure didn't know anyone by that name in town.

"Kirby Mudge. He was Klaus's assistant here. He pretty much ran the operation, business-wise."

It looked as if Cameron was about to launch into something and that in itself was fine, but Koznowski stopped him. "Wait now, you saying you think this guy might be our suspect, then?"

The coroner shrugged. "I don't really know. I think it might be possible. I honestly don't know what I think. Maybe." He looked toward the low ceiling. "It just seems strange he's not here. You see, he's always here—he has an apartment upstairs. But he wasn't around when I came here this morning." He thought about it. "No, I'm sorry. It's wrong for me to be pointing fingers. But even if he didn't do it, he's someone you need to talk to. He knows everything that goes on here."

"Ah, now, don't go kickin' yourself there, Doc," Koznowski said, shifting his body in the narrow pew so he could pat the coroner reassuringly on the arm. "Believe you me, this stage of the investigation we can use all the leads we can get." He opened the notebook and began writing something down. He continued speaking as he wrote. "Now, was there any bad blood there, do you think? Any, ah, wha'cha call a possible motive here?"

Cameron frowned. "Klaus ... I mean, we got along just fine. He was my friend." Some concern passed across his face. "But I guess it should be said that he wasn't always the most ... pleasant person to be around. He could be harsh. I know he didn't always treat Kirby very well. Even in front of customers."

"And there were no other employees?"

The coroner shook his head again. "No one permanent. They brought in a lot of temps to handle the front desk and such, but they generally didn't last long. Half left because they couldn't take the atmosphere, the others because they couldn't take Klaus. He'd hire local cabdrivers to drive the hearse, bring in an agency to do the billing, things like that, but for the most part Kirby ran the operation. Handled customers, made removals, set up and cleaned, everything."

"Mm-hm." Koznowski made another note. "So what you're sayin' was that one day Kirby mighta been, y'know, pushed a little too far."

Cameron shrugged again. "I don't know. Kirby doesn't seem the type, but if he did do it—" He stopped abruptly. When he spoke again his voice was nearly plaintive, even as the county medical examiner took over. "I found Klaus around nine forty-five this morning, and from what I could determine, in a very preliminary observation of the scene, he'd been dead at least an hour at that point."

"So if it was Kirby," Koznowski filled in as he made a few more notations, "he's got himself a two-hour lead on us by now."

"Something like that, yes. At least two."

"All right then." Koznowski closed the notebook and replaced it in his pocket. "You suppose we'd find any kinda pictures of this guy around here? Something we could use? Otherwise I'll be needin' you to come on over to the station an' talk to Jenny Abler to do a sketch—"

From down the hall outside the chapel, Koznowski heard two excited voices and his guts tightened slightly.

"*Chief?*"

"*Yah, Chief, you down here?*"

With an apologetic glance at the coroner, Koznowski pulled himself to his feet, squeezed into the aisle, and pushed the door open a few inches. "Yah, down here. What is it?"

Out of breath but giddy as fools, Ziegler and Knudson scampered down the hall toward him like two children who'd just figured out how matches work. "Hey! Chief!" Knudson blurted. "We found something!"

"Yah," Ziegler clarified. "We was searching the building like you said, an' we found something."

"Well, what?"

"It's upstairs!"

"Yah, we was searching the building just like you said an' we found something upstairs!"

Koznowski blinked at them both for a moment, then turned back to Cameron, still sitting behind him. "Doc? You might want to come along here, just so's I have a witness."

Before the sheriff and the coroner were both fully outside the chapel and into the hallway, Ziegler and Knudson were already running back toward the stairs, their cackles trailing behind them.

"Which is exactly why I need you to search an' secure the whole dang building here when you show up, and not, y'know, an hour later." Koznowski was still chastising his two officers a few minutes later. "Jeeze, eh?" He glared at them both, his loose fists resting on his hips. "Now you're a hundred percent sure there ain't no more bodies around?"

"Oh, you betcha, Chief. All secure," Knudson said. Ziegler remained silent, tears flowing freely from both eyes. The furniture in the office looked expensive and comfortable. The thick carpeting was maroon, as were the dark velvet drapes blocking the afternoon winter sun. The wide desk was polished and black. One of the two heavy, leather-upholstered armchairs facing the desk was on its side. The walls were lined with filing cabinets, and atop the blotter on the desk was a single, artfully positioned gold pen holder. The chairs, blotter, and several of the cabinets were splattered with blood. The body lay between the desk and the drapes, the carpeting and the drapes both helping mask just how much blood had spilled. Koznowski noted that they probably also helped muffle the sound of the blast.

"Yah, I just don't fucking believe this," Koznowski muttered quietly to himself. "If you'll pardon my French, there."

Both Dr. Cameron and the unobtrusive identification badge pinned over the left breast pocket of the victim's shiny black suit coat identified him as Kirby Mudge, twenty-four. Like Unterhumm, he had been shot twice in the back at close range with what appeared to be a shotgun. His thick eyeglasses lay broken on the carpet next to his head.

"Well," Koznowski told Cameron. "So much for your silly theory, eh?"

Any initial hopes Koznowski had this might be a neat, clean, easily filed murder-suicide vanished quickly, as no murder weapon was immediately apparent at the scene (and they'd looked under the desk and everything). There hadn't been any weapon downstairs, either. At the very least it's extremely difficult to shoot yourself once in the back, let alone twice. And it's even harder still to shoot yourself twice that way, then stash the weapon someplace, then come back and die.

"Ziegler, yah," Koznowski turned to the weeping officer. "You might as well head downstairs and tell the crew they're needed up here next." He thought a second. "Y'know, why don't both of you go down there."

Once they were gone, he stepped away from the body and gestured Cameron over next to him. "You know him well?" He nodded toward Mudge.

"Naw, not much, like I said. Not as well as Klaus. My guess is Kirby started here maybe two years back or so?" He looked away from the body and slipped his thin pale hands into his pockets. "See, my usual rounds bring me by here every Tuesday to get vital statistics re—" Remembering he wasn't talking to a professional he corrected himself. "Death certificates signed. I still have Hattie's right here." He removed one of the hands from its pocket and patted his coat. He took another sad look at Mudge's corpse. "It was Klaus's signature I needed, but I usually saw Kirby at least briefly . . . I just can't fathom all this, Leonard. Not here. So young like that."

"Yah, tell me about it," Koznowski said. "So Doc, answer me a question." There was a new tightness in his voice. "You came here this morning, but there was no one downstairs, you said. So why'd you never come up here to the office? Seems like it'd be the thing to do, eh?"

Dr. Cameron sensed the hint of suspicion in Koznowski's voice and didn't care for it. He knew this wasn't the time to push back. He also guessed any defensiveness on his part wouldn't look good on paper. They were both pretty tense and shaky right now. The best way to handle things was to tell the whole story again, as calmly as he could, while the sheriff took notes. So that's what he did.

". . . So when I saw Klaus's body, I called your station immediately. Then I waited. I think I was in shock. After that the idea of exploring the building just never came to mind, I guess. That's my mistake right there. I'd looked for Kirby earlier and he didn't respond. I wasn't really thinking of anything after I found Klaus."

"But why, y'know, go into the room down there when you got no reply, but not up here? I mean"—Koznowski was just making guesses—"wouldn't all the reports and the like be in his office, here?"

It occurred to both of them, but only vaguely and distantly, that Kirby Mudge's corpse was not six feet away from where they stood, his blood still drying in the carpet fibers. There was probably a better time and place for this Q&A business, but they were in it now.

"I just needed a signature." Dr. Cameron took a breath and half glanced over his shoulder. He would have liked to drop himself into one of those comfy chairs but knew he didn't dare. Jesus, what a day. "Sheriff, let me tell you a little something about Klaus. See, Klaus didn't interact well with . . . how to put this? With the living. Weird as it may sound to you, he preferred the dead. They were quieter, he told me. He thought the living made too much noise and asked too many stupid questions. So he hired Kirby," he almost pointed, but stopped himself, "to deal with the families, the paperwork, the suppliers, while he spent his days down in the prep room, embalming. If you ever needed to find him—like I did this morning—that's where he would be. He was down there sixteen, seventeen hours a day. That was his only true joy in life."

Koznowski heard Ziegler, out of breath, call him from the bottom of the stairs. He stepped to the open doorway. "What?"

"They just found something down here, Chief. I think you should come look!"

"They find the murder weapon?"

"*No!*" Ziegler called back. "*Better!*"

"You know what I think?" Knudson was saying when Koznowski entered the prep room. "You ever hear about them wha'cha call Goth kids? They're all like into death an' shit like that? Weird little fuckers. They worship Satan an' shit. That's what this is all about."

"Oh just stop with that, eh?" Koznowski snapped. "Wha'dja find?"

Deputy Vandenberg pointed to a spot on the wall behind the chair where Cameron had been sitting earlier.

The scrawled brown letters could have been written with blood, but Koznowski couldn't tell. If it was blood, it looked as if whoever wrote it ran out before they finished. Or maybe they forgot what they wanted to say and just gave up.

The *R* was in question, as was the *M*, and there were smudges to the right of the *S* hinting something more was intended, but in crooked, misshapen letters, what was there seemed to read HEED THE WORMS.

"Heed the worms? That what it says?"

"Good enough guess for me."

"What the fuck does that even mean?"

"Got me. Doc?"

A quiet voice behind Koznowski whispered, "Goth kids."

"Oh, just shut up with that, Knudson. Any idea Doc?"

The coroner, confounded as everyone else in the room, shook his head and made a small helpless sound as he stared at the message.

"Wait a second," Koznowski said, sounding weary and perhaps a little frightened. This was all very quickly turning into far too much for him. "This ain't a crappy joke on someone's part is it, there? Ziegler? Seems about your speed. Yours or Deke's, but he ain't here."

Ziegler shook his head vigorously. "Not me, Chief. Swear. Ain't hardly been in here. They wouldn't let me stay. Then Ellsworth there, he said—"

"Guys, jeeze, if this is a joke wouldja tell me now? I got two bodies on my hands here as it is and don't need a third."

Nobody said a word. He looked from one face to the next. Finally satisfied he said, "Okay then. Looks like I need to deal with this here too . . . Jeeze what a mess this all is . . . Deliah, get a sample so we can see if that there's blood or what, and if so whose. And get lots of pictures. Maybe, I dunno, somebody at the university can analyze it or somethin', eh. And don't forget we got another body upstairs there." He began heading for the doors. "Gonna be a long damn day. I better get a call out to LeAnn."

"Chief?"

Koznowski turned to face Deputy Vandenberg. "Yah?"

"What do we do with her?" She pointed at the body on the table.

Koznowski stared. He blinked once before turning to Cameron. "You're the damn undertaker in the room, eh, so you tell her."

III

"Healter."

Behind the wheel of the Sheriff's Department truck and otherwise pre-occupied anyway, Koznowski didn't turn his head. "What?"

"Healter Skelter."

"What the hell are you talking about?" Koznowski kept his eyes on the dark asphalt slowly curving in front of them and the scattered other cars headed their way. "You been huffin' some of that formaldehyde down there, weren't you?" The sun had set an hour earlier. For the first ten or fifteen minutes after leaving the scene and heading back to the station, neither he nor Deputy Vandenberg had spoken a word. Seven hours after the discovery of Unterhumm's body, Koznowski's team had gathered about as much evidence as they were likely to find, and Koznowski had gotten about as much information out of Cameron as he was likely to get. Even after shipping the two bodies off to the county morgue to see if Cameron could uncover anything that wasn't already pretty obvious, Koznowski still had too much paperwork to fill out. He was confused and numbed by all he had seen, and all that still lay ahead. More than anything, he was exhausted and a little sick. The silence in the cab had been a momentary blessing until Vandenberg had to go and rupture it with something else that made no sense.

"The Manson Family," Vandenberg said. "That's what they wrote on the walls in blood. One of the things anyways."

"I still got no idea what you're talking about."

"Well why did they misspell it? It's supposed to be 'Helter Skelter,' like the Beatles song? Not 'Healter.'"

"So they're bad spellers. Whaddya expect from hippies? Look, Deliah, I'm real tired, here, okay? You just makin' conversation, or what?"

"I'm thinking of 'heed the worms.' Maybe something there's misspelled, too, y'know? Maybe it's supposed to be, I dunno, 'head the worms,' or 'heed the words,' or somethin'."

Koznowski cleared his throat. "Yah, I can't really think about all this here now."

"But it might be a clue, see?"

"Yah?" His voice was sharper. "An' maybe it's not, eh? Maybe Unterhumm put it there himself. So let's just wait for the lab tests, there, an' then worry about it."

"You remember that *Fatal Vision* guy, what's his name? He wrote that stuff on the walls, too, to make it look like hippies did it. 'Acid is groovy' and shit like that. Maybe whoever wrote 'heed the worms' is just trying to throw us off the trail."

"Can't very well throw us off the trail if we ain't hiking nowheres yet."

"I'm just trying to consider all the possibilities, here."

Koznowski said nothing more, tempted for a moment to stop the truck and make her get the hell out if she couldn't shut up. Of everything that had happened that day, a blood-smeared message on the wall was the last thing he wanted to be forced to think about at this particular moment.

Vandenberg read his silence and the set of his jaw and decided it might be a good idea if she stopped speculating. Instead, she commenced pouting. She was only trying to help, is all. A minute passed in silence, save for the crackling of the radio between them and the hiss of the tires on the asphalt as they rolled through the empty landscape.

"Sorry," he said. He took his eyes off the road for just an instant. "Here's what I wan'cha to do," he told her. "You're the smartest one in the department. I mean, I don't know how you knew what that thing stickin' outa poor Mrs. Dankowski was, there . . . Hell, I was all set to call it a triple homicide, eh?" He was going to force a small laugh when an image of the nude and mutilated Hattie Dankowski flashed back at him. Christ, he was going to have nightmares about that for months.

"I just did some reading up on it a little bit ago, is all."

Koznowski smirked. "I dunno there, Deputy. First the Manson Family, then you're reading about embalming for fun. You're starting to sound like one of them Goth kids, there. Don't watch your step, Knudson'll haul your ass in for questioning."

"Guess I thought knowing about autopsies an' stuff might help my police work." She was starting to brighten up a bit, as he knew she would.

"Yah, see?" Koznowski said. "That's just what I'm saying there. Always thinking. An' so you're the only one I can trust with this." She turned her face away from the window. "Tomorrow morning first thing, I wan'cha to go back over there to the funeral home office, eh, an' start goin' through the papers. Start with that desk where we found Mudge, then move on over to the file cabinets an' such. Hold on."

She was about to ask him what he meant by "hold on" when he hit the brakes hard and leaned on the horn. Vandenberg's seat belt held her in place for the most part, but her arms flew up defensively, searching for any kind of support. Through the windshield she saw the flash of the brown rabbit, its black eyes bright in the headlights, darting off the dark highway and back into the fields.

"Sorry 'bout that," Koznowski said as he hit the gas again. They were passing Svenson's Taxidermy and Guns (the place with the giant fiberglass badger on the roof), which meant they were only about a half mile away from the station. "Didn't need to deal with any more death today."

"It's okay," she said, only mildly shaken. "Just glad you didn't hit a patch of black ice there, or you would have . . . So what, ah, am I looking for over at Unterhumm's?"

"Oh, clues. Evidence an' such. Y'know, the usual. Anything that might be pointin' a finger at someone with a beef. Angry customers. Anything with 'heed the worms' written on it."

"Or 'head the worms.'"

"Whatever, yah."

Deputy Vandenberg allowed herself to smile. "And what'll you be doing?"

"Apart from being sheriff?" He flicked the turn signal as they approached the main driveway. "Well, gotta say at this particular moment in, y'know, time, I'd rather not be thinkin' about it. Few people I need to talk to, I s'pose.

First thing when we get in here, though, I gotta call Kirby Mudge's parents in Indiana, let 'em know their boy's been gunned down like an animal."

"Whoa," Vandenberg offered after a moment of silence. "Bummer." Then, in an effort to quickly change the subject, she asked, "So you ready for deer season?"

Koznowski pulled the truck into its spot by the back door and killed the engine. "Never been hunting in my life."

"Really?" she asked. "Are you sure you're from Wisconsin?"

✠

LeAnn Koznowski stepped from the kitchen to check on her husband, who'd been on the couch wide awake for over an hour. In all their years of marriage, and all his years as sheriff, she'd never seen him acting like this before, except maybe for that time in the hospital. It frightened her, because she had no idea what to do. Anger she could understand, and physical pain, but depression was outside her experience. "Oh, hon, now c'mon," she said, snapping on the table lamp near his head. "You gotta eat some supper."

"I'm not real hungry right now, sweets."

"I made a casserole, though. I left the peas out this time, too."

"It'll keep."

She bit the inside of her lip and her eyes wandered around the small but comfortable living room as she tried to figure out what she should do next. "Hey," she eventually said. "I know." She headed back into the kitchen. He heard the refrigerator door open and her returning footsteps. "How 'bout a big glass a this, then? Five an' Alive juice? I picked it up today over at the Red Owl. That'll make you feel a little better, eh? Alive an' such." She shook the carton so he could hear the muffled sloshing of the juice or whatever it was.

"Do we still have that vodka to put in it?"

Her smile faded and she stepped around to the easy chair nearest the couch, still carrying the bright orange carton. "Oh, now, Len, that's not like you talkin'. You know well as I do what the doc said about you drinkin' when you got out of the hospital. You skipped bowlin' practice tonight, you ain't eatin'? You just been layin' there like a lump."

Koznowski sighed. "Been a long day."

"I know that, hon, but tomorrow'll be even longer, you don't eat somethin', an' so."

He turned to look at her. "These things ain't supposed to happen here."

"Yah, I know that too, Len. But I guess this time they did. So's you can either keep layin' there like a lump bein' all Mister Mopey or you can deal with it."

He slowly pushed himself upright. "Yah, guess so." He stood and held out a hand. "Here, gimme that Five whatever."

With a relieved smile, she handed him the carton, and he stood. He limped into the kitchen, set the carton on the counter next to the sink, and reached for the amber pill bottle he kept on top of the microwave. After shaking one of the small white pills into his palm, he opened a cabinet over the sink and pulled down a milk glass, clunking it on the counter so LeAnn would hear. He half filled it with juice from the carton, then quietly reached into the cupboard above the refrigerator and snatched down the vodka bottle, filling the milk glass nearly to the top. After replacing the bottle just as quietly above the fridge, he dropped the pill on his tongue and raised the glass.

"And how perfectly goddamn delightful it all is, to be sure."

By ten thirty the next morning Dr. Cameron already had full autopsy results for Koznowski.

"That was quick there, Doc," Koznowski told him.

"They weren't exactly tricky cases. Neither had any discernible medical conditions. Nothing major, anyway. No lethal amounts of drugs or alcohol in the system. No car accidents. No cancer. Both men died as the result of multiple gunshot wounds to the torso and chest. In both cases the weapon was fired at close range from behind."

"Any idea about the make of the gun?" Koznowski knew it was a long if not impossible shot.

"Ah, sorry, Leonard," Cameron said. "I just deal with the aftermath. That's more a question for your ballistics people. And even then with no weapon and no shell casings or anything?"

"Oh, yah," Koznowski snorted into the phone. "Yah, I'll get our team right on it, there."

"Well," Cameron said, recognizing the sheriff could use whatever he could get at this point. "If I said anything at all, it would be nothing more than a guess on my part—completely nonprofessional speculation. But keeping that in mind, I'd say it was probably a double-barreled thirty-thirty. Pretty standard weapon around here. Find one matching that description in two-thirds of the households across the county."

Koznowski figured that would be the case. And with everyone gearing up for deer season, most were probably within easy reach. "Yah, thanks, Doc. It's at least a little something. I'll get your report and the pictures an' whatnot to Randy up in the lab here. Not sure how he is on ballistics, but he might be able to come up with something, eh."

Before he could hang up the phone the coroner stopped him. "Oh, one other thing. That packing material in Unterhumm's mouth?"

"Yah."

"Placed there after he died. Again, just standard cotton packing, no prints or anything. None on the body, either."

"Yah, well, that figures, eh? Weren't any prints anywhere down there, save for Unterhumm's and Kirby's."

"This really is turning into a doozy, isn't it?" the coroner commented.

"One word I can think of for it, yah. Anyways, thanks for the speedy delivery there, Doc. Appreciate it."

He hung up the phone with no more than he'd had the previous afternoon. He decided his next stop—for any number of reasons—should probably be Unterhumm's friend the priest. To hear Cameron tell it, he and that priest were the only two people for whom Unterhumm had even the slightest bit of patience. Living people, anyway.

✠

The hangover didn't creep in until later that afternoon as Koznowski was driving back toward Beaver Rapids, and when it did it crept in hard.

After parking the truck in the St. Timothy's lot and getting directions from that decrepit old Father Molloy, he headed back outside and around the church to the rear parking lot in search of the gymnasium. Over the years, and without Koznowski's noticing, St. Timothy's had evolved into a much more expansive complex than he could've imagined. At least the chill air on the walk from the church itself to the gym helped clear his head a little, even if it didn't do much for his throbbing legs. Legs aside, there was one solid advantage to winter in Kausheenah County. Every time the temperatures dropped into the thirties, and he recognized this every year anew, it helped smother the stench of the sulfur fumes from the paper mills. Lived there all his life and never did get used to the stench.

After trying, without a whiff of luck, the reception hall, the rectory, the storage warehouse, the classroom building, and the garage, he eventually tracked down the square, unmarked gray brick of a gymnasium. Koznowski knocked a few times, but receiving no response he pushed open one of the solid metal doors and found himself in the middle of a basketball practice. A group of roughly a dozen boys, all thirteen or fourteen years old, all dressed in rumpled gray gym uniforms, were lined up in the middle of the court running layup drills one after another. His first thought was to wonder when it was, exactly, that churches started coming complete with full-sized, fully equipped gymnasiums. Who decided they needed things like that, and who paid for them? Weren't they supposed to, y'know, be feeding the poor and such? His second thought was that every goddamn gymnasium in the world smelled the same—an unholy blend of sweat, bleach, dirty steam, floor wax, and vinyl. To Koznowski, it all added up to the stink of failure. Moments after stepping inside and letting the door slam behind him, he could feel the pain slipping back through his sinuses and the base of his skull. All those squeaking tennies and pounding basketballs and that unavoidable smell, bringing back all the gym class nightmares of his youth, only compounded the hangover.

Off to the side near the bench was a lean, dark-haired man in his late thirties or early forties. Despite the shorts and the University of Minnesota sweatshirt, Koznowski presumed this had to be Father Timothy Avalone, so intent on the practice he hadn't noticed the door opening, the blast of cool air from the outside, or the approach of Sheriff Koznowski.

Avalone continued pacing the sidelines, clapping loudly and hurling abusive encouragement at his players, who were hitting maybe one out of every five of their collective attempted layups.

"C'mon, Johnson, put a little heart into it! And that goes for the rest of you too! What are you, a buncha old ladies? C'mon! Move your buttskis and focus on the basket! How the hell you expect us to beat the shit outa Our Savior next week if you're hobbling around out there like you need walkers?"

Not wanting to interrupt the man while he was on a roll, Koznowski waited for Avalone to take a breath. "Ah, Father Avalone?"

Avalone only half turned his head, clearly too involved in the practice to be bothered. "Yes?"

"Yah, Father Molloy told me I'd find you here. Sorry to interrupt an' all but . . ." He fished a wallet out of his pocket and flashed his badge. "Sheriff Koznowski, Kausheenah County? Yah, I was wondering if I could talk to you about Klaus Unterhumm."

Behind the priest, a few of the gangly, awkward, and sweaty boys—some of whom Koznowski now realized he recognized—had started elbowing each other and nodding toward the pair.

"Oh," Avalone said, offering a smile. "A pleasure to meet you. Why don't you let me wrap up with this buncha losers here, and I'll give you my un-divided attention." When Avalone turned back to his team and blew his whistle sharply, Koznowski winced and nearly screamed.

"All right you fags! Gimme three laps then hit the showers! And while you're doin' that try thinking about how you're gonna do a hell of a lot better tomorrow!"

As the boys grumbled and reluctantly fell into the rough semblance of a line before they began trotting around the gym, Avalone scooped a white towel from the bench and draped it around his neck. "If you'll excuse me for just a moment, Sheriff, I'm gonna go clean myself up a bit too, then I'll meet you back here and we can go talk in my office. More comfortable up there."

✠

The office on the second floor of the rectory building next to St. Timothy's was much more lavish than Koznowski would have expected for a junior priest. An enormous oil painting of a white-robed Jesus sitting on a stump (or maybe it was a rock) surrounded by adoring children of all races domi-nated one wall, while a smaller painting of an arrow-riddled Saint Sebastian hung opposite. Wall space not occupied by artwork was filled with either bookshelves or varyingly ornate crucifixes. The floor was covered in thick navy blue shag carpeting, and a gold-colored vase filled with red and yellow roses adorned the oak desk. The picture window behind the desk looked out over a soccer field pockmarked with patches of snow.

"Can I get you a drink, Sheriff?" was the first thing Father Avalone said upon unlocking the door and leading Koznowski inside.

"Yah, uh, no, thanks." He was a bit thrown by the offer. It probably would have eased the shrieking in his head some, but given as he was conducting a murder investigation he figured it best to pass. Plus he was for some reason hesitant to accept liquor from a man of the cloth. Father Avalone, who was already on his way to the liquor cabinet in the corner, paused and turned back, smiling.

"Well if you change your mind, just give the word." The priest was an enthusiastic, broad-gestured man who'd switched out his shorts for a pair of well-worn blue jeans, but he was still wearing the same University of Minnesota sweatshirt and tattered sneakers he'd worn at practice. He offered Koznowski a chair beneath Saint Sebastian, then dropped himself in the chair across from him. "I don't normally dress this way," he explained, tugging lightly at the sweatshirt. "Not when I'm up here anyway, but I didn't want to keep you waiting. Y'know, the boys down there aren't so bad so long as they keep their minds focused. That's not always easy for thirteen-year-olds."

"Yah, I can imagine, what with starting to notice girls and such. But they looked pretty good to me, what little I saw."

"Thanks. Been working with them a long time now. Some since they were nine or ten. I think you probably heard I run the youth program here. Weekly youth group meetings, prayer meetings on Sunday after Mass, confirmation classes Wednesday evening, soccer and softball teams in the spring and summer, basketball in winter. We play Our Savior down in Janesville next Thursday."

"Yah, good luck there," Koznowski said, not much caring as he unzipped his coat.

"I must say, I'm grateful the Lord gave me this outlet at a time like this." The almost jubilant priest who'd ushered Koznowski into the office was suddenly more serious. Koznowski had been thinking Father Avalone seemed a bit lighthearted for a man whose best friend had just been blown away.

"A little physical exertion, y'know? Good for the head and the spirit."

Koznowski reached into his pocket for his notebook and pen. "Uh-huh, yah . . . Well, first let me say I'm real sorry there about the loss of your friend. But given the circumstance, I hope you're understanding why I need to ask you a few questions." He opened the notebook to a blank page. "We honestly don't have much by way of leads at this point, padre, so I was hoping you might be able to point us toward some. You bein' his friend an' all."

Outside the window, the low gray clouds from earlier that morning were beginning to burn away, allowing the grainy November sunlight to leak into the room.

"He was my friend, Sheriff," the priest said, all the backslapping joviality gone now. "I was quite possibly his only friend. Closest thing he had to a family too. That's why I wanted to see him so badly yesterday. When I saw all the patrol cars out front and the yellow tape, I knew something was wrong."

"Yah, sorry I couldn't let you in," Koznowski told him. "But it was a little late for last rites anyways. Plus, him being your friend, you didn't wanna see him like that. It was pretty grim. Hell, I didn't want to see him that way myself, and I didn't even know the guy."

Father Avalone leaned forward in his chair. "Sheriff, before we go any further with this, I was hoping we could share a moment of silent prayer for the departed souls of God's children, Klaus and . . ."

"Kirby Mudge."

"Yes, Kirby, thank you, who are now sharing in the glory of Jesus' countenance in their heavenly home."

He closed his eyes and folded his hands. Koznowski, uncomfortable with the whole idea (this being a homicide investigation and all), nevertheless did the same.

"Amen," Father Avalone said quietly after a few long moments, then leaned back in his chair. "Thank you, Sheriff. Something else I should perhaps clarify for you."

"Mm-hm?" Koznowski asked, above all else simply relieved the praying was over.

"If at times I don't seem as outwardly devastated as someone might normally be after a dear friend is murdered, remember that I am a man of faith, and I know in my heart that Klaus has gone to a much better life with Our Lord and Savior. So while I may be saddened by the loss of my friend, I do know that this loss is only temporary, as I will see him again one day. And on that day we'll walk together without fear or pain in the glory of the Lord."

"Uh-huh, yah, good," Koznowski said, wondering how, exactly, a mortician would occupy himself in heaven. "So are you willing to help us out, here?"

"He was my friend, Sheriff. Somebody out there has broken both God's law and man's by taking him away so terribly and violently. And while I know this person will one day face God's judgment, until then it is also important that man's law be upheld as well. You can count on me to offer whatever help I can until you find the son of a bitch who did this."

"Yah . . ." Koznowski's eyes shifted quickly. "Good." He poised his pen over the notebook. "So, then. Can you tell me when you last saw the deceased?" Koznowski knew he'd lifted most of his lines from *Dragnet*, but it still sounded good to him.

Father Avalone nodded. "We'd just been out Sunday night, after I finished giving the eight o'clock Mass. He met me here, and we got a couple drinks over at the Dew Drop." It sounded like he'd been watching a few cop shows himself.

As Koznowski jotted that down in his notebook he said, "Makes for a pretty funny picture, don't it? To me anyways. Priest and an undertaker walk into a bar. Sounds like the first line of a joke, eh?"

Father Avalone's face lightened a bit. "I said the same thing to Klaus once. I'll tell you nobody ever screwed with us there. But it's really not so odd, you think about it. We're both in pretty much the same business—preparing people for the hereafter and helping those left behind to cope with the loss. We often worked together, Klaus and I."

"Yah, from what I hear, though," Koznowski said, "Doctor Unterhumm there wasn't exactly what you'd call a people person."

"No, there wasn't much denying that," the priest had to admit. "Maybe not, but he was an artist at what he did. It made things much easier for the families. In that alone he was doing his part." He thought a few moments. "You ask me, Klaus was a man who deeply loved humanity. It just came out in different ways. You need to love people in order to do what he did with such care."

"Yah, well, ya may be right there, padre, but lemme ask ya." He reviewed his notes, which now consisted solely of the words "Dew Drop." "When you were, y'know, at the Dew Drop Sunday, did he say anything? Give you any kinda hint at all that someone might be wanting to, y'know, shoot him? Or cause him any kinda bodily harm?"

The priest was shaking his head before Koznowski was finished asking the question. "Nothing at all. But to be honest, I guess I did most of the talking that night. Sometimes, y'know, I get a few beers in me and I just won't shut up. So if there was a threat or something that was worrying him—y'know, bothering him that night—I guess I never gave him the opportunity to relieve his burden. I guess sometimes I'm not a very good priest."

"Mm-hm," Koznowski said as he scribbled "won't shut up" under "Dew Drop." "What about generally—either Mudge or Doctor Unterhumm? Any families you know have a beef with the way they handled a funeral, anything like that?"

Outside the window, the clouds were swallowing the sunlight again.

Father Avalone once more shook his head. "No, not that I can think of. I can't say I knew Kirby very well, but whenever I did speak with him he seemed a very gentle, sensitive soul. He treated every family who came in with a great deal of care. I can't imagine anyone being displeased with him for any reason. I just . . . I'm finding it very difficult to understand any of this." For the first time, the priest's eyes began watering as emotion burbled to the surface.

"Yah," Koznowski said, "I guess I can understand that. Doesn't make much sense." The priest wasn't turning out to be quite as helpful as he'd hoped. "So . . . what about something earlier? He came over from Germany? Is that what Doc Cameron said?"

"Vienna."

"Okay then, Vienna, around sixty-seven or so. From what I'm finding he worked in a little college town up in Massachusetts there for a good few years before comin' out this way around eighty and setting up shop an' so. That sound about right?"

"Right," Avalone confirmed. "The Lord brought me to Saint Tim's not long afterward, in eighty-two. That might have had something to do with why we became friends. We were both new here."

"Mm-hmm . . . but what about those other years? He ever talk about Massachusetts or Vienna."

Father Avalone took a deep breath. "It's something I've been thinking about since yesterday," he said. "Something that's been nagging me."

Hoping he was finally on the verge of something here, Koznowski poised his pen again in anticipation.

"While he never talked about his time in either place in any great detail, I should tell you Klaus was what you might call a rabid anticommunist."

The sheriff wrote nothing. "Anticommunist?"

Avalone nodded. "He was very outspoken. Made Joe McCarthy look like a piker."

Koznowski was quiet for a moment. "Uh-huh. So you saying here the commies mighta done him in?"

"Just throwing it out there as a possibility, Sheriff. Klaus was very vocal about his hatred for the communists, and he may have made some powerful enemies in the years before he arrived here."

"Uh-huh." The sheriff reluctantly jotted "commies" below "won't shut up." "An' did he mention any specifics about any enemies in the, ah, Communist Party, there? Any names?"

The priest spread his arms. "Not a peep. Apart from his general feelings, he didn't go into any details about it. But boy did he ever hate them. I wouldn't be at all surprised."

"Right. Thanks. The Communist Party don't really have much of a . . . ah . . . wha'cha call a foothold here in Kausheenah County, but we'll certainly keep it in mind, eh?" Koznowski began to close the notebook. This was plain silly.

Then a brief, puzzled concern washed over Avalone's face. "Wait. There was one thing."

Koznowski didn't close the notebook completely just yet, but now if the priest suggested maybe it was the Mafia or the CIA or anti-Castro Cubans who killed Unterhumm and Mudge, swear to God he was gonna get socked.

"He did mention once that he'd received some death threats. I don't think they came from the communists, though, or he probably would've mentioned it."

Koznowski rolled his eyes and let the notebook flop back open. *Now it comes back to him.* "Yah, that might be a little something to go on, eh? What can you tell me?"

"I'm afraid that's all. This was last year, I think? Maybe a little earlier? I'd forgotten about it until right now."

"And?"

"All I can tell you is that he didn't seem too concerned. He laughed about it, actually. I don't think I'd be doing much laughing about it, but he did. He said almost every funeral director in the state got them."

"I don't remember him reporting anything to the Sheriff's Department, but I can check the records."

Father Avalone smiled slightly. "That . . . wasn't really Klaus's way, I guess. He was a very self-reliant man."

"Yah, but with death threats an' such, that could be a federal issue. And now I really wish he had, 'cause it would gimme some place to start, here."

"I'm sure if you ask one of the other funeral directors in the area, they'll be able to tell you more."

"Well," Koznowski looked up. "That's a start, I guess, eh? More'n I had before I came in here."

Father Avalone beamed. "Good then, I'm glad I was able to offer at least some little assistance. He was my friend, remember, and so anything I can do to help justice be served . . ." His voice drifted away for a moment. He shook his head slightly. "But if you'll excuse me, I need to go begin making funeral arrangements."

"You're handling Unterhumm's yourself?"

"Who better than someone who knew him? I also need to talk to Amos Squire about arranging to ship Kirby's earthly remains to his parents in Indiana. The coroner was supposed to be sending them both over to Squire's funeral home sometime today or tomorrow."

Koznowski took another glance out the priest's window and saw it was getting dark fast. *Communists. Jesus.* He thanked Avalone for his time and zipped up his coat as he headed for the office door.

"May the Lord guide your investigation to a speedy resolution, Sheriff."

"Yah, thanks." He paused and turned back while reaching for the knob. "Oh, one more thing."

Father Avalone was already opening the glass doors of the liquor cabinet in the corner. "Yes?"

"You ever heard the phrase 'heed the worms' anywheres before?"

Father Avalone paused, his hand still on the knob. "Heed the worms?"

"Yah. I mean, is that from the Bible or something?"

The priest thought some more. "Not any Bible I know, but there are a number of translations, and I'd be happy to look into it for you. Got most of those translations and concordances right here." He nodded toward the bookshelves.

"That'd be super, padre. Thanks."

"Why do you ask?"

"Oh, just something we heard about down at the station. Probably no big deal I'd say. I'm just kinda curious."

The following morning Deputy Ellsworth drew patrol duty, which he always found a relief. Helluva lot better than sitting at his desk filling out forms. Patrol was where you had a chance to hit some real action, and after that murder scene a couple days earlier he sure as shit needed some.

Things had been quiet as usual since leaving the station at six thirty (okay, patrol or not, there was precious little by way of "action" to be found around Kausheenah County). But then at eleven fifteen he received a call from Leona, asking him to check out reports of an unconscious man in a vehicle at the Grease Pit burger joint over on Paper Mill Road. It seemed the management was less concerned about the man's well-being than about his car, which was blocking the drive-through window.

Although Ellsworth had been headed to the Grease Pit himself anyway at the time, he flipped on the lights and the siren (he always grabbed any chance he could to do that), hitting the gas for that last half mile, bounding the cruiser into the parking lot that served the Spookie's discount furniture store, the Krimple's, and the Grease Pit, screeching to a halt just shy of the mound of dirty snow piled there after the last storm.

Leaving the lights flashing and the cruiser parked haphazardly across three spots, the deputy stepped from the car and strode purposefully toward the burger joint, still honing the Hopalong Cassidy stroll he'd been trying to perfect since he was six.

The Grease Pit was a squat, lopsided orange and brown structure ringed with enormous picture windows that allowed the curious to easily see how much the customers inside were enjoying themselves. It had remained an unchanged Kausheenah standby since first opening in 1967. There was nothing special about the Grease Pit, really, but the statue out front—a fifteen-foot-tall smiling pig in a chef's hat holding a tray of enormous hamburgers overloaded with mysterious green toppings—was hard to resist. Every two or three years or so, some rambunctious and bored drunks would get it in their heads to steal the pig ("Greasy," as the locals had christened him) and spirit him away for purposes unknown and perhaps indecent. He was never gone for more than a few days, usually finding his way back to the Pit (occasionally even ending up on the roof) once the thieves came to understand how difficult it was to hide a fifteen-foot-tall pig with a tray of burgers.

Greasy did the job, though, even that early in the day. Ellsworth noted as he approached there were at least ten cars backed up around the building patiently waiting their turn. It would have been very easy and undoubtedly much faster at that point simply to exit the car, enter the restaurant, pick up a takeout order there, and leave, but who wants to give up drive-through convenience, especially when it's that close?

Those who were waiting, Ellsworth thought, would likely be waiting a while longer. The dented olive green 1973 Buick at the window, from his perspective anyway, didn't seem to have a driver. Missy, the sixteen-year-old dropout who worked the window on Tuesdays and Thursdays, waved at Ellsworth as he drew closer, then pointed down into the car. Ellsworth touched the brim of his hat in response, poised his hand near his weapon, and cautiously approached the vehicle.

Peering inside the passenger window he saw there was indeed a driver. A Caucasion male, early twenties, his head down on his forearms, hands still loosely clutching the steering wheel. On the passenger seat next to him lay at least half a dozen empty and crumpled tallboys. Ellsworth could also hear the REO Speedwagon playing on the idling car's stereo.

"How long's he been here?" the deputy asked Missy, who was clutching a soggy and presumably cold bag of burgers and fries. She was calmly sucking on a vanilla malt, which may or may not have been part of the original order.

"'Bout twenty minutes or so. Dan's pissed, gotta say."

"Uh-huh? Well, then, let's just see what we can do here, eh?" Ellsworth assessed the situation, circled the car, pulled his nightstick from his belt, and rapped it firmly against the driver's window.

The kid inside sat bolt upright in his seat, snapped his head around in apparent bewildered panic, briefly fixed his bleary and watery eyes on Ellsworth's own, then turned his attention to the stereo, cranking "Take It on the Run" to deafening levels. He then began playing air drums and bobbing his head to the beat.

Ellsworth and Missy watched.

The Squire Funeral Pavilion was on Cravenswood Avenue, and it was the only other mortuary in Beaver Rapids. Now, Sheriff Koznowski guessed, it was the only one in Beaver Rapids until somebody decided to take over Unterhumm's place. That had to be good for business.

There were three or four cars in the parking lot out front. Figuring they might be customers he parked the truck off to the side out of an inexplicable deference. He just hoped it wasn't Hattie Dankowski's family. Not that they had to know anything, but he'd still feel weird about it. He checked in with Leona one last time, then headed inside.

As he passed through the double glass doors it struck him whoever designed this place must've designed Unterhumm's as well. Who knows? Maybe there was only one guy out there who specialized in funeral homes, and so they were all the same. Same antique furniture, same muted lighting, same carpeting, same heavy air. Even the same layout, more or less. This time, though, a downbeat Muzak version of a Carpenters song was playing quietly over the hidden loudspeakers and there was someone seated at the reception desk.

Koznowski's first thought was that this young woman here liked her Morticia Addams Halloween costume so much she decided to wear it all year round. A long, tight, vintage black dress, a silver crucifix necklace, silver earrings, and a pair of jangling silver bracelets. Her face, save for the bloodred lipstick and the heavy mascara encircling her eyes, had been caked with what might've been any circus clown's white greasepaint. It also seemed to him that in all her fuss to get ready for work that morning she'd forgotten to comb her hair. These damn kids today and their goofy . . . things.

"Ah, yah, huya," he said. "Sheriff Koznowski of the Kausheenah Sheriff's Department? Wondering if I might be able to talk to that Mr. Squire, there, for a minute. Got some official business. Thanks."

She seemed to sneer at him for an instant, though it was hard to tell under all that makeup. "Please have a seat over there," she pointed with a long blue fingernail, "and I'll see if *Doctor* Squire is available." She disappeared behind a door as the sheriff removed his hat and moved toward a pair of chairs against a peach-colored wall.

There were a few others milling about the lobby, quiet, somberly dressed men and women in their thirties he took to be employees. Several were consulting clipboards, others kept checking their watches.

Koznowski waited patiently, looking around the lobby and listening to the gentle canned music dripping out of the ceiling somewhere. Apart from the color scheme and the woodwork, it really was set up very much like the competition, and again he wondered if there was one and only one plan available if you wanted to open a mortuary. Maybe it was a legal thing.

He didn't mean to eavesdrop, but as he sat and waited the voices—a young woman's, primarily—began seeping around the corner from a meeting room on the other side of the peach wall.

". . . and if you like, while you're working on that, I can get an announcement in tomorrow's paper. That's another thirty-five. For the announcement."

There was a bit of quiet shuffling and murmurs of assent. "Okay, then, let's see what we have here. The flower arrangements are eighteen-fifty, the prayer cards—that's fifty of them—are seventy-five, plus an extra fifteen for the three you want laminated ... and envelopes, and the obituary is a hundred twelve, plus seventy-five cents for each additional word ... There's room rental for the viewing—that's two-fifty—and the guestbooks are eighty-two each, and the casket itself—you showed me the model you want ... and the sealant in the vault ... hmmm ... that's another fifty-seven hundred for that. Then, since you wanted the service to be on a weekend, the men who open and close the site—they work for Cravenswood—get paid overtime. Then there's the truck to haul the equipment over and away, and the driver gets overtime too on account of the weekend ..."

As she spoke, he could hear fingernails clacking on what must've been a plastic desktop calculator. Whoever was in there with her was saying nothing at all.

". . . overtime too. Plus the organist's fee, and another two hundred for the ladies working the kitchen at the luncheon afterward ... And you said you wanted a canopy? Okay, I'll need to look into that, see if one will be available on Saturday, but assuming it is . . ." There was a flurry of clacking. "That brings the total here for the full service and entombment to ... thirty-eight thousand seven hundred eighty-two. But that's without the memorial marker or the engraving. That's gonna take a few months, so we'll work that out later. Now, if you'll just sign here ... and here ... and here ... Oh, and will this be cash or credit card?"

He had become so engrossed and terrified by what he was hearing he didn't notice the return of the spooky receptionist. When she spoke, and when he snapped his eyes up and saw her, he nearly screamed, convinced for an instant she was either one of those zombies from that *Carnival of Souls* movie or the Angel of Death herself, there to carry him away.

"Doctor Squire'll be with you in a moment," she said. "He's just wrapping up in the prep room, then needs to check on the smiling bags of death. He said you could wait in his office."

"Check on the, ah, *what,* now?" Koznowski was starting to think coming here had been a terrible mistake.

The receptionist's hand flew to cover her embarrassed grin, her eyes opening in mild shock through the raccoon mascara. "Oh my God, I can't believe I said that. I'm so sorry, it just slipped out. It's been so crazy around here these past couple days. Boy, am I glad you weren't a customer." She laughed nervously, a sharp, mirthless giggle that ended abruptly. "That's what Doctor Squire calls body bags after they've been hosed out and we hang them up to dry. They hang open and . . ." The words slowed as she realized she was saying far too much. "They . . . look like they're . . . smiling, I guess." She cleared her throat.

"Yah, I see," Koznowski said. "Guess that's some a that wha'cha call your undertaker humor, eh?" As she spoke he was starting to see through the makeup. She seemed awfully young and pretty to be involved in a business like this, but maybe it helped explain the getup.

"I guess," the receptionist said, wanting desperately to get off the subject. "Will you follow me, please?" She took a few steps up the carpeted staircase, then stopped and turned to see the sheriff staring with some trepidation at the path ahead. Something winced inside him.

"The office is right up here," she pointed. Koznowski nodded and followed slowly.

She led him upstairs and through the casket showroom. As he passed, he looked around with curiosity. Dozens of caskets made of oak, redwood, mahogany, bronze, steel, and one sparkly blue job made of plastic. He paused and rapped on the lid. The coffin rattled.

"That's our most affordable model," the pale young woman said, her eyes revealing the lie behind her smile.

"Really," Koznowski replied. "I'll keep that in mind, an' so."

On the other side of the showroom was an unmarked door. Behind the door was Amos Squire's office. It, too, was much like Unterhumm's, except for the carpeting and the drapes, which were a deep forest green. Like Avalone's office, the walls featured artwork Koznowski assumed was supposed to offer solace to the mournful. On one wall was a painting of a newly resurrected Jesus emerging from the tomb as two elderly women dressed in black look on in abject terror. On another wall was an unusually bloody painting of Hippocrates performing what appears to be gallbladder surgery on a young boy. The other big difference was the skull prominently displayed on the desk. A pair of aviator shades had been balanced in place over the eye sockets and a black cigarette holder was pinched between its teeth. Koznowski took a seat facing the skull but said nothing about it. "Thanks," he told the receptionist.

"He'll just be a minute," she said, before leaving and closing the door behind her. He could not hear her departing footsteps.

As promised, a few minutes later the door opened again and Amos Squire entered, wearing a lab coat over an open-collared shirt.

"Whoopsies," he said, walking past the sheriff's outstretched hand, snatching the skull off the desk, and slipping it neatly into a drawer.

"Excuse me," he said as he slammed the drawer shut. "I honestly don't know how that keeps getting out of there." He swung himself into his expensive-looking high-backed leather desk chair. "Well now, Colonel, what can I do you for?"

Koznowski glanced at his still outstretched hand and let it fall to his side before taking his seat once more. Squire noted the look on his face.

"Oh—sorry for missing your hand. As a Toucher of the Dead, as they call it, most people try to avoid shaking my hand anyway, so I guess I've fallen out of the habit."

Koznowski's first impression was that Squire couldn't have been more than fifteen. Energetic fellow. "Yah, that's okay then," he said. "So you probably figured I'm investigating the murders of Klaus Unterhumm and Kirby Mudge. I was hoping to ask you a few questions."

"Oh, you betcha. Anything," Squire said, spreading his arms. "Doctor Cameron sent them both over yesterday afternoon, late. I haven't had a chance to see them yet, but should be starting my work this evening."

"That was quick, eh? This whole thing seems to be movin' real quick, 'cept for my end."

Squire looked concerned. "No suspects yet?"

"Working on it." Koznowski shifted to his left haunch and pulled the notebook from his pocket, flipping it open to the page following his meager jottings from the interview with the priest. "All right, then. Did you know the victims well?"

"Klaus?" He squinted slightly at the sheriff to let him know it was a pretty idiotic question. "Well, consider the situation we were in, Colonel, as the only two funeral directors in town. We couldn't get away from each other even if we wanted." Squire kept the curtains behind him pulled. Overhead, one of the bulbs in the light fixture flickered and buzzed. "And I'll say this straight out just to lay it on the table. Klaus Unterhumm was a son of a bitch, and anyone who tells you any different is a liar."

"Yah, heard as much." Koznowski made a note. "So you're saying then there was some competition between the two of yas."

Squire closed his eyes patiently. Sometimes he was amazed at how slow people could be. "No, I'm saying just the opposite. Small as Beaver Rapids may be, for businesses like this there's plenty of work to go around. Sometimes when things got busy, I'd send a removal to him and vice versa."

"Removal?"

"Sorry. That's mortician speak. Deceased, deaths, cadavers, whatever you want to call it. It's work. As they say, it's the one business that never has to worry about a slump. And being on opposite sides of town as we are—were—it made things very easy. People on the east side came here, people on the west went to Klaus. He opened in eighty, I think it was, but did just fine for himself."

As the undertaker spoke, Koznowski began developing an idea. "Yah, for a long time—ever since I was a kid—your family's place was the only game in town, y'know, funeral-wise. But without Unterhumm right across the way, there—y'know, in the picture—that just means more business for you again, right?"

Oh, he just wasn't very good at this "cop" thing. He never should've shown his hand that quickly.

Squire's eyes cooled. "I hope you aren't implying anything by that. For the record, as big a son of a bitch as he was, I liked Klaus. I don't own a shotgun, and I'm as anxious for you to catch whoever did this as you are—"

Koznowski's right eyebrow went up. "Where'd you hear it was a shotgun?" That was one of several details they hadn't made public. That and the "heed the worms" thing. "I thought you said you hadn't seen the bodies yet."

Squire didn't flinch. "Cameron told me when we spoke yesterday. Actually it has me a little worried. Shotguns can be bad news for morticians, you know? Not worried about Klaus so much—he's being cremated. But I'd like to do a good job on Kirby. He was a nice kid and I want to give his parents something to remember. But if he was hit in the face?" His own face revealed it wasn't a rhetorical question.

"He was shot in the back, like Unterhumm."

"Oh, thank God," Squire said, his shoulders relaxing. Then he caught himself. "Well, you know, from a professional perspective."

The sheriff made another notation. "Mm-hmm."

Perhaps realizing he was digging himself into a hole, Squire began to scramble. "But back to your whole question about getting more business. I mean, sure, Klaus's murder might mean more business for me in the short run, but it also means a lot more work." The mortician shifted in his seat and looked Koznowski in the eye. "I'll be honest with you, Sarge, I make a decent living. But at the same time I'm a fairly lazy man. I don't wanna work twenty-four-seven the way Klaus did. I like being able to go home and relax with my family, and can't wait for another funeral home to move in. Jobs are piling up downstairs, they're all on tight schedules, and I'm already tired."

"All right, then," Koznowski backed off, scratching out the word "suspect" on the open page. "Didn't mean to go implying nothing. Just asking some questions, here." He glanced at his notes. "Now, apart from professionally, you know him well? Either Doctor Unterhumm or Kirby?"

The young mortician considered his answer, touching a finger to his lips before he spoke. "I don't think anyone ever really got to know Klaus all that well. He was a very private man. It's not like we ever hung out together or anything like that, if that's what you mean. Might call him for advice once in a while, but that's all."

"What sort of advice, you think?"

Squire shrugged. "You know, tough cases. Injuries to the head and face—what I was worried about with Kirby—stuff that's difficult to mask with mortician's wax and rouge. He had some great ideas, I guess from being in the business as long as he had. See, what we do here, really, is make souvenirs for the living. A hopefully pleasant final moment together." He leaned back in his chair and idly played with a pen. "I might be good at what I do, Sergeant, but Klaus was a master, a true artist and craftsman."

He leaned forward as if about to share a secret. "Maybe I shouldn't tell you this." Koznowski leaned forward himself. "Morticians have a bagful of tricks. Little cheats that can make a loved one presentable. If someone lost a hand in a farm accident, say, we can replace it with a roll of socks and wrap the good hand around it. Or if someone has no teeth, a flattened tube of toothpaste can give the face some structure. It looks perfectly presentable. But Klaus? He went beyond all that. I don't know how he did it—it might've been black magic for all I know—but he could make anyone, *everyone*, look alive again."

"Yah," Koznowski said. "I been to a couple viewings over there. They were really something. Go to most funerals these days, hell, the body looks like some kinda, I dunno, washed-up New Orleans whore."

Squire blinked and paused, then almost reluctantly nodded, sitting back. "The really amazing thing is he did it all himself—the dressing, the hair, the cosmetizing... I might trim the nails and shave them, but when it comes to the more womanly things like applying the makeup and arranging the hair I bring in a couple girls. Hate to think what I'd be like applying makeup, y'know? Send them out to the viewing looking like Bozo."

For a moment Koznowski flashed back to the girl at the front desk.

"... He was a genius and an inspiration, and I will miss him. Nobody else like him anywhere."

"He was as good as all that, you think it might've been a case of wha'cha call professional jealousy. I don't mean you here, but some other mortician in the area?"

Squire shook his head. "No, I can't really see that. No one liked Klaus, no, but we still all wanted to be him, know what I mean? He was the master, and we all hoped to be as good as him, to maybe learn something from him. Can't do that if you kill him."

Figuring this was about all the eulogizing they needed that afternoon, the sheriff remembered why he'd come there in the first place. "Okay, then. I'm, ah... yah. Now, if... Lemme ask one more thing. Father Avalone over at Saint Tim's there mentioned something about death threats Unterhumm and all youse undertakers got. You know anything about that?"

Squire lowered his head almost to his desk and put his hands lightly to his temples. "Oh, God. Those." He looked up again with an odd, cynical smile on his face. "Yes I know about them. Klaus got them. I got them. Nearly every funeral director in Wisconsin got them. They showed up for years."

"Yah, an' so?" This might be his first solid lead after the whole "Kirby Mudge" theory fell apart. Not counting Avalone's commie angle.

"Some got only two or three. Others got six, eight, more. It seemed random. They all said the same thing, though. I mean, they were photocopies. It was some religious nut. I think it was a Bible quote or something."

"You happen to have one I can look at?"

Squire shook his head. "No, sorry, I threw them away as soon as they came in. Last one was just a couple weeks ago. Don't know if Klaus got one then or not. We talked about it at the state convention in Madison a couple years back, and nobody took them seriously. Just some wackadoodle religious crap."

"You remember what the notes said?"

Once again Squire's shoulders bounced slightly. "Oh, I don't remember exactly. I . . . like I said . . . I think it was something from the Bible. Something like we hadn't heeded the word of the Lord, that we—morticians, I'm presuming—were an abomination or something to that effect. Then it closed by saying we should start preparing our own funerals."

"And nothing else? No explanation why they had this beef, there, whoever it was?"

"Not really, no. But who knows with these people?"

That "heed the word" rang a bell. Maybe that was the link, and maybe Deliah was right after all. "So what you said just now was in the notes. You used the line 'heed the word of the Lord.' Was that wha'cha'd call an exact quote? I mean, was that in the note, there?"

Squire raised a curious eyebrow and frowned. "I . . . really don't know if that was exact. It was something like that. Why?"

The sheriff added a few notes. No need to give him too much. "Just a hunch. But if you don't know if it's exact or not, well, then, guess I'll just leave it there." Why do people always throw evidence away? "You ever report them threats to the police?"

The mortician shrugged again, a habit that was starting to annoy Koznowski. "Maybe a few of them did. I never took it seriously enough to report it. Like I said, Colonel, it's been going on for years and nothing ever happened."

"Yah, until now, eh?"

✠

The sheriff wrapped things up a few minutes later, figuring he'd gotten all he was going to out of Squire, which wasn't quite as much as he'd gotten out of the priest.

"Here," Squire said as Koznowski zipped up his coat and plopped his hat on his head. "I'll walk you down." Before he did, he pulled open a drawer and replaced the skull on his desktop. "Got a few distributors coming by later," he explained. "They always get a big kick out of Myron."

"Yah, I can imagine. That'll do 'er then."

As they strolled back through the coffins, Squire asked, "Did you hear Father Avalone is insisting on giving Klaus a full funeral Mass?"

"Yah, I think he mentioned something about that."

Squire shook his head. "Even though he's getting cremated. If Klaus was still around he'd have a fucking fit."

"Not the religious type, then, Unterhumm?"

They left the showroom, turned the corner, and headed for the stairs.

"Not in that way, no. The really sad thing, unfortunately—besides my prep job, which no doubt would never live up to his standards—is that I couldn't fulfill his final request."

Koznowski grabbed the railing and considered the staircase. At least going down was easier than coming up. "Yah?"

"Yeah, see, he wanted a full Viking funeral. Father Avalone mention that little bit of trivia?"

"Can't say as he did, no."

Below them in the lobby, a family of five was preparing to leave. They may or may not have been the ones Koznowski heard through the wall as they received the second bit of bad news they'd heard in recent days. They all looked stunned. It might've been grief or it might've been sticker shock. What happens to those folks who simply can't afford it? Guess that's about the time you decide Grandma would be happier wrapped in a sheet and dumped in the woods.

"So what the hell am I supposed to do?" Squire asked. "Just go pick up a Viking ship over at Krimple's, right? Drag it out to Lake Winnebago, put him in it, and set it on fire?"

"Yah, I think there are prob'ly some state and local ordinances that, ah..."

"Yeah, sorry about that one, Klaus. Ain't gonna happen. Best I can do is put a toy ship in there with him and hope he finds it in himself to forgive me."

Through the front doors, they both saw it had started to snow.

"Comin' down again," Koznowski observed.

"Yup," Squire agreed. "Think Gus'll be ready to go this season?"

Koznowski zipped up his coat a little more. "He ain't, I'll go over there an' sober him up myself. Done it before."

He turned and stuck out his hand, then quietly slipped it into his pocket, hoping it looked natural. "Well, Mister . . . Doctor Squire, ah, thanks for taking the time, there."

"No trouble at all, Sarge. Anything else I could do, just call. And I hope you catch whoever did this soon."

"Yah, makes two of us," Koznowski replied, squinting through the glass doors toward the sky. "Sure hope it don't keep comin' down like this."

After the sheriff stepped outside, Squire watched him for a moment, then turned to see Clorella, the receptionist, staring at him. He smiled, approached her desk, and quietly explained why the "stupid fucking hick" was there in the first place. More than anything it was an effort to stop the spread of unnecessary rumors around the Funeral Pavilion. He knew what kind of mouth she had.

He patted her reassuringly on the shoulder, opened a door behind her, and headed down a short flight of stairs. Turning a corner at the bottom he followed the brightly lit hallway to the two stainless steel swinging doors leading into the prep room.

Before taking a full step into the room he froze and screamed.

"*Dwight*! Stop that!"

A small, unshaven man in a rumpled orange hunting cap, his pants gathered around his ankles, was on one of the embalming tables, atop the still body of an elderly woman.

Dwight looked over his shoulder at Squire, his mouth agape. "But . . . but Mr. Squire," he sputtered, "this is what you told me to do!"

"*Yes*!" Squire screamed, still furious. "But not now! *And for godsakes not Mrs. Dankowski!*"

IV

Unterhumm, Mudge, and Hattie Dankowski (poor dear) had all been cared for, but it took another two days, once all the excitement had quieted down, before someone (well, the coroner) had the idea to take a look and sure enough. That's when the remaining bodies still awaiting preparation in Dr. Unterhumm's cooler were finally removed and transported across town to Squire's. Most of the families, thankfully, were quite understanding. More so than Dr. Squire, that's for damn sure. Bill and Carol Cieszlwicz, the local husband-and-wife crime scene cleanup team (who honestly weren't that busy most of the year), still hadn't made an appearance at the funeral home but promised they would be there by Saturday or maybe Sunday after the game.

Deputy Vandenberg, meanwhile, wearing a pair of rubber gloves to prevent any contamination of would-be evidence, was spending her second day sorting through the thousands of files in Unterhumm's office. She hadn't given his apartment down the hall anything more than a cursory once-over, but it didn't seem to hold much by way of clues. Just a bed and nightstand, a hot plate and toaster next to the sink, a closet containing three black suits and half a dozen lab coats, and a bookshelf filled with old medical and history books, most of them in German.

Her focus in the office had been on the filing cabinets, and those hadn't offered much, either. Copies of bills for services rendered, transfer orders, sticky, weird-smelling photostats of death certificates. There were also a few forms she didn't fully understand, so she set those off to the side. In all honesty, she hadn't the slightest idea what the hell she was supposed to be looking for. None of these things, even the things she didn't understand, seemed like evidence in a murder case. Just regular business papers. She'd much rather be back at the station with the chief, tracking down leads and whatnot. Then again, maybe this had its advantages. It was tedious work but at least it got her away from all the idiots on the force. Why the chief had ever hired a moron like Ziegler, she couldn't say. Then again, maybe she could. There was that whole family thing to consider. Still. What a stupid fucking tard he was.

She pushed herself up from the floor, moved across the maroon carpet still crunchy with Kirby Mudge's dried blood, and took a seat behind the desk, itself still sprinkled with dried spots of dark brown blood. There were three drawers to her left. She tried them all and found the bottom one locked. She opened the middle drawer and withdrew a handful of manila folders, which she flopped on the stained blotter. Opening the top one, she saw six pieces of paper, each with an open envelope paper-clipped to the upper left-hand corner. The envelopes had all been addressed to the funeral home. She flipped the first envelope back and read the note.

✠

". . . He is the resurrection and the light, and whoso believeth in him shall not die, but shall have everlasting life. Amen . . . Now if you'll please rise and celebrate the Lord's gift of life by turning to number three twenty-seven."
There was a soft rustle and shuffle and groan as everyone eventually made it to their feet. Father Avalone wore a white robe as he stood on St. Timothy's altar and looked out over the pitiful congregation. It was the same crew of fifteen faces, mostly elderly, who came to every funeral whether they knew the deceased or not. At the foot of the altar, Klaus Unterhumm lay in a closed casket made of cobalt steel and iron. It was waterproofed, rustproofed, bombproofed, galvanized, and polished. Before the service it had been draped in a white silk cloth adorned with the red cross of the Crusaders.

The priest knew Unterhumm was not going to be buried in the impregnable casket. After the service Klaus's earthly remains would be delivered to Squire's on-site crematory, while the casket itself would be returned to the showroom floor. He also knew Klaus was not in the least interested in funerals, and if given the opportunity likely would not have attended his own. For the brief period he would be on display prior to that afternoon's cremation, however, Father Avalone wanted to make sure Klaus was provided with the very best.

Father Avalone also knew Klaus was not a religious man (let alone a Catholic), that he had repeatedly referred to such practices as "primitive idiocy." But as the priest had always tried to explain to him, the funeral Mass was for the living, not the deceased. That being the case, dammit, Klaus was going to have a Mass, if only for Father Tim's sake and no one else's. Besides, he thought, it would be kind of funny. The sort of ironic final joke that would've made Klaus shake his fist and sputter in guttural German.

Leonard Koznowski was sitting in the last pew, his hat on his lap, scanning the faces of everyone who'd made a point of attending Unterhumm's funeral. You never could tell when a killer might show his (or her) hand. Problem was he knew all these people. He'd been to enough local funerals during his time on the force to recognize the Funeral Club (as they were unofficially known). Christ, most of these people couldn't stop their hands and head from shaking long enough to sing a hymn, let alone point a shotgun and pull the trigger.

That damn shotgun, he thought again. They still hadn't found it. He had the idea that once they found that they'd have their killer. Even if he did find a suspect he knew was guilty but tried to go to court without that singular piece of physical evidence, where the hell would he be? Back in the shithouse, is where.

He again looked around. No, there wasn't a strange face there, and none of these people killed two morticians less than a week ago. Unless that Ellie Langowicz over there did it, poor thing. Koznowski watched as she tried to turn a page. No, it wasn't Ellie. Recoil alone would've sent her through the wall.

These folks here wanted to stay as far away from funeral homes as they could for as long as they could. They wouldn't venture into one alone simply to kill someone. Too close. They only went to funerals every week to remind themselves they were still alive. He grabbed his hat and tried to quietly slip out the back door before the song ended.

✠

When they were first married, oh some twenty-odd years earlier, LeAnn just thought Lenny was being a stubborn so-and-so. He seemed to have an awful lot of absurd (that's a fifty-cent word for "stupid") theories about things that didn't really matter—like the proper way to cool a cup of coffee or make ice cubes. Even what table they should or shouldn't sit at when they went down to Buzz's. Nothing, no amount of logic or contrary evidence, could shake his beliefs. After a few years she came to accept his quirks as nothing more than quirks. They didn't get in the way much except at home. You saw him in public, you'd never know he could be obsessive and demanding when it came to certain issues that never occurred to most folks, especially folks around Kausheenah County. They had better things to think about than parallel parking and lightbulbs.

It wasn't until their fifteenth anniversary or thereabouts that LeAnn came to understand these little quirks of Lenny's were as close as he came to having a religion. He steadfastly clung to dumb ideas about the most efficient way to shovel snow the way some people clung to the Virgin Mary or the Lord's Prayer. They were his way of coping with a world that often made no sense.

Take breakfast cereal. He insisted his breakfast cereal be in the form of discrete pieces that would more or less maintain their form throughout the duration of the meal. Pieces that could be counted if need be (though he rarely went that far). No flakes, nothing that would turn to a mush. He liked individual pieces he could look at in the bowl. His reason for this was simple. With individual pieces, you always knew when you were finished, and when you were finished you had eaten everything that had been given you. With things that went all mushy, or pieces that were so small they could not be distinguished from one another, you were never really sure. You always left something behind in the bowl which then got washed down the drain. It was not only wasteful, it involved guesswork and some fairly loose judgment calls. Lenny liked the certainty of Cheerios, if not the cereal itself. It allowed him to maintain a sense of order and control. As a result, LeAnn stopped buying corn flakes, raisin bran, and any other cereal he considered morally lacking.

He also considered pomegranates immoral, simply in terms of their work-reward ratio. It should never require that much effort, he told her, to eat a damn piece of fruit. That was less of an issue, though, as very few supermarkets in the area carried pomegranates. She was relieved he didn't feel the opposite. It saved her a heck of a lot of driving. She loved him and she would've done it, but jeeze.

✠

When Koznowski walked into the station half an hour after sneaking out of St. Timothy's, he saw Deputy Vandenberg was there and looking awfully perky. She could be perky when the situation called for it. He'd seen it work to her advantage.

"Guess what I found?" she asked before he had a chance to sit. In her right hand were several pieces of paper.

"Death threats from some religious kook, eh?"

"*No*," she said, ready to one-up him. Then she stopped and looked crestfallen. She slapped the letters on his desk and started walking away.

"Oh," Koznowski said, "don't be looking so gloomy there, eh? These are just what I was hoping you'd find. You done good, Deputy."

That seemed to help some as he took a seat and scooped up the letters. Vandenberg reconsidered her snit and returned to his desk. "Yah, this is super." He read the top letter. It had been typed on what appeared to be an old manual typewriter. Some of the letters were much darker than others, and the *a* and *m* keys dropped a bit.

> *Because you have heard not the words of the Lord, I take from you your sons and daughters into early graves. Prepare for burial yourself.*

"Well, there goes that theory," Koznowski muttered to himself. He flipped through the other pages, finding them identical. "Pretty blunt, there, ain't it?" he said to Vandenberg. "You have these checked for prints, now we both been handling them like a coupla monkeys?"

"Yeah," she said. "They're clean except for, y'know, the mortician's."

He knotted his brow. "Yah, figures, eh. But still, if we can just find this typewriter here, we might have something to go on." He looked to Vandenberg hopefully. "Hey, you didn't find nothing in the files about that worm business, didja?"

"No." Vandenberg pointed to the papers in his hands. "But y'know there is that." She tapped one of the envelopes. Koznowski glanced at her, then down at the envelope. Someone had stamped a return address in the upper left-hand corner.

> *Pollex Christi Ministries*
> *P.O. Box 28*
> *Prar du Morte, WI*

"Oh. Well that's convenient, then, ain't it?"

"Yeah, that's what I thought."

"Who the hell puts a return address on a death threat, you suppose?"

"Maybe someone stupid," Vandenberg guessed. "Or maybe it's a red herring."

"Either way, it's the only lead we got, so we should jump on it like a bear on a . . . well, yah, you know, whatever bears jump on. We'll be like that."

Vandenberg beamed and very nearly gave Koznowski a hug. He was still looking at that return address in mild disbelief and didn't notice her.

"Yah, so it looks like I'm gonna have to take a little road trip down to Prar du Morte."

⁜

"Yah, y'know I have trouble sortin' out fender benders. So now I get this damn thing here dropped on me and . . . I got no damn idea what the hell I'm doing here. Buncha flopping around, is all."

"Oh now, just you hush," LeAnn said quietly. "That ain't the kinda thing we need the folks in town hearing, what with everyone all antsy as it is, an' so. And besides it ain't true. You're a real good sheriff, hon."

Given he was heading out on a road trip the next morning to try and collar some potentially deadly murder suspects, Koznowski thought it would be nice to take LeAnn out to Buzz's for the perch fry. Just in case, y'know, he was killed in a shoot-out with some religious fanatics down in Prar du Morte.

"Yah, you think so?" he asked. "Watch this." He turned in his seat and shouted toward the bar. "Heya, Tom!"

A hefty man in a pullover sweater and a green and yellow knit cap turned and smiled. He held a short-neck beer bottle in one hand. On the bar in front of him rested an empty paper plate covered with grease stains, smeared ketchup, and fried fish crumbs. "Heya Len, heya LeAnn. Didn't see youse two come in."

"That's 'cause your face was down in that perch there, eh?"

"Best in the county, eh?"

For all their shouting, nobody around them seemed to mind, or even notice.

"Hey, Tom, lemme ask you," Koznowski said. "Hey, do I know what the hell I'm doin'?"

Tom paused briefly, the heels of his Red Wing boots hooked on the rungs of his bar stool as he stared down into his beer bottle. "Len, we known each other a long time now. Since we was kids," he shouted back over the half-crowded restaurant. "An' I can honestly say, there, I can honestly say you ain't known what you was doin' since you was eight, so why the hell should anything be any different now? Why th' hell else you think I keep votin' for yas?"

Koznowski gave him a thumbs-up and turned back to LeAnn, a victorious glint in his eye. "See?"

From the outside, Buzz's appeared to be nothing more than an abandoned, ramshackle wood-frame farmhouse just off the highway about ten miles west of Beaver Rapids. If you didn't know better, you could drive by without noticing. Inside, however, Buzz's was a single open and airy room, with creaky, warped wooden floors and dark paneled walls adorned with monstrous mounted fish caught by local fishermen and donated to the restaurant. A scarred and handsome old bar lined one wall and six picnic tables, each topped with a sheet of white paper, scattered condiments, and a couple ashtrays, filled the rest of the space. A gathering quilt of gray, still cigarette smoke clouded the overhead lights. Sophisticates from Milwaukee or the Cities would probably call it "rustic," but to folks in Kausheenah County it was just Buzz's. There was nothing fancy about it. Dinner came on paper plates and cutlery was usually optional (unless you got the broiled trout). A teetering stack of folded paper napkins arrived with each order, and the only menu was written on a chalkboard behind the bar. There were never that many choices anyway, which was okay because the people who went to Buzz's generally knew what they wanted long before they stepped through the squealing screen door. Buzz's served up the best fish in the county, and the twice-weekly perch fry had people standing in line out in the gravel parking lot, no matter how cold it was, waiting to get in.

It was early enough yet Thursday that the Koznowskis had a table to themselves, which offered at least the illusion of privacy.

"I got absolutely no idea what to expect down there with these religious nuts. What the hell they want, nothin'. But I gotta go down there an' find out. Hopefully come back with a killer, eh?" He lifted his beer and took a sip.

LeAnn was about to say something when the waitress showed up with their perch. "Thanks, Debbie," she said, grinding out her cigarette in the black plastic ashtray.

"Enjoy it, Sheriff . . . Mrs. Sheriff," the waitress said before heading back to the bar. They took turns dolloping the ketchup onto a corner of their plates, and LeAnn dug the two small slices of buttered rye bread from beneath the pile of fish and fries, laying them on one of her napkins.

Koznowski was lifting that first cluster of yellow crinkle-cut fries to his mouth when his bench jumped. He turned to find Ronnie Seymour seated next to him, leaning in earnestly. He felt his throat tighten. "Oh, heya, there, Ronnie. Ah, so how's that bowling average holding up? You still up around two forty, two forty-three?"

"Heya, Sheriff," Ronnie said. "Gotta ask ya."

As the sheriff feared, Ronnie had no time for idle chitchat. He was wearing a battered once-blue baseball cap, the brim pulled down low over his eyebrows. His hands were permanently grease-blackened, but his shirt was always pristine. Above his drooping mustache his eyes were worried. Koznowski just wanted to eat his damn dinner in peace.

"Shoot." He set the fries down and reached for a napkin.

"I know you can't really say a whole lot about a wha'cha call a . . . ongoing investigation there, but I gotta tellya, my ma's pretty freaked out by the whole thing, y'know? This whole thing with the murders? So you got any suspects yet? Any news I could tell Ma just to calm her the hell down a little? I won't tell nobody else, promise." He raised a hand. "Just that last two days, she's scared to go out—not to the backyard or nothin'. Drivin' me a little nuts."

Koznowski weighed his options. Having known her as long as he had, he sometimes thought it might be best for everyone in the area if Mrs. Seymour didn't leave the house. Crazy old bird. But that wouldn't exactly be fair to Ronnie, who still had to live with her. He popped a french fry into his mouth and chewed. They always started out a little soggy, but now they were getting cold on top of it. "Tellya what, there, Ronnie. You tell your ma we got ourselves a real solid lead just today, an' we're investigating it now. You can also tell her it ain't no one in town here she needs to fret over, so that oughta help, eh?"

Ronnie's worried expression didn't change. "Yah, really? You ain't, y'know, just jackin' me around, are ya? 'Cause Sheriff, I mean, we alls know you ain't exactly had to deal with nothin' like this before. An' since the accident an' all, y'know, folks they understand, but we're all a little worried. Not as much as Ma, maybe, but still."

Koznowski stared at him for a moment. "Right. Yah, so lemme ask you. Did you know either of the victims? Just askin' here."

Ronnie made a vague gesture. "Yah, that's where they took my pa, over to Unterhumm's."

"Oh yah? I didn't remember that one. Did they, y'know, do a good job, ya think?"

The air slid out of Ronnie as he thought back six years. "Only so much you can do with a combine accident, I s'pose, eh. But yah, I guess. We kept some pictures. Never really met that Unterhumm guy. I never knew the other one at all neither. It was another guy there when we went."

"Yah," Koznowski said, looking toward the floor. "What I figured. Seems nobody around here knew much about 'em." The sheriff just wanted to get back to his dinner, which was fast soaking through the plate. Across the table it looked like LeAnn was about finished already, dammit. "Yah, so, you just tell your ma that everything's gonna be fine, eh? We'll have it wrapped up in a jiffy, there."

Ronnie looked less than convinced. "Yah, you say so, I guess."

Koznowski ignored his tone and expression. "Yah, good, eh? So now go eat your perch an' don't worry about your ma."

Watching Ronnie as he headed back to his table, LeAnn waited until he was well out of earshot before turning back to her husband, who was glumly eating a soggy fry. "See?" he said.

"Oh, now you just hush. Don't tell me you let that get to you."

He was no longer in any mood for one of her pep talks. He shook his head quickly before reaching for some perch. The breading was already starting to slide away in hunks, revealing the gray, dead fish beneath. It was useless. "Just need to take account of everything, here."

LeAnn squinted at him. "Oh, don't go tellin' me you think Ronnie's a suspect."

"I have a suspect," Koznowski reminded her. "Just need to, y'know, take everything into account, eh?"

"Oh, you. I cannot believe you'd let that get to you an' so. And right after you was foolin' with Tom over there."

"Hearing it from Tom's one thing," he said. "Hearing it from Ronnie's another."

"Just listen to you. Now don't you go gettin' so worked up over this you go gettin' yourself in another accident tomorrow, eh? 'Bout lost you that last time, an don't wanna do it again. You're still walking funny, an' I don't wanna be spendin' another eight months sittin' in the hospital feedin' you pop." She smiled, but he knew better. He also knew they shouldn't have sat at table three again. They always got into a little snit when they sat at table three. LeAnn told him he was being all crazy, but it was true.

V

Before heading out on the twenty-five-mile drive to Prar du Morte (pronounced "Praddymort") Friday morning, Koznowski stopped by the station. He'd asked Deputy Vandenberg to find out what she could about these Pollex Christi Ministries people. What they were all about, how many members, any criminal complaints, and most important of all where he might find them once he got into town. He also wanted to grab a cup of coffee before he left. He hated stopping on the road.

After he filled a paper cup with the scorched, dusty, weak coffee from the office pot, Vandenberg handed him an address written on a small piece of paper. He read it, confused. "The Village Inn Mall?" .

"Yeah?" she said. "It's like a strip mall deal. They rent out one of the spots there three, four days a week. Rest of the time it's usually used for A.A. meetings, stuff like that."

"Yah, super. Thanks." As he took a seat behind his desk, he flipped the paper over and found the other side blank. "You got anything else, there?"

"Well, yeah." She consulted the legal pad upon which she'd written some notes in a curlicue script left over from her junior high years. "But not a whole lot . . . I guess they been at this whole 'death threat' thing for a while now. Eight or nine years, maybe? But there've been only a couple official complaints about it." She flipped a page. "Oh, but here's something interesting, eh? Our Mr. Unterhumm there filed a complaint back in eighty-one. Never followed up on it, an' it's looking like no action was ever taken. But when he filled out the complaint form? It says here he wrote, 'I don't care if they kill me, so long as I'm allowed to finish my work first.'"

She looked up. They were both silent. Koznowski was about to take a sip of his coffee but paused. "Well that's kinda curious, eh?"

"Yeah, I thought so."

"No idea what he meant by all that?"

"No, uh-uh."

Koznowski stared at her for a moment. "All right then," he said. "Wonder if he finished it, whatever it was."

"Dunno. Hope so." Vandenberg glanced at her notes again as Koznowski folded the piece of paper with the address and slipped it into his breast pocket beneath his badge.

"Got one more thing here, Chief. Nobody else remembers this, but I guess there was another mortician over in Shawano who died four years back or so."

Koznowski stopped what he was doing. "What?"

"Yeah, an' he had some letters there, too, I guess."

"How was he killed?" Things were starting to come together. He could feel it.

"Oh, well, guess he had a heart attack. Something like that. He was eighty-one. But still, eh?"

The sheriff exhaled. "Yah, that's . . . super, eh?" He stood and began slipping into his heavy jacket. It was another chilly one out there, and there had been another inch or two of snow overnight. "That's real good work on short notice, there, Deputy. All that stuff's a big help. So how's them files coming over to the funeral home?"

"Y'mean since yesterday afternoon when you asked me to find all this?" she said, holding up the yellow pad. "Yeah, I ain't really made a heckuva lotta progress."

Koznowski almost smirked. "Oh, yah. That's right, ain't it?"

"Yeah . . . but you mean you want me to go back there?" She didn't care much for that idea one bit. The place was starting to give her the willies. "I figured the death threats would be, y'know, what you were looking for."

"Well, yah, but you found them death threats, so who knows what else you might find, eh?" He zipped up his jacket. "Besides, someone's gotta be there tomorrow to let them Cieszlwiczes in to clean up." He grabbed his hat. "Might as well have someone there who's doing something."

"Sure thing, yeah," she said, trying to hide the sigh. Koznowski limped toward the door, leaving the half cup of coffee behind on his desk. "You be careful out on them roads, eh?" she called after him. "No telling how long it'll take Gus to sober up an' get his plows out."

"Oh, you betcha," he called back. "Too early in the year for this much snow, eh?"

✠

Although the storm had dwindled to a mere sprinkling by about six that morning, the snow raised by the cars on the highway and the dust blowing off that eighteen-wheeler in front of him forced Koznowski to flip on his wipers and use his fog lights. He was gonna have to have a little chat with Gus about hitting the Yukon Jack too hard on the nights snow was forecast. He didn't get his plows and salt spreaders out after a snow—even a little snow like this one—it just led to more headaches for the Sheriff's Department.

Ah, he knew Gus, though. His wife had died three years previous during a snowstorm, so now these days whenever he saw that first flake he started hitting the Yukon Jack, just the way she had that night. Only difference is Gus usually has the damn good sense to stay at home and pass out when he does. Heck of a mess for everyone else, that's for sure.

It took Koznowski nearly two and a half hours trapped behind that extremely cautious truck driver to reach Prar du Morte. Sometimes there were disadvantages to driving a vehicle with blue lights on the roof. He kept an ear to the radio the whole way, but it sounded like the roads were pretty calm. Guess most everyone in Kausheenah County knew well enough by now to wait for Gus and his boys before they decided to go rushing off anywhere.

Prar du Morte wasn't a whole lot, town-wise. About four, five miles out the farms started getting smaller and closer together. The barns, tractors, and silos disappeared, replaced by two-story houses with long gravel driveways. Then there was the mile-long strip where the highway widened and you had your shops, cafés, the drugstore, the post office, and a few taverns. On the other side of the commercial stretch was the Resurrection

Episcopalian Church, then as you continued on south the houses start growing farther apart again and the farms reappear.

It was along that commercial stretch that Koznowski found the Village Inn strip mall without too much trouble. It was made up of a beauty parlor, a Sav-Less grocery, the bank, Francine's Cards and Gifts, and a community space, left open for use by recovering alcoholics and potentially murderous religious zealots.

He pulled the Kausheenah County Sheriff's Department four-by-four into the almost crowded lot and parked next to a rusting pickup. He nudged his glove back and looked at his watch. It was a little after twelve. "Sure do wish I knew what the hell I was doing," he said aloud. He checked in with Leona back at the station to let her know where he was, then stepped out of the truck.

Finding the makeshift church wasn't difficult. All he had to do was follow the sound of the singing, if you could call it that. If that sound was coming out of the bank, he thought, he was in more trouble down here than he realized.

As he crunched through the hard packed snow of the parking lot, a few of the shoppers heading back to their cars with sacks full of pre-Thanksgiving groceries gave him quizzical looks. It wasn't often they had much call for law enforcement around there.

Outside the beauty parlor next to the community space, a well-bundled man in his thirties was shoveling the snow off the sidewalk, piling it around the front end of a beat-up '79 Chevy.

"Heya there, officer." The man paused in his shoveling and pulled the red scarf away from his nose and mouth. "You goin' to the prayer meetin' there?"

Koznowski stopped. "Yah, chilly day for shovelin', eh?"

"Oh, you betcha. Gotta get done, though. Better now'n later when everyone's walked all over it."

"Yah, that's true there." Koznowski started to reach for the door, behind which the singing or whatever it was seemed to be reaching a crescendo. He could hear a shrill woman's voice wailing high above the others and some kind of music creeping around beneath it all that didn't seem to quite fit.

"Y'know," the man went on, "I ain't been over to Resurrection there in about three years now." He nodded farther down the road to the visible steeple. "Yah, see? One night back there I went over to my brother's place. This is my older brother Jerry I mean. He lives not too far away from me, an' his wife was makin' some supper so they asked me to visit, y'know? They're nice folks that way. Have me over an' stuff. So I walk over there about five or so—it was summer then—an' we have a real nice supper."

The sheriff could feel his toes growing numb despite the heavy leather boots and the three pairs of wool socks. He wanted to tell the handyman here that he was on official business, no time for neighborly gum flapping in the cold like this. But this seemed like the kind of guy who'd want details, so he kept his mouth shut.

"Then after supper, see, while the wife is cleanin' up the dishes an' such, my brother an' I split a doobie out in the backyard. Like I says it was summer. Oh, they got a nice backyard there, I tellya. Big swing for the kids an' all. So's anyway, I thanks Marlene—that's his wife, she's a sweetheart—so's I says good night."

Koznowski was about to interrupt him.

"But when I'm walkin' home, see? This was in the summer, so it's a real nice night out. Not too hot yet, y'know? No skeeters or nothin' 'cause it's been real dry. So's I'm walkin' home, see, an' then right over by Doug Haansen's place, I realize that, like, everything in the universe is connected, that . . . that this universe is inside each of us. An' that's when I realized, see, that if the whole universe was inside me like that, then I must be God. An' so I figures, if I'm God, why th' heck am I goin' to church? Right?" He banged the shovel once on the sidewalk to knock some of the snow loose. "That's why I don't go to church no more."

Koznowski forgot about his frozen feet and stared at the handyman. "Why in the hell you telling me this?" he asked, honestly curious.

"W'I'm just sayin'," the man said. "Whatever you're lookin' for in that prayer meetin' there, you can find straight from the horse's mouth right out here on the sidewalk, eh? I sing a heck of a lot better too."

It was a long few moments before Koznowski said, "Well all right, then." He finally grabbed the door to the community center as the handyman resumed his shoveling.

There was a great shuffling among the congregation as the sheriff stepped inside. He was accompanied by a shear of frigid wind that sliced through the room until the door hissed shut again. It was warm in there, and the thick air smelled of sweat, stale cigarette smoke, and insecticide. The singing had ended. To the right, an elderly woman sitting before a small keyboard looked defeated. An electronic samba beat continued chirping with no melody to accompany it. At the front of the room, a tiny, bird-faced woman in glasses and a long white robe rocked from side to side, her eyes closed, her clawed fingers reaching toward the ceiling. Propped on a flimsy wooden easel behind her, a yellow posterboard sign read, in hand-drawn block letters:

> *Pollex Christi Ministrys*
> *Rev. Euglina Boefinck*
> *Preeching the One True Creed*
> *Since 1978*

Sheriff Koznowski wondered idly why they would choose a name like Pollex Christi when they seemed to have such trouble spelling to begin with. Unless the name was spelled wrong too. No matter, he guessed, so long as they knew what they were talking about.

"Do not be deceived, my children," the Reverend Boefinck was saying in a sharp, unpleasant voice. "Do not let these masters of death, these purveyors of falsehoods—these destroyers of the soul—lie to you! It is Satan who speaks through them, preaching an unholy gospel of laws and public health statutes. It is the Gospel of Annihilation! We all know that Satan is a liar, my children, and these are all lies! You can buy salvation, but it is not in the form of an airtight, waterproof coffin. You buy salvation for yourselves and your families only by helping spread the word of the One True Creed, and by making it clear to your loved ones that if you want to walk with the Lord when the mighty day of judgment comes, this ministry must be kept alive!" A tight smile curled her mouth but her eyes remained closed. "And when that day of judgment comes, my children—oh, I can see it!—when that day comes the Lord will restore each and every one of you to wholeness and beauty like we've never known on the surface of this sinful planet . . ."

A husky blond teenager was working his way up and down the four narrow aisles of folding chairs, holding out a paper sack into which each congregant was dropping a handful of coins or a few bills.

"If we," Rev. Boefinck continued as the collection was taken, "those few of us in this room today, if we're the only ones walking with our Heavenly Father on that glorious day, then so be it. Let those others who refused to hear the word lay stiff in their boxes, unable to move or cry out, to say 'I'm down here!' For they were deceived by Satan and do not deserve to dwell in the Heavenly Kingdom for eternity."

"*I'm down here,*" the congregation mumbled in something approximating unison. "*Amen.*"

After being handed the pitiful sack by the blond youth, the preacher shook it lightly and finally opened her eyes. Apparently the service was over. The old woman with the keyboard seemed grateful to finally snap off that incessant samba beat, and the worshippers stood and began gathering their coats and hats. Some were alone, Koznowski noted, while others had dragged the whole family along, including a number of children who should've been in school on a Friday morning.

Probably home schoolers, the sheriff thought. *Look the type.* As he stood in the corner waiting, he studied their faces. None of them looked straight off the bat like a potential murderer, but you can never tell. One family in particular stopped him. The son, about twelve, was a scrawny lad. His wide-eyed and dour face seemed too small for his skull and his chin came nearly to a point. What struck Koznowski as strangest of all was that, though still a preadolescent, the boy already had a mustache. At that tender age, he already looked like a seedy bookie.

His older sister had an enormous jaw. An enormous forehead as well, the brow overhanging and permanently shading her widely spaced eyes like some kind of rock formation. Her blond curls resembled a poorly knitted doilie slapped awkwardly atop her square head. But she was smiling a sad, crooked smile. She looked like she was always smiling, unlike her brother.

Koznowski forced his eyes away from the misbegotten children and stepped through the departing congregation toward the preacher. Every one of the twenty or so members of the congregation seemed to be misshapen somehow. Some were missing eyes and hands. Two were in wheelchairs. A couple more were on crutches, and one of them was missing a leg, the empty and filthy pant leg dragging on the floor. There were at least two pronounced goiters he caught, one woman had an oozing cyst or tumor the size of a golf ball on her upper lip, and another had drooping sacks of flesh like misplaced scrotums swinging from her temples and beneath her chin. It was little wonder this kook was promising them they'd be whole again some day, and little wonder they followed her. Apart from grunts and sighs, none of them had spoken a word since the service ended. Koznowski began to wonder if there was something wrong with the water down here. Some chemical runoff from the paper mills to the north or something. Better to avoid the water altogether if he could.

"Reverend . . ."—he glanced at the cardboard sign—"ah . . . Boefinck?" He pulled the wallet from his pocket and flipped it open to reveal his identification. "Sheriff Leonard Koznowski, Kausheenah County Sheriff's Department. I need to ask you some questions, iffen you don't mind."

The blond boy appeared immediately at her side. "The Blessed Reverend speaks only when the Lord speaks through her." He seemed quite serious about this.

Koznowski looked from the boy to the woman then back to the boy. Then back to the woman, whose thin lips were pressed so tightly together they were turning white. "Well all right, then, I guess," he said. "That case I'll be needing to ask the Lord a few questions." He reached into his breast pocket and slipped out a copy of one of the death threats found in Unterhumm's desk, unfolded it, and showed it to her. "Do you recognize this letter?"

Euglina Boefinck's head lolled to one side and her eyes rolled back. For a moment she went limp and it seemed she was about to collapse to the filthy carpeting like a neglected marionette. Koznowski began reaching out to catch her but she stiffened again, her fingers curling inward and arms slowly rising. Her lips began to tremble, and a soft, nasal babbling sound emerged from her mouth.

Concluding the reverend preacher was having a grand mal seizure, Koznowski leapt into clumsy action, knocking folding chairs out of the way to clear a space for her to flop around without injuring herself too badly. "Lie down, ma'am!" he shouted at the woman. "You don't wanna, y'know, hit your head." Then he turned to the blond youth, who was suddenly standing beside him. "You got a towel or something there? Something for her to chew on, I mean." The blond kid seemed strangely impassive given the circumstances. "Don't just be standing there, c'mon!" The Reverend Boefinck, he noticed, was still on her feet.

"The Lord says, 'Of course I recognize the letter you idiot. I dictated it.'"

Koznowski's frantic and spasmodic attempts at first aid quieted. He looked to the woman, who was still mumbling a string of nonsense syllables, then to the boy, who had spoken. "What's that, now?"

"The Lord is speaking through the Blessed Reverend," the boy said calmly. "I'm translating for you."

The baffled sheriff looked again at the woman, still on her feet and muttering away. If she was having a seizure, it was unlike anything he had ever seen before. "Really?"

"The Lord asks that you stop all this nonsense and start listening to the words of the Most High." He cocked his head upward, awaiting the next divine message.

Koznowski looked at the boy, then at the woman. "Yah, okay then. But you're saying she's okay, there. No kinda, y'know, neurological trouble?"

"The Blessed Reverend is merely an earthly vessel for the Lord God Almighty."

The sheriff frowned, sniffing a con. "She was speaking English there just fine-like when I came in."

"That was different."

Koznowski wasn't liking this game. "Yah, okay, gotcha, sure." He nodded, playing along nevertheless. "So she heal people, too, being a vessel an' all?"

"Of course she has the gift of healing, as given through her by the Lord." Beside them the Reverend Boefinck continued gibbering quietly.

"She heal any of them folks who was here earlier?"

"Most of them, yes."

"Whoa," Koznowski said, recalling the poor thing with the face scrotums. "Hate to see what kinda shape they were in before, eh?" This was ridiculous, and his legs hurt. "So can I sit, d'you suppose? I'm thinking we'd all be more comfortable that way, eh?" He bent and righted a few of the nearby chairs he'd knocked over.

"Look, is this gonna take long?" the suddenly agitated teen asked. "I gotta get to practice."

"Gonna take as long as it takes, there, junior," Koznowski replied, moving a few more chairs.

The boy led the preacher woman to one and she took a seat, still babbling in a whisper. The kid was going to have an awful lot of catching up to do if he wanted to translate all that. Unless most of what Koznowski was hearing was just static coming down from heaven (which is what it sounded like to him).

The sheriff took a seat facing her. "So ma'am . . . ah, Reverend Boefinck," he said, unsure how to address her (or God, for that matter). "Did you know that sending threats like that through the mails there is a federal offense?"

In response, the Reverend Boefinck spouted several more holy grunts and syllables, and Koznowski waited patiently for the boy to fill him in. He wondered how long it took them to work this routine out.

The teen was growing more tense, his voice a hint sharper. "The Lord says he is well aware of your earthly laws, but that they don't exactly apply to him. And besides, the letters weren't sent through the mail. They were all hand delivered."

"But . . ." Koznowski felt increasingly foolish directing his questions to the woman and then waiting for some snot-nosed high school student to translate. She wasn't Cambodian, for chrissakes. "It's still against the law to threaten to kill people, smart guy. And what is your name, anyway?" he said to the teen.

"Ezekiel Hoseah Boefinck," he answered flatly. He'd started to tap his right foot, anxious to be done with the questions. "And the Lord suggests you show the letter to a judge or something. Others have tried. When the Lord composes a letter, He knows what He's doing. They don't say anywhere that anybody in the Pollex Christi Ministries is gonna be doing any killing. It's just a warning from God Almighty."

"It's still against the law."

More noise spilled from the tiny woman's small, tight mouth.

"The Lord asks," her son inquired. "Haven't you been listening, dummy? It's the One True Creed."

"Oh, Jesus H. Christ, that's it. Enough." Koznowski made a cutting motion with his left hand. "You're gonna put an end to these shenanigans right now. I'm either gonna talk to the Reverend Boefinck here all straight, or I'm gonna run both of youse in right here and now and charge you with . . . foolishness. An' if the Lord wants to meet us at the station to serve as your counsel, well, that's up to him."

Rev. Boefinck's body shuddered violently and she opened her eyes. Beside her, Ezekiel cast an exasperated look toward the wall and clucked his tongue loudly. At this rate he would never make practice. The woman stared at the sheriff, seemingly dazed. "All right Ezekiel," she said. "Go start folding up the chairs. I'll wrap this up so you can get to practice on time, sweetheart."

"Yah, I figured as much," Koznowski said.

As her presumed son stepped away to start folding the gray steel chairs, the clouds began breaking over the parking lot outside the window, allowing the cold afternoon light to filter into the dingy room.

"So you all set?" he asked the Reverend Boefinck, now that she'd fully returned to earth. "Feeling okay there? Now let's try this again, eh? What of it there, you recognize this?" He snapped the letter in front of her, angry at himself as much as with her for having wasted so much damn time playing along with their nonsense.

She sighed. "Of *course* I recognize it. The Lord God Almighty dictated it and I typed it."

"Mm-hmm," Koznowski said, folding the letter and returning it to his pocket. "The man who received this one received six identical letters over the past few years."

She nodded slightly, satisfied. "That sounds about right."

"Uh-huh. So that's all God has to say? The same damn thing over and over?"

"If the message doesn't take, yes." She didn't seem in the least concerned about any of this.

"Yah, but I'm just curious, here. Seems to me, right, that if it didn't take that first time he'd mix things up a little. Y'know, try a new angle folks might take to better?"

"The One True Creed doesn't need a new angle."

They were both silent for a moment.

"Yah, okeydoke, then," Koznowski said. "Were you also aware the mortician who got all those letters and his assistant were murdered this past Tuesday up in Beaver Rapids?" He watched for a reaction, but saw nothing. Behind her, Ezekiel was roughly gathering the chairs, clanging them into leaning stacks against the wall.

"No, I was not aware of that. I do not concern myself with such earthly things. But I can't say as I'm much heartbroken to learn there's one less undertaker in the world."

"Yah, super, then," he said, ready to snap the cuffs on her right there. "Very Christian of you. So tell me, does this One True Creed of yours include, y'know, killing folks? Just trying to establish wha'cha call motive here, y'understand."

Boehnck glared at him through the square lenses of her glasses. Despite the clearly simmering anger, when she spoke her voice remained even. "The One True Creed, Sheriff, is from the Holy Bible. The direct word of the Most High. And it states that embalming and cremation of the dead are an abomination unto the Lord, a desecration of these holy vessels we will need again on the day of Judgment."

"Yah, fine," Koznowski said. "But that doesn't really answer the question there, does it?"

There were a few more moments of tense silence as he waited for a response. "So that's it? That's the One True Creed? No embalming?" He almost started laughing. "I mean . . . I mean all that other stuff there in the Bible and *this* is what you got out of it?"

The Reverend Boefinck was not amused. "Where would we be today if the Savior Jesus had been embalmed? They destroy the organs and fill the body with wax. If they'd done that to Jesus, He couldn't live again. He wouldn'ta been able to even move, so He couldn'ta been resurrected, could He now? If He wasn't resurrected, then we aren't saved from our sins." She stared at the sheriff in triumph. "And like Jesus, if we're embalmed, how can we be risen from the dead on the day of Judgment, when all our bodies"— she waved her arms generally toward the empty room, obviously slipping back into character—"will be risen from the grave to stand before the Lord God Almighty. You just tell me how could that happen if we have no organs anymore and can't move 'cause we're all fulla wax like that?" The more she spoke, the more animated she became, the more he caught the northern Wisconsin accent sneaking back into her voice. She'd done a good job of burying it up to that point. "And you been cremated, what'cha gonna do then? No corporeal body at all? No nothin'? Just ashes blown away? No sir it says in the Bible the dead should be wrapped in a clean white cloth and placed in the ground. That's all. End of story."

"Ah-huh," Koznowski said doubtfully once it was clear she'd finished her sermon. "So this is why you been threatenin' morticians all over the state, eh?"

Rev. Boefinck was well rehearsed in this, either in preparation for this specific situation or simply as part of her general routine. "Those people who mutilate the dead bodies for money are nothing but agents of Satan who are preventing millions of good and faithful Christians from experiencin' the true resurrection an' life everlasting. Our job here at the ministry is to spread the Truth and the Light and such. Those letters were not threats. Merely warnings directed from the Lord Most High. Suggestions that they change their wicked ways and leave the work of Satan behind."

He hadn't driven down to Prar du Morte that morning in hopes of getting into a goddamned theological debate. His question for this woman was a very simple one. "An' so you murder those undertakers who don't take your advice, is that the deal?"

The question did not throw her. "I am a mailman for the Lord, Sheriff," she said firmly. "Not an assassin for Satan."

That sounded to him like another well-prepared answer.

Ezekiel, meanwhile, leaned the last of the unoccupied chairs against the scarred, smoke-darkened wall and returned to stand behind his mother, arms folded. He alternately glared at the sheriff and glanced at his watch. It struck Koznowski they were both playing it like they'd been through this conversation before.

"Yah, lemme ask you, then," Koznowski pressed. "Where were you Tuesday morning?" He had the estimated time of death from Cameron, which is why he didn't ask them when Tuesday morning. He was waiting for an opening.

With a heavy and annoyed breath, Rev. Boefinck replied, "We have a prayer service that goes from six to ten every Tuesday and Thursday morning. Eight to twelve Wednesdays and Fridays. After Tuesday's meeting is when those drug addict people move in here to have their thing with their cigarettes."

"And you had a meeting this past Tuesday."

"The Lord God wouldn't allow me to miss one, Sheriff. The spreading of the One True Creed is far too important. So, yes, I was here. If you don't believe me—I know what you cops are like—you can ask anyone around here. Ask that blaspheming barber next door." She gestured through the wall with contempt. "He opens at the same time."

"And your boy was here?" He nodded at Ezekiel.

"Sheriff," she sighed. "Yes. We were both here. Now I suggest you take your questions and go looking for the real killer. But I will say without the least guilt or shame I'm not one bit sorry he did what he did, whoever it is."

The front door opened, and a blast of frozen air blew three forsaken souls into the storefront, gaunt men with hollow eyes and camouflage hunting jackets who cast quick, nervous glances at the sheriff and the good reverend woman as they shambled toward the folding chairs.

"Now if we're free to go," she added, nodding toward the men. "We need to clear the room for the alcoholic meeting. Hey Sheriff, maybe one of *them* did it, huh? So why don't you go persecute them for a while?

He was just no damn good at this, that's all there was to it.

After taking down their full names and the names of their parishioners and promising he'd be back, Koznowski prepared to leave the storefront. That would be a relief. There was a heavy air of disappointment about the place, as if everyone who stepped foot through the door had deposited a bit of their own personal failure in the room for safekeeping. Now it seemed he was about to leave a bit of his own.

He paused before opening the door and made a small show of carefully pulling on his gloves while pondering the parking lot beyond the glass. "Well," he said with a sigh, making sure it was loud enough for everyone in the room to hear. "Guess I'll just have to go heed the worms then, eh?"

He whipped his head around hoping to catch even the slightest hint of recognition in their faces. Rev. Boefinck was staring at him, confused.

"What?" she asked.

"It's all right," Koznowski said as he reached for the door. "It's nothing. I'll be in touch."

"God be with you, Sheriff, regardless," the preacher said before turning back to the table where that day's offering waited in the paper sack.

Koznowski crunched through the parking lot and climbed into his truck feeling the weight of his disappointment in his stomach and his legs. He turned the key to let the truck warm up for a few minutes. Thick white exhaust billowed from the tailpipe. Give the aching in his legs a chance to ease up some, too, once the heat took hold. He stared through the windshield across the white parking lot at the storefront. For a moment he was tempted to hit the gas and plow the truck through the fucking window, but that probably wouldn't help much. Besides, roll he was on, he'd probably hit the gift shop instead.

He was still absolutely certain she was the one he was after. Somehow the Reverend Boefinck or some of her followers were directly or indirectly responsible for those two murders. It was just up to him to prove it. Not an easy thing to do when you didn't have any tangible evidence apart from some letters that may or may not be threats. He didn't even have enough to bring them in and hold them until he did have what he needed. He sat helpless and unmoving behind the wheel, unsure where to go, what to do. No, he sure wasn't very good at this.

"Well, horseshit," he whispered. He checked in with Leona, revved the engine a couple times, then headed back to the station, praying Gus had finally gotten up and moving in the meantime.

He'd never had much time for the religious thing. Not since he was a kid, anyway. After that it was all over. He guessed he could understand the people who got it and needed it, for whatever reason, and he had nothing against them. Even these Pollex whatever people. Whatever trips your trigger, right?

And those poor sonsabitches in there sure needed something, what with their damned inbred kids and deformities and all. As a church, he supposed it made as much sense as some of the others he'd heard about. Except maybe for that "killing undertakers" part.

No, religion just wasn't for him, is all. Seemed a little silly, especially for someone in his business. He may not've seen too many murders (or any before these two), but he still saw crap enough out there to give a man pause. He'd felt the same way long before he ever thought of getting into law enforcement. Sometimes he wondered if it had anything to do with his school.

He passed a pickup headed in the opposite direction. A small buck, maybe a six-pointer, was tied to the roof, a visible tag flopping from its bound front legs. The animal's head bounced on its loose neck over the windshield, and four arrows quivered upright from its side. As he drew closer, the driver honked his horn and flashed his lights at Koznowski. He peered through the windshield and saw two hunters excitedly pointing toward the roof. One raised a celebratory beer.

The sheriff knew better than to pull them over and slap them with a citation. This time of year in these parts he did the best thing he could do. He flashed his own lights, gave them a thumbs-up, and let them drive on. One thing about the snow, it made the hunters happy. Given hunters made up ninety percent of Kausheenah's population, an inch or two of snow in the woods tended to make everyone a little easier on everyone else.

What had he been thinking about again? His school, that's right.

Other schools in the region had mascots like cougars, falcons, grizzly bears, tigers, pirates—fierce and savage beasts of one kind or another. Not back at Beaver Rapids High School. Nope, they weren't satisfied with some piddly little mortal beast with puny claws and fangs. They skipped the middle man entirely and went straight to the top.

Sure they called their football, basketball, and track teams the Blue Devils, but when you got right down to the gritty the school mascot was Satan. Walk down the main hallway or go into the cafeteria, or step foot in the gym, and the walls were covered with pictures of Satan. Everywhere you looked there he was, staring down at you like Big Brother while you ate your lunch or tried to reach your locker before heading upstairs to social studies. How can you go through three, four years like that, inundated with leering images of the Master of All Lies every single goddamn day and not let it seep into your head somehow?

It would be easy, he supposed, to point at Satan's influence during his high school years as an explanation for his lack of faith as an adult. Sometimes that's even what he told people when the question came up (which it rarely did), but he fell back on that story only because he didn't want to tell the truth.

As he drove past Ed Lachman's farm, he saw Ed out by the barn with some of his cattle. Koznowski knew what was going on. Happened every year around this time. Ed was out there with a stool, a bucket of white paint, and a brush.

He was moving from beast to beast and, in block letters large enough for Koznowski to read from where he sat, was painting COW on both sides of each. Ed had lost too damn many head over the years to hunters who, so consumed with bloodlust, could no longer distinguish between a ten-point buck and a dairy cow.

The sheriff leaned on his horn and waved. Ed waved back with the paintbrush.

Koznowski could pinpoint the very moment he first let go of religion. The night he tried not to think about anymore. He was seven years old, never told anyone what happened, and never told anyone that he'd given up on religion. As the years passed the feelings grew only more adamant, and by the time he graduated (already having decided to become a cop) he thought religion was for the desperate, the lonely, the dull-witted or otherwise helpless. He knew—somehow he just knew—there was nothing else out there, nothing beyond this life and this world, so we better make the most of it here. Unfortunately most of the damn fools didn't seem to feel the same way.

In later years people of assorted faiths would tell him Satan was making him think that way, and sometimes, well, he had to wonder.

Still, after only a few years on the force and having seen the sorts of things staunch churchgoers could do to each other, he held more tightly than ever to his idea.

This case, though. It was turning into much more than he'd bargained for. Plus his legs were starting to hurt again in spite of the heat in the truck. Keeping one hand on the wheel, he slid the square silver pill box out of his pocket, popped the lid open with his thumb, and laid it on the seat. He snatched up two of the tiny white pills and dropped them under his tongue.

Up ahead he saw the Big Carp, eighteen feet of bottom-feeding fiberglass wonderment, curled and jumping like a marlin. No one knew why the owners of the Slab City bar opted to park a giant carp in front of the place, or maybe no one bothered to ask. Maybe it was simply one of those things no one ever stopped to really think about for too long. It was just the Slab City Carp. To Koznowski, though, it meant he was only a mile from the station. He always looked forward to seeing that stupid carp.

VI

"Heya, Deke, you look like you just got fished out of a mousetrap."

Keller looked up from the typewriter, where he'd been pecking away with one finger. His eyes were red and his uniform was stained and rumpled. "Some things just ain't meant to go together, that's for damn sure."

"Oh, yah, don't I know it." Koznowski was holding a sheet of paper. "Hey, and forgot to ask. You bag yourself a twelve-pointer last weekend?"

Keller's eyebrows came together and he was silent for a confused moment. "What the hell are you talking about, there, Chief?"

"Well you're a hunter, right? Always going on about heading up north with your dad and brother."

Keller paused again. "But . . . deer season don't start till next weekend."

The sheriff glanced at the calendar on the wall behind the deputy and saw a red circle around the twenty-fifth. Now Koznowski was confused. "But I been seeing deer strapped to cars all up an' down the highway. Saw a nice one on my way back today."

"Them's bow hunters. It's bow season now. Guns come out next Saturday."

"Really?" Koznowski asked. "Always thought they were the same thing."

"Nope. You been sheriff here how long now and don't know when deer season is?"

"Yah, well." Not caring to push this line of conversation any further, Koznowski turned his attention to the paper in his hand. "Okay, then. Now, Deke, here you go." He handed the stupid smirking deputy the list, glad he'd chosen Keller for the job. Damn smartass kids. "This here's a list of everyone we know of who's associated with Pollex Christi Ministries. Need you to run a check on alla them."

Deputy Keller eyed the list warily, then looked at the sheriff. "Alla 'em here, Chief?"

Koznowski gave him a quick roll of the eyes. "Yah, Deke, alla them. That's why I said alla them. Jeeze Louise. Every name on the list." To be fair there were twenty-six names on the list, but still. It was going to take some doing down in records.

"Aw, jeeze hey, that's a lot." Keller glanced at the list again. "But I suppose."

"Yah, super then. Glad you're willing, there." Koznowski sometimes wondered how they'd ended up with so many goddamned whiners in the Sheriff's Department. It sure didn't used to be that way. Maybe these days they should keep kids in high school until they turn twenty-three. Either that or pitch them into the real world at fourteen. Maybe then they wouldn't be such mollycoddled, sniveling little dips by the time they reached his department. Every time he asked them to do something it was whine, whine, whine.

He stopped and gave his head a brief shake. He was getting off track. "And Deke, now, I mean I wantchata look for everything down there, eh? Assaults, reckless driving, domestic disturbances, weapons charges. We're looking here for a fella who might be, y'know, the violent type. Check 'em out for any kinda mental problems there, too, drug addicts, regular kooks. Anything at all."

"On alla them."

"Yah on alla them, like I said. Cripes, Keller, you got shit in your ears?"

Keller was reading down the list again. "What's the deal? Mosta these names don't even sound Polish."

"Just go do it, eh? Please." (That lady from the State Labor Relations Board who'd come by a year or two back told Koznowski he had to start saying "please" and "thank you" more often when asking his officers to do their fucking jobs. He was surprised she didn't tell him to bake them a damned cake every time they turned in a report.)

"When'd you want this back?"

Koznowski gave him a look that told the deputy exactly when he wanted it back. "If you stop just standing there flapping your gums, you'd be gettin' it done a lot faster, eh?"

Keller slowly pushed himself to his feet, reading the list through again as if he couldn't believe what he'd been asked to do. He stopped suddenly, eyes still on the page, and called after Koznowski, who was returning to his desk. "Hey, Chief? This here Ezekiel Boefinck . . . you're not talkin' about *the* Ezekiel Boefinck, are ya? Y'know, E.Z.?"

The paperwork was starting to pile up on Koznowski's desk. As he lowered himself into the chair, he didn't even want to look at it. Some people got no goddamn consideration. Here he is, hands full with a double homicide and they're still out there driving drunk and getting in bar fights and slapping their wives around. "I'm sure I don't know."

"Blond kid, 'bout seventeen, just under six feet?"

"Yah, I s'pose that'd be him."

Keller's face brightened. "Jeeze, Chief, don't you recognize him?" Koznowski said nothing but was suddenly curious. "He's the star running back for the Hawks. He's the one took 'em to state last season. This season, too, they win their next two games. His picture's in the *Chronicle* most every darn week for something—plays football, baseball, basketball. All these school awards? Hell, damn kid's gonna be an' Eagle Scout soon, they say."

"That so?"

"Oh, you betcha. I'm real surprised you don't know him. Like I says, he's always in the paper, there."

"Yah, guess I should read more careful then. His ma's a crackpot."

"Jeeze, Chief, I can't believe you ain't hearda E.Z. Boefinck. That's what they call him—'E.Z.' for Ezekiel an' also 'cause he makes it look so *easy*, see?"

"Okay that's super. You should pay extra attention to him."

Keller studied the sheriff, an odd concern on his face. "Hey, Chief. I mean, you're gonna catch the Pack this Sunday at least ain't'cha?"

"Vikes three o'clock, so long as I ain't needed here."

"Okay, that's a relief at least," Keller said. "Don't know when huntin' season starts, don't know E.Z. Boefinck. I was startin' to think you might be turnin' a little fruity on us or somethin'."

"Just go find out about them names, Deke, won'cha? *Jeeze*." Koznowski continued sorting through the mess of papers on his desk.

It was four fifteen on Friday afternoon and it was already getting dark outside. Those officers who weren't out patrolling the highways were fielding complaint calls about Gus. His own drive back from Prar du Morte that afternoon hadn't been that bad, roadwise (easier than the trip down, that's for sure), but the folks over on the side roads where there'd been some drifting were having a time of it. He'd already made two calls over to Gus's place to find out what the story was, but he got no answer either time. Foolishly or not, it left him hoping things were at least getting under way. If not, the next step would be sending Ziegler over there to make sure Gus wasn't passed out in the tub or dead. Of course, sad as it was to think, if he was dead it would probably make everyone's life a little easier.

"Hey, Leona," he called from his desk. "You talked to the mayor yet?"

"He called three times so far," she shouted back.

"But you talked to him, right?"

"Oh, yah?"

Koznowski nodded. "Good. That means I don't gotta talk to him."

"That's not what he says."

He honestly didn't care much about the snow situation. They'd seen worse. It was just two and a quarter inches, for godsakes. He had worse things to think about. Three and a half days after the murders and he was as lost as ever. There were other cases coming in to deal with—a couple drunk and disorderlies, a couple domestic disturbances. Plus he had to start making security arrangements for the county's Thanksgiving Day parade in Beaver Rapids. Not that there was ever much need for security at a parade consisting of two high school marching bands, several tractors and other pieces of farm machinery, a small float carrying that year's Beaver Princess, some volunteer firefighters in a convertible throwing candy to the crowd, and a group of kids walking down the street carrying balloons, but there you go. There were always a few folks (he could already name them) who showed up drunk, and the scramble for the tossed candy had led to the occasional minor scuffle. But with this murder case hanging over his head he couldn't focus on any of the other bullshit. If he didn't have it wrapped up soon, everyone he saw at that damned parade was gonna be giving him the business for it. Who needs that on Thanksgiving? Just go eat your damn turkey and shut the hell up.

✠

This is just dumb, Deputy Vandenberg thought to herself as she flipped through another file folder stuffed with funeral bills, receipts, and invoices. *Here all goddamn weekend. He knows who did it, he says, so why am I still sitting in this fucking place looking for clues?* She was anxious to get back to the station and do something real on this case.

It hadn't bothered her at first, but after four or five days, being alone in the Unterhumm Funeral Home was starting to get to her. A couple times, especially when she'd been there late, she could swear she'd heard footsteps. When she went to investigate, though, there was never anyone there. She wished she knew how to turn on some music or something. That canned funeral home music probably wouldn't help much, but if the chief wanted her to come back tomorrow, maybe she'd bring a radio from home. Pick up one of those Walkmans, maybe.

On the desk behind her there still sat a small stack of files she didn't really understand. Most of the things she'd seen were pretty straightforward—fees for caskets and embalming and cremation and urns and room rentals. The kind of bill she saw when her brother died. These other ones, though, were odd. Instead of fees for funerals or cremations, they seemed to involve parts of bodies, not whole people. Bones and organs instead of "Harold Johaansen." A few—quite a few—didn't have any names at all attached to them, only numbers. And instead of being addressed to the surviving families, these had been sent to medical schools and hospitals, even a couple army bases. It was strange, even if they weren't exactly what you'd call "clues." The bills were a lot bigger than regular funeral bills too. She couldn't make sense of it. It was probably nothing, but best not to overlook anything. She'd show the chief, see if he knew what they were.

Tired of looking at files, she stood, stretched, left Unterhumm's office, and wandered down the carpeted hallway to what she guessed had been Kirby Mudge's little apartment. Must be weird living where you work, she thought. Especially if you work at an undertaker's. The building was so deathly quiet even the sound of her own footsteps on the carpet seemed to get sucked away into the walls.

The door was unlocked. By all initial appearances, Kirby's room was as bare as Unterhumm's, with a bed, a hot plate, a small refrigerator, a telephone. That was something Unterhumm didn't have, she noted, a phone. Kirby also had a small television. She sat on the edge of the bed and snapped it on for a moment. Black and white and the reception was terrible. That was the thing about this town—if you didn't spring for cable, your TV reception was for shit. She snapped it off and idly opened the nightstand drawer. Three plastic amber-colored bottles were tucked inside along with some pens and rubber bands and a lighter. She examined one of the bottles. Valium. And someone else's name was on the prescription.

Guess it's too late to bust him on possession, she thought, but she'd still return them to the station as evidence.

Curious now, she began poking around the room more thoroughly—in the closet and the dresser and the fridge. With some effort, she yanked open the dresser's middle drawer. On a hunch, she dug beneath the rolls of dark socks and the neatly folded stacks of underwear, where she found Kirby's porn stash. There wasn't much of it, but what was there told her more about Mr. Mudge's personal proclivities than she or anyone needed to know. She didn't know people were even capable of doing some of those things, let alone would want to take pictures of it. She left the magazines where they were, covering them once again with the socks and underwear before shoving the drawer closed.

While she was there, she took a quick peek under the bed. She wasn't expecting to find anything but dustballs and so was mildly surprised to find a black metal strongbox. It wasn't large, so she slid it out and examined it.

Well, it was a box, and it was locked all right. A small label on the lid read MEAT.

I sure hope he ain't really keeping any meat in there.

She leaned in and took a cautious sniff. Thankfully, she couldn't smell rotting meat or anything else. It was probably nothing—just more gay S&M porn or something—but she decided to take that back with her too, along with the prescription bottles and the files. She glanced around the room again, but there didn't appear to be any other obvious places to poke around. Kirby's place had certainly been more interesting than Unterhumm's, at least for a few short minutes.

She looked at her watch. Yeah, she figured she'd put in enough of a day here. She'd drag all this shit back to the station and see what they could make of it there.

✠

Dwight didn't like it when important people like the policeman stopped by to talk to Mr. Squire. Mr. Squire always got very nervous when that happened, and when he got nervous he always took it out on Dwight. He knew other important people were coming again sometime soon. A few minutes after the phone rang that morning, Mr. Squire came downstairs and told him to hide in the chilly room with the metal tables and the dead people. It was the usual thing. Dwight was supposed to stay down there until Mr. Squire came and got him, and if he heard Mr. Squire bringing someone downstairs with him—he always stomped on the stairs in a special way to let him know—Dwight was supposed to hide in one of the cooler drawers, just like a dead person. He wanted to hide in the smiling bags of death, but Mr. Squire said no, that it had to be the drawer. He didn't like hiding in the cooler drawers. It wasn't the smell so much—he liked the smell—but it was cold and sticky in there, and Mr. Squire always sprayed him down with a hose after he was allowed to climb out. Just to clean him off, Mr. Squire said.

So far that morning Dwight had been lucky. He heard the important people show up but they hadn't come downstairs yet. He pulled an empty drawer open, just in case. He knew what he was doing. Dwight always knew what he was doing. Mr. Squire knew that, and that's why Mr. Squire asked him to do things that maybe other people wouldn't do. Dwight was good, and when he did good Mr. Squire was nice to him. He'd been mean that morning, but when the important people were gone he knew Mr. Squire would be nice again.

He looked over at the new lady who'd come in the night before. Mr. Squire was supposed to fix her that afternoon. If he was real nice he might leave Dwight alone with her for a little bit. He knew he didn't dare do anything now. Not after what happened last time.

He leaned his broom against the wall, took a furtive look around, then tiptoed over to the table where the lady was lying. She wasn't real old. Dwight leaned over her face and stared at her. Then he leaned in more closely and smelled her breath.

Giggling, he tore himself away and skipped across the room to grab the broom.

✠

"What're you talking about there, 'clean'?"

"All clean as a whistle is what, Chief. No bullshit. Not a parking violation, no barking dog complaints, no nothin'. Though most of these folks are farmers, so I guess complainin' about a barkin' dog would be pretty dumb, eh?"

Koznowski closed his eyes. "You only been at it a day, Deke. You couldn'ta gone through everything, there."

"Well, yah? There's nothin' there, see, so that's why it went so quick."

Koznowski stared at Keller. There's just no way a group that size could be completely clean. It's impossible. "You're sure you did this proper? You talk to Jackie in records? 'Cause I'm telling you, Deputy, I don't care how far back you have to go, you miss anything on this it's gonna be your hide."

Keller was growing defensive and pitiful. "I was down there with her most all day. Give her a call an' ask. An' it was no fun, I'll tell you that. You ever spend five, six hours in a room with her?"

"Woman gets lonely down there, likes having someone to talk to."

"Yah, she farts a lot too."

Koznowski raised his hand. "All right, I believe you, there, but I mean, you bet I'm gonna call Jackie an' check. I'm just letting you know I believe you."

"Thanks a lot there, Chief." He almost turned to leave. "Hey, I was thinking about somethin' while I was lookin' up all these folks."

"Mm-hmm?" Koznowski was scanning the names again, a neat red check mark next to each one on the list. He guessed that bit of record keeping was Jackie's doing. He still couldn't believe every last one of them was spotless. That right there was a little suspicious. No one's that clean. Even he wasn't that clean, and he was the damned sheriff.

"So I was thinkin', if like you say these folks believe that the only ones who're gonna be resurrected by, y'know, God or whatever are the ones who ain't been embalmed, then come Judgment Day the only ones, pretty much anyway, the only ones who're gonna be resurrected are hookers who been killed an' dumped by the side of the highway. Who else is left, right? Well, them an' these Polack Christi folks."

The sheriff looked up at the grinning deputy. "Deputy, that's . . . ah . . . yeah, you should bounce that one offen your ma at dinner tonight."

"She's makin' a hot dish!"

✠

"Well Captain I'm not the kind of woman who takes pleasure in tellin' deceitful lies, so I won't say I'm happy to see you again."

"Yah, lyin's a sin," Sheriff Koznowski agreed. "I wouldn'ta believed you if you'd said you were happy to see me. But I'm hoping you understand that I got a job to do, here, so just keep tellin' the truth like that, an' it'll be a lot easier for all of us. Now, two men been murdered, an' it's up to me to figure out who did it. Right now, since we're being honest, you're the only one who had any kinda motive. An' it's 'sheriff,' iffen you don't mind."

Rev. Boefinck was staring at him through the screen door, her small mouth pinched with anger and distrust. "That's the devil feeding you those lies. The devil who's out to destroy me."

"Yah, that may very well be," Koznowski replied, "but at the moment I'll take what I can get. Now, might I step in for a few minutes of your time, please, ma'am? It's chilly out here, an' you leave that door open much longer it's gonna be chilly in there too."

"You gotta warrant, there?"

"Naw, can't say as I really do. Let's call this an informal visit, eh? But you wanna warrant, believe you me I could be back here with one faster'n you can spit."

She reluctantly stepped back and Koznowski entered the aging two-story farmhouse. There was no farm around it anymore, just a few weary trees out front, open, untended fields out back, and the nearest neighbor was a quarter mile down the road. It smelled of old dog and righteousness in there. He stomped his feet on the black rubber mat to shake off the snow. "Thanks. So where's your boy, then?"

"At practice," she said coldly, arms folded. He guessed she wasn't going to pull her "speaking in tongues" routine here, not without someone around to translate.

"He must practice a lot, from what I hear, eh?" Letting his eyes adjust to the dim light he saw the house was not exactly what he expected. Missing were the crucifixes, the shrines, the statuaries, and other religious iconography you might expect to overcrowd the living room of the leader of a lunatic sect. There were shrines and icons, yes, but instead of Jesus, Mary, or assorted saints they all revolved around her son Ezekiel. Trophies, pennants, photographs, and framed newspaper clippings covered the walls and the shelves. A plaster statue of a football player painted to resemble Ezekiel rested on the kidney-shaped coffee table. Posed and action shots of Ezekiel in a baseball uniform, a football uniform, a track outfit, a hockey uniform, and a soccer uniform were propped in a wooden display case. In fact, Koznowski noted, there didn't seem to be a single religious item anywhere in sight. That would've been a strange oversight for any of the houses around here, most all of which contained a prominent cross or two in the front room. To be missing from a preacher's house? There was something wrong here.

"One of my deputies was telling me that your boy is really something," Koznowski said, hoping to dissuade Rev. Boefinck from giving him the evil eye. "Sports-wise, I mean." He admired the shrine. "A real golden boy, he said, eh?"

"Get thee behind me, Satan," Rev. Boefinck proclaimed at him. "You can flatter me and my child all you want, but true as your words are I will not succumb to your attempts to seduce me, for you are the master of lies."

Koznowski closed his eyes. "I'm just trying to make nice here, Reverend Boefinck. He's obviously a very talented boy."

"Oh, he's more than talented. Captain of every varsity team in school, student body president, and in June he'll be graduating at the very top of his class. Plus he's about to become an Eagle Scout." Although the words themselves were those of a proud parent, there was a harshness to her tone, and it seemed to Koznowski she was trying to grind it all in his face. It didn't much bother the sheriff, who'd never even tried out for a team of any kind when he was in school.

"Wow, huh? Ain't that something? Can I ask what happened to his dad?" That was another thing Koznowski noticed. There were no family portraits in the room, and in those few photos of her with Ezekiel, there were no adult males anywhere to be seen.

"He's around, you might say. He's always been with us, even if we don't see him."

"So you raised the boy all by your lonesome? It's rare, y'know, for a single mom to raise a son who's any good at sports. Ever notice that? Normally they turn out, y'know, a little off. You must be very proud." He followed the pictures down the wall, secretly aiming for the couch.

"Oh, I'm more than proud. And he's more than all those awards and honors put together." She was still speaking as if trying to make Koznowski feel bad about himself. "I know that's why you're here. It's the way you've always worked. You want to build him up, make him think all these earthly accomplishments are important. But they're not. It's part of my job in doin' the Lord's work to keep him humble."

Koznowski looked around again at the trophies and awards and framed news clippings. "Yah, gotta say, you're doin' a real super job there, ma'am, an' so—you mind if I have a sit here?" With a swallowed groan he took a seat on the couch, which, if far from comfortable, was still better than standing. "Now please take a load off there yourself." He gestured at a chair. "I'd like to ask you a few more questions, as they say, about your church an' some a your congregants, there. Like, I notice you don't have prayer meetings on the weekends. That's pretty different, eh?"

VII

Driving back to the station, the sheriff couldn't believe how much time he'd wasted these past three days questioning useless deformed knotheads one after the other. He'd split up the names on the list with Keller and Vandenberg, but it didn't make things any easier. The Reverend Boefinck's flock, for the most part, consisted of inbreds, the cross-eyed, a goodly handful of retards, and a quadriplegic. The rest were just hapless simpletons. They sure loved the reverend woman, though, and could quote her mumbling, incoherent sermons verbatim (a good thing, too, considering it was the direct word of God funneled through Rev. Boefinck's larynx). It was easy to see why they'd been attracted to her message in the first place. If the squalor they lived in was any indication, most of these people wouldn't've been able to afford a traditional funeral if they wanted one. Better to come up with some excuse to avoid that final humiliation altogether. A white sheet and a hole in the ground were much more economically feasible, and if you could legitimize them with some kind of wackadoodle religious faith, all the better.

Most important for Koznowski's present purposes, however, not only did none of the congregants own a shotgun, none of them seemed capable of pointing and firing one even if they did.

"Well, crap," Koznowski muttered. He kept his eyes on the highway, which cut a gently arcing path through the stark, barren fields around him. It felt as if he were standing out there in the snow, scanning the white, featureless horizon in every direction, looking for some kind of landmark. He knew he was missing something basic, something obvious, but there was no one around who could tell him what it was. "Crap, crap, crap."

✠

"Heya, Chief, what's news?" Keller said as he passed the sheriff's desk, leading a disgruntled citizen toward his own.

"Hmm?" Koznowski mumbled. He'd been concentrating on the files Vandenberg brought in from Unterhumm's. He was still trying to make sense of them when the phone rang. The voice on the other end was familiar, but not so familiar he could put an immediate name to it.

"Mockery from the *Chronicle* here."

Aw, jeeze Louise. Knut Mockery, editor of the *Kausheenah County Chronicle,* was one of those guys who liked to pretend he was a real big city reporter when in fact his local community weekly tended to concentrate on the team standings in the local bowling leagues, which restaurants would be cooking up a vat of booyah that weekend (it was always anyone's guess during the winter), how the area high school teams were doing, and what kind of entertainment had been offered at Gustafsen's nursing home (last week it was the Kinder Klompers). The high school teams usually dominated the front page of the eight-page broadsheet, but if you stopped for gas while passing through Beaver Rapids you usually made it into next week's *Chronicle*.

This double murder business was a dream come true for Mockery, and because of it he wouldn't leave Koznowski alone. The longer the investigation wore on, the bigger a pain in the ass he became.

"Yah, I really don't got the time here, Knut."

"Oh, come on, there, Chief. The people have, y'know, a right to know what's goin' on here. You have anyone in custody yet?"

Koznowski squeezed the bridge of his nose and tried to keep his voice friendly. It was like talking to a hyperactive child. "Now, I know you're real excited about this whole murder thing, Knut, but you gotta just cool your jets there for a while. You know darn well I can't be saying nothin' about an open investigation."

"But you're still the sheriff of Kausheenah County, ain'cha?"

Somewhere down the line, swear to God, he was gonna pop Mockery a good one right in the nose. Out of the blue one day, just see him in the Telstar Diner or the Dew Drop and bam. Until then he had to try and be friendly, sort of. "No need to get all huffy there, Knut. You're a professional, you know the procedure. You gotta go through the public affairs office, there. She'll tell you all anybody here can tell you, an' I can keep on doing my job here, instead a, y'know, gabbing on the horn all day."

"Millie?" Mockery was tired of getting the brush. "C'mon, Chief, you know damn well that Millie—bless her an' all—is eighty-three years old. Sweetheart that she is, the last case she can remember—no, make it more like the *only* case she can remember—happened back in nineteen fifty-seven. Before you were sheriff, even. Every goddamn time I call up for a little info, here, she's goin' off tellin' me about the break-in at the old Kryzpackski place. I know that story well as she does now."

"Yah, she does love that story, don't she? She knows more about that case than anyone alive, I'll tell you that much."

"Please, Chief, gimme a break here. This story's a thousand times bigger'n that stupid break-in ever was."

"Not according to Millie it ain't."

"Yah, but don'cha think the people gotta right to know if there's still some kinda killer on the loose? For chrissakes, Chief."

"Protocol takes precedence over procedure, Knut. You know that. Can't give any suspects a heads-up here while we're investigating 'em, don'cha know."

The reporter's tone quickly shifted from pleading to abusive. "Yah I know all about that. An' I also know, an' you do too, there, that you weren't elected sheriff on accounta your whachacall powers of deduction or your crime-fighting skills. You were elected on account a you were a nice fella, an' folks here figured you'd let their DUIs slide and wouldn't come down on 'em too hard if they took a deer outa season. But give you a real crime to deal with—"

Koznowski had heard plenty and hung up. "Yah, stick it in your ear." He reminded himself to tell Leona that the next time Mockery called she was to patch him straight through to Millie, no matter who he was asking for or why.

He knew there was some truth in what Mockery had said, a truth that would probably appear in some form in the next issue of the *Chronicle*. He also knew it was up to him and no one else to prove the little weasel wrong.

Koznowski slid open his desk drawer and felt around for a while in search of his pill box before remembering it was still in his pocket. In his guts he knew Pollex Christi Ministries was involved somehow. He just needed to figure out the "somehow" part.

"Look lady, if I had all day I'd be an astronaut," someone shouted above the other voices in the office, breaking Koznowski's reverie. He looked up and around the room, only then realizing how busy it was. He'd been so wrapped up in those files and then that jackass Mockery he hadn't noticed all the people coming through the door and all the ensuing hubbub. The sheriff stood and headed for the bathroom to get a sip of water from the sink (he didn't trust the water cooler, and LeAnn knew why), snaking his way through the desks and coats and stray chairs to the door on the far wall.

"I don't know why one of 'em was carrying a frozen turkey," Bob Dunlop was telling Sgt. Lacroix. "One of 'em just was, is all. They come into my barbershop and tell me to hand over all my money. And one had a turkey."

"So what'd you do?"

"I gave it to 'em, whaddya think? I didn't know what they had a mind to do with that turkey, but I didn't wanna find out so's I gave 'em the money. Then after they get the money, they demand I give 'em haircuts too."

Lacroix looked up from his typewriter. "Haircuts?"

"*Yah,* haircuts."

"Well, do you know who it was?"

Dunlop's voice rose. "Of *course* I knows who it was! It was them damn VanBoxel boys! Been given 'em haircuts since they could walk!"

Lacroix typed something into the complaint report and hit the return bar. "And how much did they get away with?"

"Six bucks," Dunlop told him, then paused. "It'd been a pretty slow morning."

A woman in her late forties was leaning on her elbows at another desk. "It had to've been that Mary Sweeney," she was saying. "Who else would go after my shop windows with a hammer that way? You know her."

"Yeah," Sgt. Fugate nodded. "Yah, we all know her a little too well around here. But did you actually see Mary smash your windows?"

At the front desk, a hefty balding man in a knit Packers cap was pleading his case to Leona. ". . . then I come out of the Pay-Less over on Chitaqua— needed a new pair of boots, don'cha know. So I come out of the Pay-Less and find out one of your people here gave me a ticket. For what, I can't say, but I just wanna tell you there's no way in hell I'm gonna pay it."

He handed the crumpled ticket to Leona, who flattened it on her desktop. "Well, first thing, there, Angus," she explained, "callin' 'em my people is a slight exaggeration. Not mucha one, but still. An' second here." She studied the ticket. "You'll need to take this up with Sergeant Rasmussen, and he's . . ." She turned and scanned the room, then swiveled back. "Presently with another citizen, so you'll need to set yourself a spell over there." She pointed to a row of three folding chairs against the wall, two of which were already occupied. "Best I can do for you, hon." She handed the tattered ticket back to him.

He scanned the room himself before crushing the ticket in his palm and stomping toward the remaining chair in his new squeaky boots.

In a far corner of the office near the break room, Sgt. Rasmussen pulled his arms away from the typewriter keyboard and dropped them to his sides. Across from him, a pale young man in his twenties was staring at his own knotted hands. He looked frightened, or sick, or both.

"Look," Rasmussen said. "You're wasting both our time here. This is out of our jurisdiction. You need to go down to Eagle Bluff, tell them about it. And you're saying this was ten years ago to boot? I don't know what they'll be able to do with that, but hopefully it'll be more than we can, which is nothing." He yanked the police report out of the typewriter, tore it in half, and jammed it into his overfull trash can. The pale kid watched with hopeless eyes but didn't say a word.

Over at Sgt. Hogstune's desk was Fink Anderson, a fisherman who lived up in the woods around North Overshoe Lake. The man looked pissed. Most folks in the area knew Fink at least by reputation and, seeing him sitting where he was, would've assumed he probably got drunk again and caused a ruckus. He was a big guy, Fink was, with a scraggly graying beard and a glass eye that always seemed to be staring a few degrees off to the right. He could cause quite a ruckus if he set his mind to it.

"I'm tellin' ya, there's somethin' up there," Fink was saying. "In the water. Y'know, the lake."

"Well, something like what? Fish? Yah, we know about them already, Fink." (Sgt. Hogstune was not always the most sensitive or tactful of officers when it came to handling complaints.) "You still a little loaded after this weekend?"

"*Fish?*" a furious Fink erupted. "I'll show you goddamn fish. I'll show you somethin' . . . It was somethin'," he said, reaching toward the floor behind the desk, "that could do *this.*" He held up a rowboat oar. A neat, semicircular bite about nine inches across had been taken out of the paddle.

The sergeant considered the oar. "Isn't that more of a problem for the DNR?"

Fink's good eye grew wide with rage. "DNR my ass! It's gonna be all your fuckin' problem soon!" he shouted, waving the oar around. "Far as I know this might be a problem for the fuckin' army!"

Hogstune assumed the persona of a second grade teacher. "Now, Fink, you gotta put the oar down or I won't talk to you anymore. And stop yelling. It ain't gettin' us nowhere. But first put the oar down."

Still drying his hands with a brown paper towel as he stepped from the bathroom, Koznowski paused to watch the scene.

Hogstune's gonna get that oar straight up his ass, he thought. What the hell was going on today? He'd never seen the station like this before. It was like the whole damned county had turned into Black River Falls while he was sleeping. He shook his head slightly and headed for his desk.

It had taken only a handy butter knife to open the black strongbox Vandenberg found stashed under Kirby Mudge's bed. Inside was a single sheet of letterhead stationery. Across the top was printed:

ASS. M.E.A.T.
Association of Mortuary Entrepreneurs, Aestheticians & Technicians

Handwritten in elaborate script beneath it was a simple list of names.

> *Dr. Klaus Unterhumm*
> *Dr. Amos Squire*
> *William G. Dobbs*
> *Robert Makurji*
> *Dr. H. West*
> *Dr. Harry Burke*
> *Fr. Timothy Avalone*
> *Kirby Mudge*

While the handwriting was apparently the same, the names seemed to have been written at different times and with different pens. There was little mystery surrounding who these people were and why most of them were so linked, given the letterhead. It wasn't as clear why Father Tim would be part of some fraternal order of morticians, but it was easy enough to ask him. Easy enough to talk to the others too (except of course Unterhumm and Kirby). The other thing that wasn't immediately clear was why such an innocuous piece of paper had been so carefully locked away and hidden under a bed, but he'd find out soon enough.

When he reached his desk, he found Deputy Ellsworth sitting in his chair reading one of the files Vandenberg had brought back from Unterhumm's office. "Heya Ellsworth, dreaming again?"

Ellsworth looked up from the file. "Oh, heya, Chief. Just dropping off a report."

"A report? Oh yah?" Koznowski folded his arms and leaned on his desk. "What's this now? Some diabolical crime?"

Ellsworth pointed at the sheet of paper. "Ida Boyes, over on Route Seventeen? Says someone's been deliberately, ah . . . 'unnerving' her cows."

Koznowski was quiet for a moment. He reached for the report but didn't pick it up. "Unnerving them?"

"That's what she says, yah."

Out of curiosity more than anything, Koznowski picked up the report and glanced at it. "Mm-hmm. Super, yah. Well, I s'pose we should put all our best men on it, eh? Keep round-the-clock surveillance on her place an' such."

"Yah, that's what I told her," Ellsworth said. "But I told her they'd be, like, working undercover so she probably wouldn't even see 'em around. But not to worry, they'd be there."

"Good man," Koznowski said. "Keep it up you'll have my job one day, eh? Maybe soon, way things're going. But, ah, until that day comes? You wanna get the fuck outa my chair?"

As if only then realizing where he was, Ellsworth quickly dropped the file he was holding and scrambled from the seat. "Sorry, Chief. But I was looking at some of them forms Deliah found, and she's right. They're, like, kinda weird."

The sheriff took his rightful place and exhaled. "Yah, thanks a million there for keeping it warm. Now what's this you're saying?" He looked around the desktop with some concern. "Hey, you eat my beer nuts while you were playing sheriff?"

Ignoring the question, Ellsworth reached for the stack of files and snatched the top one away, flipping it open. "See, my uncle Gomer? He used to work at a hospital in Kaukauna,"

"Yah? So why am I uncomfortable with the idea of anyone's Uncle Gomer working in a hospital?"

"Well, it was Kaukauna anyways. But he used to deal with these. They're receipts for, like, sellin' body parts to medical schools an' stuff like that?"

Koznowski frowned. "Yah, that I can see. But I thought they were organ donors."

The deputy shook his head. "Oh no, this here is definitely a for-profit operation. No donatin' goin' on here. You check out these prices? Eight, ten thou a pop here." He pointed at the top sheet. "Shit, these people are gettin' my salary for a leg bone, look at that. But weird thing is, this sorta thing's usually done in hospitals. Y'know, when things are still fresh an' all? That's like the whole idea with transplants, there. You gotta get these things right away, kidneys an' such, or they don't work. So it's kinda weird for a morgue to be doing it, don'cha think?"

"I honestly don't know."

"Yah, guess there's a lotta shit about this sorta thing we don't know, eh? I mean, Uncle Gomer was handlin' all this fifteen, twenty years ago, an' everything I know I picked up from him. He was usually kinda drunk when he was at our place, too, so who knows? Any case, I bet stuff's, like, changed a lot since, eh?"

"I'm thinking you're prob'ly right." Koznowski was taking the file back from Ellsworth when his phone rang. He stared at the device with sour disgust. "If this is that ass Knut Mockery again, I want you an' a few of the boys to go over to the *Chronicle* and arrest him for something." He picked up the phone. "Sheriff Koznowski." A moment later he squeezed his eyes shut and slapped the heel of his right hand hard against his forehead. "Hello, Mr. Mayor. Yah, real good to hear from you."

While the sheriff was preoccupied, Ellsworth grabbed another of the invoices and examined it. Then another. Confusion seeped into his features. In the corner box, where someone was supposed to type a donor ID number, someone had typed "00/0000." Not just on that one either. He flipped through all the pages and found all the donor numbers had been entered as "00/0000." That was odd. But these were for things like femurs, vertebrae, epidermal tissue . . . Plus they'd apparently been sold to hospitals and medical schools around the country. Three whole cadavers went to U.S. Army bases.

". . . Yes, hello Mr. Mayor . . . No, not at all, Mr. Mayor, I've just been following up on some leads. Lotta things to do in a murder investigation, your honor, and . . . No, no, I haven't forgotten 'em, Mayor . . . Yes, the new security plan for the parade was distributed among the troops this morning. We're ready to handle anything . . . Yes, even that. Just leave it to us . . . Yes, you, too, Mr. Mayor."

"*Stupid ass,*" he whispered after hanging up the phone. He shot a look at Leona's back. He was gonna have to do something about her.

With a sigh, he pulled open one of his side drawers and began fingering his way through the manila folders, finally pausing and sliding out one labeled "1987 Thanksgiving Parade Security."

He opened the file and flipped through the enclosed pages. Closing the file and grabbing a pen, he scratched out "1987" at the top of the folder and scribbled "1988" beneath it. He slapped the folder off to the side. "There," he said, "that's done. Pass these along to Leona when you leave, wouldja? Ask her to distribute copies?"

Ellsworth was too engrossed in the invoices to pay attention. "There's something weird goin' on here," he said. "I know some of these guys here. John VanderLeiten, Tim Ruggles . . . these are all folks who died in the past couple years."

"Yah, guess that's why we found 'em in a mortician's office, eh? Wouldda been pretty creepy iffen they weren't dead yet."

When his phone rang, Koznowski groaned. "Goddamn mayor prob'ly lost a button." He shot another glance at Leona, who merely smiled and waved. Behind her, Fink was slamming his way out the front doors, still clutching the oar in one angry calloused fist.

He picked up the phone tentatively. "Sheriff Koznowski," he said. It wasn't the mayor. The sheriff listened, and as he listened he frowned. Eventually he said, "What the hell? You might have to run that one past me again, there, sir . . . Uh-huh, uh-huh . . . But Doctor Squire was taking care of that. You spoken with him? . . . Oh, yah, very respectable operation. Been here for generations now . . . But I'm not real sure what you'd think I . . . All right, yah. Yah . . . Aw, jeeze." He reached for a pen but did nothing with it. "Well what about the airport, there, you check with—?" He frowned again. "Yah, okay, yah . . . I needed to talk to him anyways. Middleton, right? Shit . . . I'm real sorry about this, it's real awful, there . . . Yah, sure. An' yes of course I'll be letting you know what happened."

When he hung up the phone he looked deeply troubled.

"Heya, what goes on there, Chief?" Ellsworth asked. "Looks like you just ate a toad or somethin'."

The sheriff sighed but did not look up. "That was the Middleton Funeral Home in Indianapolis. Kirby Mudge's coffin got back home yesterday so's his folks could give him a proper burial . . . but Kirby wasn't in it." He slid open his desk drawer and began fumbling about the rubber bands and the paper clips and a stray harmonica in search of the pill box. "All they found inside was a couple sacks of flour."

VIII

"It was a long goddamn day, I'll tell you that much." Koznowski emptied the rest of his second beer into the glass as LeAnn slid the tray holding the pot roast onto the table. "Thanks, hon. Looks great."

"Yah, Ezra Cobb over to the Piggly Wiggly gave me a deal here. But what about the Mudge boy? That's so sad." She took a seat across from him as he began scooping potatoes onto his plate. He was about to say something when the doorbell rang. He froze.

"No," he said firmly as he resumed his scooping.

LeAnn was already rising from her seat, dropping her napkin on the table as she did. "We can't really ignore her."

"Hell we can't. I can. Watch."

"But the lights are on an' so. She knows we're here."

Koznowski continued filling his plate with angry determination. He did not look at her. "I don't care. It's the third night this week. Doesn't she have any other neighbors she can mooch off? They probably don't answer the door, that's why. Because they're smart."

LeAnn hesitated, shooting a nervous glance into the living room. "Just hush now. She'll hear you." The four-chime doorbell rang again.

"Good." He raised his voice and turned his head in the general direction of the front door. "Fat goddamn mooch!"

She lifted one finger to her lips and waved him down with her other hand before leaving the room. He stared into his plate, fists clenched. Betty from down the street was one of those creatures who seemed to be operating under the notion that if she ever stopped talking, even for a second, she'd die. It didn't matter if she had no idea what she was talking about (which she never did) or even if she had nothing at all of interest to say (which was always the case). She just kept talking. How he dreamed of shooting her in the head. That'd shut her up.

In the other room, he heard LeAnn unlock the door and pull it open. "Oh, hi Betty."

They had all goddamn day to gab, but two, three nights a week there she was again, and always right at the moment they were sitting down to supper. It was like she had some kinda fatass radar. Never brought anything, never offered anything, never made a move to help out when it was time to clean up. Barged in and stuffed her ugly face, yapping the whole while. Then afterward she sat there like some slob of a moose, still yapping while Koznowski and LeAnn did the dishes. Fat fucking cow.

"Hi LeAnn! Saw your lights on so I thought I'd stop in and say hello! Sure is getting chilly outside. Y'know they say we got some snow coming. Way it feels now I wouldn't be surprised for a second if it did. Mind if I take off my boots? You know, I think I better anyway." She cackled that same meaningless shriek of a cackle that drilled into Koznowski's skull like an awl.

His hand slid down to where he'd usually find his sidearm. Dammit, he'd left it in the other room. Instead, his fingers dug into his pocket in search of the pill box. He popped two more of the tiny white pills, washing them down with the rest of his beer.

"Len and I was just setting down to supper here," he heard LeAnn say.

"Oh? You got room for one more?" She left no room for LeAnn to suggest any alternative scenarios, not that she would. Koznowski clenched his jaw, shoved himself back from the table, and nearly toppled his chair as he headed for the fridge to get another beer. "See, I was just coming back from the doctors and gracious if that wasn't something. I have to tell you all about it. He says, well, you remember that rash I told you about ... ?"

✠

Dwight moved around the table, hooked his gloved hands under Charles Benton's armpits, and heaved him into a half-sitting position as Squire checked the drainage tubes. Above the surgical mask and behind the plastic face shield, Dwight's frightened eyes darted around the room.

"I honestly don't know. I've shipped a hundred loved ones to dozens of different states over the years. Even other countries. Nothing like this has ever happened before." He smoothly inserted another tube into Mr. Benton's carotid artery and tapped a small red button on the device next to him. "Okay, Dwight, if you'll please lay him back down carefully now and begin massaging the neck and extremities. You know the procedure." Squire turned away from the body on the table to face Sheriff Koznowski, similarly dressed in a surgical mask and hairnet, but standing as far as possible from the proceedings in a corner of the prep room. "Have they talked to people at the airport yet? That'd be my first guess. You know what kinda thugs they have working in baggage."

"Yah," Koznowski said after swallowing. Even with the distance, the mask, and the white smears of Carry-On under each nostril to cover the odor, he wasn't feeling very well. He'd been trying but failing to keep his eyes on his shoes, but something drew them back to Charlie Benton. "That's, ah . . . ah . . . the general consensus over there. They're talking to 'em now. I'm sure they'll find him. Still don't know who in their right mind would wanna steal a body like that."

"Got me there, Chief," Squire said as the inevitable shrug snuck out from beneath the lab coat. "Satanists? Yeah, but I'm sure you're right. Just some sort of simple mix-up somewhere along the line. Poor Kirby's probably down in Paraguay by now. Happened to my luggage once."

Behind him, Dwight was gently, almost lovingly massaging the thick, soft throat of the obese man on the table.

"And again I'm sorry to make you come down here while I'm working," Squire continued. "You said it was important, but I'm afraid this is important too. Mr. Benton's family will be coming by tonight at seven for a viewing."

"Oh, yah, sure. I understand. Hope you don't mind if I, ah, just stand over here and, y'know, don't watch?"

"Of course, but it is a fascinating procedure. See, what Dwight's doing now"—he gestured at his assistant who, in Koznowski's mind, might just as well be hunchbacked—"is flexing the arteries and veins, especially in the fingers and feet, to squeeze the embalming fluid down there. See, since the heart's no longer working we need to—"

"Uh-huh, super," Koznowski interrupted, not really wanting to know any more about it. "Now I was wondering if you could maybe help me out with another little thing here." He reached into his satchel and slid out a sheet of paper. LeAnn had picked up the brown fake leather satchel for him at the JCPenney during a shopping trip to Green Bay a few years back. Once at home she'd sewn on a KCSD patch to make it look official. He honestly hadn't found much use for it since then, but when he pulled it down from the closet, dusted it off, and took it with him that morning she'd felt vindicated. "Got something here, a list of names from something called the Association of Mortuary Entrepreneurs, Aestheticians, and Technicians. Ring a bell? We found it in a locked box under Mudge's bed.

Dr. Squire frowned under his surgical mask as he thought about it. "Sorry, Sarge. I really can't say."

The sheriff shifted his weight, wishing there was some kind of chair down here, something he could sit on. A shelf, maybe. But everything was cluttered with instruments and chemicals. "Sure about that, there? Like I said, it's a list of names, and yours is right up there. Number two as it happens, right below Unterhumm's. Plus it's on real letterhead. Look." He flipped the paper over and held it up so Squire could see. "Still no bells, there?"

The mortician stayed where he was, squinting briefly before turning back to the body on the table. He grabbed the man's left hand and began massaging. "Sounds like Klaus, all right. He was always making lists. I'm sure you found dozens of them when you were sifting through his files."

Koznowski thought about it for a moment. "Ah, no. Nope, this here's pretty much the only list we found. And like I says, your name's on it."

"Well," Squire said without turning around. "Who else is on it?" He moved down to Benton's leg and checked the flow of blood and other bodily fluids as they drained from the body into a trough beside the table.

"Yah, let's see here." Koznowski scrutinized the page, glad to have something else to look at. "Yah, we got you and Unterhumm, a Doctor Harry Burke, a William G. Dobbs . . ."

"Oh, hell, I see where this is going." He caught Dwight's attention and quietly instructed, "This is moving a little slow. Maybe try elevating the table a few degrees? Thanks." He returned his attention to the sheriff. "Those are names of local morticians. Burke is over in Plainfield and Dobbs is in

Black River Falls. I think I know what this is. See, Klaus had done some talking—blue-skying, really—about forming some kind of trade union or support group or something. I was never clear on what he was talking about, except it would be a way to bring all the local morticians together as a group, exchange ideas, bullshit like that. Nothing ever came of it. Didn't know he had a name picked out already, but yeah, that's all that is."

Glancing at the list again, Koznowski scratched his left ear. "Yah, okay. Seems kinda weird, though, don'cha think? Guy who wasn't exactly the most sociable man on earth dreaming of pulling a big club like this together?"

"Hey, Sarge, Klaus was a weird guy. I can't claim to understand how he thought most of the time."

"Yah, other thing here that don't make much sense, though. You have any idea why Father Avalone would be on the list? He doing a little embalming on the side, maybe?"

"Huh," Squire said. "Does pickling count? Can't tell you anything about that either, except Avalone was the only one Klaus did seem to tolerate, so maybe that's all that is. He was a funny guy."

"Yah, okay," Koznowski sighed. "That's all it is, don't look like it's gonna get me mucha anywhere, eh?" He slid the sheet back into his satchel and pulled out another batch. "Don't know why it was in a locked box under Mudge's bed, but yah, who knows, eh? Now . . ." He flipped through the new papers. "Got just one more thing to ask you, here, then I'll let you get back to Charlie." His eyes shot to the body for what he hoped would be the last time. "Didn't know him real well myself, but he was a heck of a bowler, tell you that." He forced himself to focus on what was in his hand. "Anyway, sorry to be so wha'cha call inquisitive here, but a case like this you gotta look at everything, eh?" He held out the papers but would not take a step closer to the table. "These mean anything to you?"

Annoyed, Squire checked the tubes one more time, nodded to Dwight, and stepped over to Koznowski. "Look, Sarge, do you have any idea how long it takes to embalm a four-hundred-pound body? This whole process gets far more complicated from here on in, especially with a body of this size. It requires serious attention and we need to be careful so . . ." Koznowski said nothing but continued holding the papers out to him. Squire exhaled through his nose as he took the seven or eight pages and flipped through them.

As he read and Koznowski watched him read, Dwight, seeing an opening, slipped a hand down Charlie Benton's pendulous belly and fondled his dead penis. He snatched the hand back quickly and tried to swallow his giggles. Neither Squire nor Koznowski seemed to notice.

Squire raised an eyebrow. "Hmm," he said. "That's odd. These are invoices for organ sales, but I don't know why you'd find something like this in Klaus's files. This sort of thing gets taken care of in the hospital."

"Yah, right?" Koznowski was relieved at last to get some kind of an answer out of this guy. "That's what Uncle Gomer said. You need these things fresh, and by the time they get to the morgue—"

"Mortuary."

"Yah, mortuary, it's too late. But look at that there." He pointed at one of the invoices. "A rib cage to the University of Delaware for eighteen thousand smackers, eh? What the hell? Musta been one superduper rib cage, you ask me."

"Yeah," Squire said after a brief pause, still perusing the invoices. "It's an expensive business." He flipped the pages together and handed them back. "But that's all I can tell you. That it's odd. It's not a business I'm involved in. And so long as you found the consent forms, well, then, there's that."

"Consent forms?"

Squire headed back to the table where Dwight seemed to have made a game of moving around the body counterclockwise, massaging each hand and foot in turn as he passed it. "Dwight, that's enough," the mortician said. "Consent forms, yes. Like anything else. Normally the family signs these in the hospital before the patient expires. But here? I'm not sure what the story is."

"Can't say we found anything like that. Not that I'm aware of," Koznowski admitted. "For things like burials and cremations, sure, but not for selling off bits an' pieces here like you're stripping down an old Pontiac or something."

Squire was pulling open a series of drawers on the side of the embalming table, then slamming them shut. "I really wouldn't worry about it all that much, Sarge. I'm sure it's nothing anyway."

"Yah, thanks," Koznowski said, returning the invoices to his satchel. "Prob'ly nothing anyway, eh? Doesn't get me any closer to finding a killer, there. Sorry to interrupt you down here while you're working an' all, but thanks so much again for your help, there." He zipped up his coat and tried to put his hat on.

"Oh," Squire said. "There's a can to your right when you leave the preparation room. You can just dump the gloves and mask and hairnet in there.

Thanks." He was no longer looking at the sheriff. When Squire reached for a long and sinister metal tube like the one he saw sticking out of Hattie Dankowski, Koznowski decided it was time for him to leave.

"So be sure and pass along my condolences, there, to Charlie's family, you see them tonight. And you hear anything or think of anything might help us track down Mudge's body, be sure and give a holler, eh?"

"Will do, Sarge," Squire said, distracted as he attached a hose to whatever the hell that thing was called. "And I wouldn't worry too much about those other things. I'm sure you're gonna crack this one real soon."

✠

"One of these things is not like the others, right, Sheriff?" Father Avalone offered a smile as he looked up from the sheet. "To quote Mister Rogers."

"Yah, kinda like finding a zebra in a herd of camels, or a pumpkin in the . . . aw, hell, I dunno. A pumpkin in the . . ."

"Slaughterhouse?"

"Yah," Koznowski said. "That'll do it."

Avalone leaned back in his comfortable leather chair. "It's pretty simple to explain, actually. Klaus asked me to sit in as a kind of spiritual adviser."

"I'd a thought maybe that wha'cha call acronym might throw you for a minute, an' so."

"Acronym?" Avalone asked.

Koznowski nodded toward the stationery. "Right at the top, there. Big letters." Avalone picked up the paper and peered at the name at the top and the acronym above that. When it finally seemed to register, he stared blankly at the page, frowning. "Oh my God." He looked up to the sheriff. "ASS MEAT? You know, I never really thought about that before. Never saw it spelled out like this. Can you imagine?"

"Yah, I can see how a priest like yourself might, ah, be a little off-put by that."

The priest set the stationery down, shaking his head. "That's Klaus's German sense of humor coming out again. Well, let's just say I'm glad I never told Father Molloy about my association with . . . um . . . ASS MEAT."

Koznowski tried to cross his legs, winced, and forgot about it. "So can you gimme a hint as to what this was all about, then?"

Father Avalone looked out the window of his office. The sun shone brightly and the sky was a hard blue. It meant things were cold outside. The unblemished snow covering the soccer field was nearly blinding. "It was just a kind of fraternal organization, really, like the Kiwanis or the Lions. Any local funeral director who cared to could join. See, as you might imagine they had a hard time talking about their profession with most people."

"Oh, yah, you mentioned that. Start talking about embalming at a cookout an' folks don't exactly gather 'round, eh?"

The priest offered a friendly nod. "Exactly. Same with the crucifixion . . . So this was a way for local funeral directors to keep one another up to date on new techniques, any legal changes, things like that they might've heard. Trade some professional secrets, discuss any relevant issues. Like any group of, oh, plumbers or barbers . . . or even law enforcement officers."

"Uh-huh?" Koznowski said, wondering why Squire had been afraid to tell him about something this boring. "So you were there to do what?"

The priest took a loud, slurping sip of his tea. He held it in his mouth for a moment before noisily squeezing it down his throat as he exhaled through his nose. "Like I said, I was a kind of spiritual adviser. If they had any questions about how the Church talks to family members in a time of grief, or how we prepare people for when they will at last be called to meet their Heavenly Father, or even how to deal with people of different faiths, what sorts of things they might expect. I think it was of use to them."

"I see, yah," Koznowski said, jotting the word "fruity" into his notebook. "An' how often'd you all get together like that?"

The priest's eyes rolled ceilingward as he thought back. "Oh, just once or twice a year. Like regular conventions only a lot smaller and we never went to Vegas. But we were in touch, a lot of us, of course."

"Uh-huh? Super, then," Koznowski said. "Sounds pretty straightforward. Well, thanks for takin' the time to clear all that up, padre. One less thing I need to be thinking about." He began to pack up his notebook and the list. "Guess it's time for me to head back out there. Cold as a . . . Well, it's cold."

"I know it must be frustrating at times, criminal investigations like this," Father Avalone said a few minutes later as he walked Koznowski downstairs to the front door of the rectory. "But it must be fascinating too. Like seeking out the answer of an extremely difficult puzzle."

"Yah," Koznowski said, more aware of the shooting pain in his right leg than anything else. "Never, ah, never been much a whiz at puzzles myself, but I see what you're saying, there, yah."

"Oh, I've always loved puzzles of all kinds. Keeps the brain active and alive."

They turned a corner and walked past the secretary's office. "They usually just make my brain hurt, don'cha know? When I go to the Telstar, I flip my place mat over so I don't even have to think about it."

Avalone offered a chuckle. "I think it's one of the things that made me want to be a police officer when I was young, the idea I'd be good at solving crimes like I was good at puzzles."

"Oh yah?"

"Even applied to the academy when I was nineteen. I ever tell you that?"

Koznowski shook his head, measuring out the steps to the front door ahead of them. "Nah, can't say as you did, there."

"It was all I wanted, really. To be a cop. But I couldn't pass the physical."

The sheriff looked at him. "Really? Seem like you're in pretty good shape to me. Coaching all them teams an' all. Hell of a lot better shape than I'm in."

"Oh, now, sure, but not when it mattered. After the academy turned me down I entered the seminary, and that's when I started getting into shape. Think I was trying to prove a point of some kind. You know? Silly human pride."

Koznowski paused in front of the doors, glad they were there at last. "Well, padre," he held out a hand, which the priest shook. "Sorry you didn't make it as a cop, but you're likely doing more good here, eh? An' for what it's worth, you've been a big help here on the investigation." He pulled his hand back and pushed his way through the door.

"Anything I can do, Sheriff. And God be with you."

Most of the other morticians on the list confirmed what Father Avalone had told him about ASS MEAT. None of them denied knowing anything about it, except Squire. That made Koznowski more than a little suspicious. Everyone agreed—even the priest—that it was nothing but a professional group, so what's there to get all twitchy about? Maybe he was late with his dues.

He chose not to mention Squire's dumb show routine to the others, figuring he'd hold on to that for himself. It might be useful. Squire and the others could duke it out at their next meeting, should it come up.

A few things (apart from the obvious) did strike him as oddball about the group as a whole. Even after two of their own had been blown away inside a mortuary, none of them seemed worried in the least the same thing might happen to them. If someone started knockin' off his deputies, or members of his bowling team, he'd be plenty worried. A little something to keep in the back of his head. The other oddball thing was that Father Tim was the only one who asked him how the investigation was going. None of the others said a peep about that. He couldn't tell if they figured he'd get it wrapped up soon—Squire said something like that—or maybe they just didn't care. None of them had even come to Unterhumm's funeral. Sure, they're busy people but, Christ, if they all thought the guy was such a genius and an inspiration, why not put in a little effort?

What a screwy lot these undertakers were. And nary a one of them— nary a one of anybody—had been able to give him the slightest damn hint about that "heed the worms" business. And written in Unterhumm's own blood, even? That was just damn crazy. Of course his line of questioning may not have been the most direct, but still.

Then there was that last guy—Harry Burke from Burke & Son's Family Funeral Emporium over in Plainfield. When Koznowski first asked him what they did at ASS MEAT meetings, Burke got real fidgety and said, "You don't want to know." When Koznowski assured him that, yes, indeed he did want to know, that it might help his investigation, the guy said, "No, I mean it. You really, *really* don't want to know." Then he snorted out a high-pitched chuckle, explained it was just a mortician joke, and told the sheriff they talked about articles and things they'd read in the trade magazines. That sort of thing. Same as everyone else. Joking or not, after hanging up the phone he jotted Burke's name next to Squire's in his notes. Goddamned weirdoes.

He checked his watch. It was quarter to five and he was still some half a dozen miles away from the station. He picked up the radio and hit the button. "This is car zero-zero checking in. Leona, sweetheart, you around?"

After a brief crackle of static, a metallic voice returned. "Oh yeah, Chief, right here don'cha know."

"Okay good, then. Now I'm on my way in there, but it's gonna take me a little bit yet. Might stop off at the Hansen's outlet, pick up some cheese. But I need you to do something for me, eh?"

"Oh, yah? What's that?"

"You got a pen? Here's the deal. Need you to try an' catch Judge Muskie before'n he leaves for the night, okay then? He usually leaves a little after five. But I need you to call him an' ask him to put through a search warrant for me."

There was another crackle on the radio. "A search warrant? Holy jeeze, there, Chief, we gettin' all Milwaukee here, or what? You betcha, though. I'm on it."

"That's super then. Now here's the details—"

"Oh wait a sec there, Chief, do you think Judge Muskie knows how to do all this?"

"He hasn't started hitting the gin yet he damn well better know."

IX

After what felt like hours, even days loitering on the cold downtown side-walk (but was in fact only slightly over four and a half minutes), the pale young man in the parka checked the address over the door one last time against the number written on the piece of paper in his hand. There weren't many people outside that afternoon, not on foot, anyway, and those few who did pass him paid him no attention at all. Still, it felt to him like every passing pair of eyes was not only studying his face and judging him by his tattered parka, but digging deeper as well. It seemed to him as if they all knew why he was there.

He checked the name carved into the stone above the number over the doorway: Eagle Bluff Police Department. There was no denying he'd found the place he'd set out to find, but now that he was here he wasn't so sure how much he wanted to go in. Going inside meant changing everything.

Somehow finding the strength of will his mother had always discouraged, he nodded to himself and pushed through the door. It was warm inside. The office was much smaller and much more drab than what he'd encountered in Kausheenah County, with fake wood paneling on the walls and what may have been real or plastic ferns sitting on the windowsills. Either way, real or fake, they all looked dead. The few officers in the claustrophobic space seemed more bored than anything. Still, for it all the operation somehow seemed much more professional than what he'd found back home.

He lowered his fur-trimmed hood and approached the front desk, where a smiling, balding man set down his newspaper. "Yessir," the desk officer said. "And how might we be of service to you today?"

The young man in the parka had made the drive, he'd come this far, and however much he was tempted to turn and smash back through the doors onto the sidewalk he knew he couldn't. "I'd," he said to the desk officer, choosing each word carefully, "I'd like to report a crime."

The tip of the officer's tongue protruded for a blink, then disappeared. His smile did not fade. "Well then, son," he said. "You certainly come to the right place, haven't you? I mean, you got a crime to report, where better to do it. The garden store across the way, there? What the heck are they gonna do?" He burst into a bellowing, chesty laugh that was almost immediately overtaken by a coughing fit. "Guess they could . . . guess they could . . ." he tried to squeeze it out between thick hacks, but it was no good. He gave up on the joke and slapped the top of his desk instead.

✠

When Rev. Boefinck opened the front door, she found that godless heathen sheriff on her porch, along with three of his presumably godless cronies. Her first impulse was to slam the door in their stupid Satanic faces. But no, that wouldn't be very Christian, she thought. Instead, the words of the Lord came back to her.

"Go to hell," she said. "An' get the hell off my porch." The heathen just grinned at her. She could smell the stench of brimstone belching out of all their rancid guts.

"Oh now, ma'am, that ain't very neighborly," Koznowski said. "I thought we had us a real nice chat last time I visited."

"What is it you want this time?" she asked, taking a look at the four of them. "You an' your jesters of Satan here still trying to crucify me and my son?" The hatred in her eyes nearly scorched the locked screen door.

"Not if you've done nothing wrong. Just need to, y'know, do everything we can to figure out who took the lives of those two innocent men."

"Innocent?" She spat on the rubber mat at her feet. "None of you are innocent in the eyes of the Lord. An' doing what they did for money? Satan's henchmen is what they were."

"I think I'd rather be a henchman than a jester," Keller whispered to Vandenberg. "Pay's better."

Koznowski's eyes shifted. "Ah . . . okay, yah, whatever you say. But see, we're talking wha'cha call Caesar's law right now, an' I have here . . ." He reached into his inside jacket pocket and withdrew a sheet of paper. ". . . a warrant to search the premises, ma'am. We would also like to talk to Ezekiel, if we might." He unfolded the warrant and held it up to the screen.

Her eyes narrowed slightly behind the thick lenses of her glasses. "You really are here to crucify him, ain'cha? Oh, yah, I can see it all now."

"Whatever you may think, ma'am, I have a warrant here, so if you'll kindly let us in, please? It'll make everything much easier."

Rev. Boefinck's hand tightened on the knob. She should've slammed the door when she had the chance. She offered a cold smile. "Yah, what choice do I have, eh? But you have to wait here a second. I'll be right back. Lemma take my rhubarb bread outa the oven or it'll burn." She closed the door firmly.

It was nineteen degrees out that morning, and the wind wasn't helping matters. Too cold for any November day and here they were waiting on a nutjob. Deputy Vandenberg stomped her feet on the wooden porch to warm them up. It didn't work. It never works. They'd all received training in this sort of thing, but they'd never done it before for real. Beneath the excitement, the thrill of finally being able to act like TV cops, there was some trepidation as well. In all the videos they'd been shown, in all the movies and police dramas, there was always some vicious drug dealer shooting at whoever was performing the search. Not that they seriously expected to encounter anything like that in Rev. Boefinck's house but, as all the training videos emphasized, you never could tell what the criminal element might do next. Inside heavy gloves, palms were sweating.

It seemed an awfully long time for someone to take something out of the oven. Maybe she neglected to mention she planned to sit down and eat it too.

"This ain't smellin' right," Koznowski said. He reached out and tried the handle to the screen door, only to find it locked. "Who keeps their screen doors up all winter?"

A moment later he heard the squeak of another screen door in the back of the house and the woman's voice shouting, *"Run!"*

Koznowski's head snapped around to see Ezekiel Boefinck whipping around the corner of the house faster than he'd ever seen a human being run before—it was almost as if he were running on top of the snow.

"Deke! Ellsworth!" Koznowski shouted, pointing. "Get after him!"

"But Chief..." Ezekiel was already at the bottom of the gravel driveway. "He's real fast an'—"

"Oh Jesus Christ," the sheriff sputtered. "Just—just take the damn cruiser." He turned to Deputy Vandenberg. "Deliah, you go 'round to the back, I'll take the front. Don't let her outa there."

The other two deputies were already revving the cruiser's engine, the back tires throwing gravel, while Ezekiel, judging from the way he came around the house, was probably down around Janesville by now. Vandenberg drew her gun and hopped off the end of the porch, promptly finding herself knee-deep in a snowdrift.

"Jesus Christ, how did he run in this?"

Koznowski drew his own weapon and was about to kick in both front doors when he remembered his legs and hesitated. Before he had to make a decision the inside door opened.

"Okay then, I suppose I got no choice but to letcha in." Rev. Boefinck unsnapped the screen door lock, then paused and looked around. "Hey, where'd those other persecutors go?"

"Reverend Boefinck, I'm afraid I'm gonna have to place you under arrest."

"Oh yah?" She seemed almost amused by this. "An' what the' hell for, Pilate?"

"Well, there's obstruction of justice for one, there, and, ah . . . aiding and abetting the attempted escape of a suspect wanted for questioning, an' let's see . . ."

As the sheriff spoke, Deputy Vandenberg silently crept into the room behind the Reverend Boefinck. Her boots and pants were covered with snow, which began melting into the carpet. She swiveled into position and took a stance, her .38 caliber service revolver aimed squarely at the preacher woman's head.

"*Drop to the fucking floor! Hands behind your fucking head! Now! Do it! Do it now!*"

Both the sheriff and the suspect screamed sharply and jumped, Koznowski's arms flying up to cover his head.

"Holy shit, there, Deputy, just calm the hell down," Koznowski commanded, his voice an octave or two higher than he may have preferred. "Jesus! An' lower your weapon. You're liable to hurt someone."

"Sorry."

Rev. Boefinck looked from one to the other in astonishment. "You both really are Pilate, ain'cha? Man alive."

The sheriff stepped into the house and holstered his weapon. "None of it changes the fact you're still under arrest, ma'am. So why don't you take a seat?"

"I reckon you think you been redeemed," she sneered at him. "But you ain't. You're Satan, that's all. Satan himself. You ain't been washed in the blood of the Lamb. You're a stench in the nostrils of the righteous."

"Yes, well, you may be right about all them things," Koznowski said, still a bit shaky. "But take a seat anyways." He nodded to the nearby couch.

In spite of her fuming holy indignation she took a seat, at which point Koznowski read her her rights, emphasizing the "remain silent" part.

"So lemme ask you," he said when he was finished. "If your boy's innocent, why'd you sneak him out the back door an' tell him to run?"

Rev. Boefinck shook her head. "Nah, I take it back. You people couldn't be devils. Devils ain't that stupid." She clucked her tongue. "I was takin' my rhubarb bread outa the oven, okay? Ezekiel was out running 'cause he runs every day before school. Y'know? To keep in practice?" She tipped her head toward the clippings on the wall. "He's got state invitationals comin' up, don'cha know? So I see him headin' toward the house, an' I stick my head out the back door to cheer him on. Since when is it a crime for a mom to cheer on her son? *Jeeze,* you people."

"But the sheriff told you he wanted to talk to Ezekiel," Deputy Vandenberg said.

"Yah, well, he didn't say right now, did he? I didn't see any reason to break his practice so's you could ask him some stupid questions about something he had nothing to do with. Not with invitationals an' all."

"Ah, crap. We'll take this up at the station," Koznowski said. "I got a search to conduct here. Deputy Vandenberg'll stay and keep an eye on you, just makin' sure you don't start training for invitationals yourself, eh? You think to try, the deputy here'll shoot you. Don't think she won't, neither. Woman's a trained killer." He looked at his watch. "Yah, I'm sure Deke and Ellsworth have caught up with Ezekiel by now. You'll be seeing him real soon."

"Hah!" the Reverend Boefinck barked. Both Koznowski and Vandenberg looked at her curiously. "You still got no idea what you're dealing with here, do you?" She seemed quite satisfied with herself and shifted back into a corner of the couch, smiling quietly into her lap.

✠

Ezekiel's room was what Koznowski would have expected from any normal teenager. The bed was unmade and the floor was cluttered with tennis shoes and discarded clothes. The one thing that did surprise him was the overflow of yet more trophies and awards. Apparently the lesser awards that didn't fit downstairs were warehoused up here. The walls were covered with plaques and certificates and ribbons, academic awards, Boy Scout badges, still more photos of the boy shaking hands with people who are handing him things. The shelves were full of cheap gold-plated trophies for damn near everything they make trophies for. It occurred to Koznowski the kid wasn't normal, in spite of all the clothes on the floor. No normal kid would push himself this way. Unless, of course, as he suspected, someone else was doing the pushing. Whatever the case and whatever the sad reason behind it all, he was coming to resent the little bastard.

He opened the closet and flipped through the shirts and pants before feeling behind them to poke into the corners where he found a hockey stick (that one had his hopes up for a second), a tennis racket, and a bowling ball and custom shoes inside a monogrammed leather bowling bag. On the nightstand next to the bed rested a personalized, leather-bound Bible filled with tiny, indecipherable notations on Post-It notes.

One thing he'd noticed was there were no pictures of golden boy here with girls. No evidence of girls of any kind apart from his mother. Kid like that? Teenage girls should be killing themselves and each other over him. Maybe Mom didn't allow it, or maybe he was one of those queer teenagers. Or maybe, looking at the awards again, he channeled all of his sexual frustration into throwing balls and whatnot.

There'd been no drugs, no empty wine cooler bottles or beer cans, no nothing. Still, there had to be some porn around here someplace. Any kind at all, he didn't care. If he couldn't uncover at least a few buried dirty pictures, Koznowski knew he was dealing with a potentially dangerous freak.

He hadn't found any in the closet or under the nightstand. All the dresser drawers were clean. He stuck a hand beneath the mattress and felt around. Nothing. Jeeze, what a loser. Maybe he'd hidden it in the bed frame.

Koznowski lowered himself painfully to the carpeting, flipped back the blankets, and craned his head to the side.

Nope, no porn there either. But there was a gun rack mounted beneath the bed cradling what appeared to be a freshly oiled shotgun. He was so intent on nailing this kid with some porn he nearly overlooked it.

Koznowski felt his shoulders relax when they passed the Slab City Carp, and he nearly went all misty when he saw the Sheriff's Department up ahead. For the last forty-five minutes he and Vandenberg had been subjected to an incessant (and increasingly profane) berating from Rev. Boefinck in the backseat. They hadn't handcuffed her, figuring handcuffing a woman of God (even a delusional and possibly murderous one) wouldn't go over real well with the townsfolk. She hadn't taken a swing at either of them, but she'd done everything short of that, especially after Leona radioed in to report Ezekiel had been arrested without incident and was presently sitting quietly in a holding cell in the basement of the station.

As he pulled into the frozen gray parking lot, the sheriff slowed the four-by-four and squinted through the windshield toward the building. Gathered outside the front doors was a cluster of a dozen or more people, most of whom Koznowski recognized even bundled up as they were. Some were carrying cardboard signs, and a TV-8 news van was parked on the other side of the lot.

"What the hey?" Vandenberg asked.

"Seems word travels fast around here, eh?"

"Wha'cha mean?"

The sheriff nodded toward the crowd, some of whom had noticed the truck and were alerting the others. "Well look at 'em. They're here I'm guessing on accounta they heard we caught a prime suspect and wanna congratulate us. Or thank us, or something. Look, a couple are headed this way even." He waved at the approaching mob and pulled the truck into his parking spot near the back door.

"I wouldn't be so sure about that," came a gleefully doubtful voice from the backseat.

"I dunno, Chief," Vandenberg agreed. "Hate to say it but she may be right. They aren't looking real happy from here."

"It's just like in the Bible," the preacher said. "They're here to demand Pilate let their Savior go."

Examining the approaching crowd, Koznowski said, "Ah, not to, ah, cast dispersions at your Bible scholarship there, ma'am, an' I may just be a jester of Satan myself, but weren't it the case in the Bible that . . . oh, never mind."

"Pilate," she muttered.

"Yah, well," Koznowski said. "I doubt very much the folks of Kausheenah County are gonna be so dumb as to be asking me to let a suspect in a double homicide loose." Still, he couldn't help but notice Deputy Vandenberg was right. They didn't look happy. The only one who was smiling was Knut Mockery, who was leading the pack toward the truck. Koznowski cracked his door open. "Okay now, you two stay put. An' you, Reverend Boefinck, you keep your mouth shut or out comes the masking tape." He opened the door and stepped outside. An arrow of pain shot up his right leg.

"Heya, Chief," Mockery shouted as he trotted across the slick packed ice toward the truck. A news camera followed the mob. "Knut Mockery of the *Chronicle* here."

"Oh, for godsakes, Knut, we all know who you are," Koznowski told the small blond man. "And you don't gotta run around with that fake press pass sticking out of your hat. It's not 1932 anymore, and you look foolish."

Mockery was too focused on his role, and on the presence of the television camera, to let it throw him. "Word has it you've taken Ezekiel Boefinck into custody on suspicion of these two murders. Is this true?"

"We do have two suspects in custody, yah," Koznowski said, snapping into public statement mode. "But I ain't had a chance to question them yet."

"Well, Chief, may I remind you he has a football game this Friday, and if he's not there, there go our chances for state?" The crowd behind Mockery cheered and waved signs reading FREE EZEKIEL, S.O.T. SAVE OUR TEAM, and GOD HATES YOU (that last one carried by a walleyed woman Koznowski recognized as a member of the Pollex Christi congregation). "I mean, it was clear you weren't getting anywhere on this case, but are you really this dumb? And is there any truth to the rumor you've laid a heavy bet on the Goodisville Grizzlies? That in short you brought in E.Z. on some trumped-up charges to cover up your own gambling addiction? Do you realize, Sheriff, what will happen to the future of the whole community if we lose this game because you were holding the star player in order to hide your own personal failings?"

Koznowski looked at his shoes, waiting to make sure Mockery was finished. Once it was clear the reporter (of sorts) had laid out his theory completely, Koznowski looked up again and scanned the angry faces. "Yah, you're insane, Knut, all there is to it. You're all insane, and I ain't even gonna dignify that with a comment. So if you'll just ask the folks to, y'know, make way, I have another suspect here I need to get inside." Koznowski turned to see the Reverend Boefinck smiling and shaking her fist to the crowd through the back window.

"Stop doing that!" he snapped.

"Reverend Boefinck!" someone screamed.

Someone else shouted, "We'll get you out of there and send this bastard to hell with the rest of them!" The crowd cheered and hissed, and it struck Koznowski that if he didn't get the woman inside now this whole scene could turn ugly. He raised both hands to the mob. "Yah, okay, careful with that kinda talk there, ma'am." He stepped around the truck and opened the door to let Rev. Boefinck out.

"Hope you weren't counting on that reelection next year, there, Chief," Mockery shouted.

With Koznowski and Vandenberg flanking her as they walked quickly to the side entrance, Rev. Boefinck extended her arms and rolled her eyes heavenward as if entering one of her trances. The mob stayed behind and as a single voice began chanting, *"Free E.Z. now! Free E.Z. now!"*

Her head back and arms still extended, the Reverend Boefinck whispered, "You'll never be able to hold him," as the sheriff scrounged in his pockets for the keys.

"Yah, so," he replied as they stood outside the locked door in the frigid breeze, his own constituents chanting at his back. He really should've pulled the keys out earlier.

✠

After locking her in the station's only holding cell with her son and Huan Tiang (who'd lost his job at Jed Karlson's Chubby Cowe feed store and was still sleeping off a three-day bender), and after dropping off the shotgun at the station's small forensics lab, Koznowski stopped by his desk. He could still hear the angry locals chanting out front. Sometimes it occurred to him the people he'd devoted his life to protecting could be a bunch of El Stupidos. He wasn't just talking about the Mexicans either. Asking him to set a killer free so he could play a damned game? How fucking nuts was that? It was like setting Charlie Manson free so he could pursue his recording career, or turning John Wayne Gacy loose so he could continue entertaining at kids' birthday parties.

His desk, which had been clean as a whistle before all this nonsense started, was becoming an increasingly incoherent mess covered with phone messages, reports, files, and paperwork that all needed his attention. It was hard to believe so much had happened in a little over two weeks. Take it day by day and it felt like nothing at all ever happened in his county. Let it build awhile and suddenly it looks like they're in the midst of a crime wave like nothing the county had ever seen before. Over the past weeks, listening to his officers and the people in the stores, it really did feel like something more was going on. But why now? Something in the air was driving people a little nuts. Some communal madness. Holiday season and all, maybe. He'd been so wrapped up in this Unterhumm case he'd been letting it slide by unnoticed. He hung his coat over the back of his chair and flipped through a few of the most recent phone messages, pausing at one. An eyebrow arched.

"Heya Leona?" he called across the louder-than-usual room. Everyone was all a-flutter over not only the protesters and having a suspect in custody but in having E.Z. Boefinck on the premises. He'd already heard a few of his people talking about autographs.

"Yah, uh-huh?" Leona called back.

"What's this message?" He held up a slip of pink paper.

The receptionist, some thirty feet away, squinted at it. "Yah got me there, Chief. You wanna gimme a hint?"

"Eagle Bluff PD?"

"Oh, yah, yah that one. I dunno. He asked you call him back when you can. Somethin' about a child molester or somethin'."

"Oh," Koznowski said, a little bewildered. "Jeepers, okay, then. They weren't asking about Denny Blodgett, were they?"

"Naw, uh-uh. Not so I think, anyways."

"Okay, good." He noticed another message slip. "And what's this one from the Wausau Psych Hospital?"

"Oh," Leona said. "That one's about Denny."

Koznowski considered the note. "Yah, figures, eh? They want my opinion, they can just keep him there." The sound of chanting leaked through the front doors again as the protesters made another round. *And while I'm at it*, he thought, *I should see if they have room for a dozen more*. Things really were going all cattywampus these days. He set the message next to the phone on top of the files from Unterhumm's office. That reminded him of something. He called over to Deputy Vandenberg, who was in the process of cleaning up her own desktop. She straightened out a pile of reports, then stepped over to the sheriff. "Been nutty in here lately," she said. "Who knew?"

"Yah, you're tellin' me . . . So Deliah. I got another mission for you. This one'll be almost twice as much fun as the last one, there."

"Hey, that's super. Sounds like a real step up." Apart from the voice, Deputy Vandenberg expressed no enthusiasm whatsoever.

"Yah, well." He picked up the stack of Unterhumm's invoices. "This might lead to nothing, here, an' it might not even be worth anything at this point, now that we got a suspect?"

Vandenberg's face drooped a bit. "This is sounding better all the time, Chief. Lets me know all my hard work's finally paying off, eh?"

"Yah, well. No need to be a smart guy about it. Here's what I wan'cha to do. I wan'cha to go through these receipts here, see? An' when there's a name attached, I wan'cha to find the families of the deceased. Then I wan'cha to call 'em up and confirm they authorized these donations. Y'know, that they said it's okay to sell off . . . ." He glanced at the top sheet. "Edie's pancreas. You think you got it?"

Deputy Vandenberg stared at Koznowski sadly for a moment. "Oh, Chief, these poor folks are not gonna be real tickled to have me calling and asking 'em a question like that."

"That's why I'm askin' you an' not Deke. Since you're a girl, see? You know how to handle things like this a little more sensitively. He'd probably just make people cry."

"Girl?" she shot back, hands moving to her hips. "I'm thirty-seven."

"Yah, great," Koznowski said. "First five say they gave their consent, then you can stop. How's that? Now if you'll excuse me I gotta go interrogate a suspect."

✠

About a quarter mile offshore on the frozen surface of North Overshoe Lake, Fink Anderson crouched in his shack over the hole he'd drilled through the ice. He had three lines down, a new fifth of Wild Turkey propped next to him, and he was still screaming in his head at those stupid bastards at the Sheriff's Department. Goddamn know-nothings. Maybe he'd go straight to the fucking army himself. Local cops won't even listen to him when it's gonna be their problem before long? Fuck 'em then, let 'em stand around with their goddamn thumbs up their asses until it's too late. When people's goddamn kids start getting eaten by this thing, whatever it is. And DNR my ass, they've had it in for him for years now and everybody knows it, so what the hell are they gonna do?

Bastards at the Sheriff's Department weren't the only know-nothings around there, neither. Everyone telling him it was too early to head out on the lake, that the ice wasn't thick enough in November, no matter how cold it'd been. Well what the hell did they know? Had they been fishing this goddamn lake for twenty years? No they sure goddamn hadn't. He had, though, and knew damn well when it was thick enough. He could smell it, same way he could smell snow two days before it rolled in. Stupid fuckers, let 'em starve then, they want to.

He twisted the cork from the bottle with a squeak and a soft pop, took a drink, and jiggled one of the lines. Been out there two hours now, and not a goddamn thing to show for it. He'd give it another hour or so, wait'll the moon comes up. If it was still running dead by then, he'd load the shack back on the truck and head home. Too goddamn cold to waste his time. Get a fire going back home, maybe fry up some baloney. He took another swallow of the whiskey and clapped his hands together.

Stupid assholes. That's what he'd do. He'd go to the army himself. Maybe call first, find out where the nearest base was, what kinda equipment they had. They gotta have experience with shit like this.

It might've just been the Turkey taking its first hold, but the water seemed to swell and lap around the edges of the four-inch-wide hole he'd drilled.

"What the hell?" he said aloud as he bent closer. Suddenly all three lines ripped hard to the side and snapped. He made a clumsy grab for them, plunging his hand into the icewater. The lines were already gone and his own stumbling, drunken momentum toppled him sprawling onto his back, thwacking his head against the shack's wall.

"Oh, shit . . . Jeezes," he groaned as he lay there, trying to decide if he should rub the back of his head or cradle the frozen hand. "What the fuck just did that?" he asked himself. He was almost tempted to laugh when he felt the very ice itself swell beneath him and heard the first pops of the ice cracking outside the shack. He forgot about his head. The immediate, reflexive impulse was to get the truck out of there. Maybe the stupid bastards were right after all and it *was* too early yet. But then he heard another sound. A sound like nothing he'd heard in all his twenty years on that goddamn lake. It sounded like something just off to his right there a ways, as if some kinda animal down there below him was trying to chew its way up through the ice. But that didn't make any goddamn sense at all.

✠

"So you're confessing, here. You're saying you did it."

"No, my mother—"

"So now you're trying to pin it on your own mother? That's pretty low, eh, Jesus. Even if she is nutty as a jaybird."

"No, that's not what I'm saying. Why aren't you listening to me?"

"But we found the murder weapon stashed under your bed, there. You're saying she put it there to frame you? That ain't real nice."

"*No!*"

"Jesus here seems to be havin' some real trouble makin' up his mind. That sure don't look good for him, eh?"

"Nah, sure don't."

Ezekiel Boefinck might have been the second coming of Christ in the eyes of most folks from Kausheenah County, but he was still seventeen, and sitting in the spare interrogation room with the yellow walls, the fake wood table, and the tile floor he was near tears. Both his wrists and his ankles had been cuffed to his chair. On the table in front of him was a boxy Panasonic tape recorder, its wheels slowly turning as the tape continued to roll. Sheriff Koznowski and Deke Keller sat across the table from him, arms folded, trying to look menacing, clearly enjoying themselves far too much. Keller might have been in awe of the kid's athletic ability, but seated across from him in an interrogation room he just wanted to see golden boy crack.

"Yah, it's really too bad your ma there don't believe in lawyers," Keller said. "That's two strikes against both of youse. But since you're still a minor, they're sendin' one by for you anyways."

"Yah, judge decides to charge you as an adult—which he will, double murder an' all—you'll need one, believe you me. Not that it'll matter, all the evidence we got." Koznowski turned to Keller. "Who're they sending?"

"Jerry Kerlin, they said."

The sheriff tried not to smile as he turned back to E.Z. "Oh, that's really too bad. But hey, Jesus, take my advice. Whenever he stops by, keep your legs crossed, eh?"

"Yah, ain't it the truth?" Keller snickered. "Looks like you're gonna be spendin' a good long time up in Waupun. Hey, here's a little more advice help you get by there. Those big black guys an' big Indians they got up there really like it when you cry. So try an' remember to cry a lot. Man, I tell ya, pretty white boy like you? They're gonna turn you into a pincushion for cock."

Koznowski nearly spit out his coffee. "Ho-lee mackerel there, Deke, where the hell'd you ever pick that one up?"

"I dunno. Just came to me."

"Yah," Koznowski said. "Sometimes I worry about you. That was a doozy, though." Both officers seemed to have forgotten the tape was still rolling, and they were supposed to be questioning a suspect. Koznowski turned back to Ezekiel. "All right, there, Jesus." He paused to take another sip of coffee and leaned back in his chair, knowing he'd just about won. *Let's see what that sumbitch Knut Mockery says when the kid confesses.* "Few minutes ago you were having some real trouble keeping your stories straight. So let's run over it again, here. See if you can stick to one or the other."

"Please stop calling me Jesus."

"Yah, it's really too bad your ma don't believe in lawyers, eh?" Keller repeated. "She forget what happened to Joan of Arc, there? Better you just confess so's we can put you back down there in the cell with her. Ole Huan, he gets pretty ornery when he's hung. All her singin' an' speakin' in tongues an' such just ain't gonna help his disposition. No tellin' what he might do."

"Joan of Arc?"

"Yah, never mind. Let's just get on with it, eh?" Koznowski shook his head slightly. On the other side of the table E.Z. bit a bloodless lower lip. "So on the night of November fourteenth you put the shotgun in the back of your car. Then you drove to Unterhumm's Funeral Home in Beaver Rapids."

"Yes," the boy said quietly.

"Okay, then you entered the premises, went to the office and killed Kirby Mudge, went downstairs, killed Klaus Unterhumm, and drove home and hid the gun under the bed."

"No. I never made it to the funeral home."

Keller rolled his eyes and his hands went skyward in supplication. "Oh, here you go again," he said. "You're being all goofy. You admit you drove up there to kill 'em, but say you didn't kill 'em. But on the morning of the fifteenth the county coroner shows up and lo an' behold finds 'em shot to death. Explain that one to a jury, there, Jesus."

E.Z.'s chains jangled and his fingers curled into fists. "I don't know how it happened. I didn't even make it to Beaver Rapids! I knew I'd never be able to do it, so I stopped and turned around."

"Yah, but with you being Jesus and all, it shoulda been no problem gettin' away with it, eh? Do it from home iffen you want, like *Bewitched* or something." Keller snickered again.

"That's what my mom kept saying. She wouldn't listen to me."

"So now you're saying your ma told you to do it. Again with the mother." One way or another, Koznowski was satisfied. They should send both of them up for life.

The boy was less frightened now than angry, churning with the frustrated rage of the misunderstood teenager. "No . . . why don't you guys ever listen? She didn't tell me to do it. All she said was I *could* do it and no one would ever catch me."

"Well, so much for her silly theory, eh?" Koznowski said.

"Yah, then," Keller added. "She might wanna stop using a return address on her death threats, y'know?"

"Yah, so, lemme ask you this. Why Unterhumm's? There's a few other funeral homes just as close."

E.Z. was quiet for a moment, staring at the table, perhaps realizing, Koznowski thought, he shouldn't have opened his big yap. "Because Mother an' me drove up there a few weeks earlier to deliver another letter . . . I knew the way." He looked up. "My mother . . . she's . . . There's something wrong with her. She thinks I'm something I'm not. All those people in church do too. And people all over. You know why I do all that stuff at school, I'm on all the teams? Even why I'm going after that stupid Eagle Scout thing?"

"Because you're Jesus?"

"Because I'll do anything that'll get me out of the house and away from her. I can't stand her and all that crap of hers. Maybe I just wanted to prove that I wasn't what she thought I was. I don't know."

"What," Koznowski asked, "by blowing a couple morticians away? Seems that woulda made her real proud."

E.Z. shook his head. "No, not by killing them. By getting caught. But I didn't kill anybody."

"Getting caught?" Koznowski stared at him. "Well, glad to see things worked out for you, there, son." He turned to Keller. "Go get Pete an' have him bring the kid back to his cell. We got him comin' and goin', especially after them ballistics tests come back."

X

"Hello?"

"Uh, hello, yes, ah, is this Beverly Kokal?"

"Yah, that's the number you called."

"Mrs. Kokal—"

"Oh, call me Bev. Everybody does."

"Okay, Bev, um . . . My name's—I mean, this is—Deputy Deliah Vandenberg, and I'm with the Kausheenah County Sheriff's Department, and I need to ask for your help on a current investigation of ours."

"Well my goodness sakes. That certainly does sound exciting, don't it, then?"

That wasn't exactly the reaction Vandenberg was expecting. She hoped it would continue over the next minute or two. "This'll just take a moment . . . um . . . I'm, ah, I'm sorry—"

"Oh, you go right ahead and spit it out there, hon," Bev said. "I've seen an' heard it all in my day, believe you me."

As the woman laughed, the deputy swallowed. "I'm sorry, Mrs. Kokal, but this involves your husband, Edward?"

There was a brief, confused silence on the other end. "I'm thinkin' you must have the wrong party here." The woman still sounded unusually chipper. "My husband Eddie died goin' on two years now. An' if you're gonna tell me he's in trouble with the law again, well, let's just say it would really be something. Then again, maybe I wouldn't put it past Eddie, right? He was always fulla surprises."

"No, I'm aware of that Mrs.—Bev . . ." It seemed as good a time as any to charge ahead and get this over with, like yanking off a bandage. Vandenberg took a breath and closed her eyes. "But I'm afraid I must ask you a very personal question. When you were dealing with the Unterhumm Funeral Home, do you remember signing any papers giving them permission to sell your . . . Edward's brain to the Mayo Clinic?"

There was more silence on the other end until Mrs. Kokal finally asked, "What the heck would anybody want with Eddie's brain? Never did him much good when he was here."

"And his pelvic bone to the Woodbridge Hospital in Rochester?"

In this second silence, Deputy Vandenberg could sense the change. Bev Kokal was no longer chipper. "Who is this?" she whispered.

"Please, Mrs. Kokal, I'm sorry, but it's very important."

"What the heck . . . is this? What are you doin' this for? What kind of sick . . . Get away from me!"

Vandenberg heard the receiver slam down violently and decided to take it as a "no."

✠

LeAnn grabbed him when he told her about the Boefincks. "Aw, hon, I was worried about you goin' down there today. That's super news! We gotta go celebrate then. You caught yourself a killer. You didn't think you could do it but I always knew you could, silly goose." She gave his belly a light pinch.

"Yah, thanks sweetie. It was pretty exciting, gotta say. The whole team worked real good. The kid's telling some crazy damn story that's sounding an awful lot like a confession, there. Judge might say it ain't exactly, but even if that happens we pretty much got him dead to rights." Looking over her shoulder he saw LeAnn had been busy decorating the small house. Usually she waited until at least after Thanksgiving, but he guessed the world was moving faster and faster all the time. Tinsel garlands had been stapled up around the doorways and a cardboard Santa and Rudolph hung in the front window. She'd even replaced her orange candles with a red one and a green one on the coffee table in front of the couch. On the mantel over the bricked-up fireplace she'd carefully placed two Hummel angels, a plastic nativity scene, and a snowglobe. She'd left a big space open over in the corner. He'd had a bit too much on his mind lately to even think about going to pick out a tree, but it was way too early yet anyway. Didn't need the damn thing turning all brown on them by second week of December.

"Oh, that's real super. I'm so proud of you, hon. Hey, what say we go over to the Dew Drop for some booyah? We ain't done that in such a time."

Koznowski made a face as he dropped his hat on the couch. "Oh, no booyah for me, no. We can go there iffen you like, but you remember what happened last time."

"Well, yah, sure," she said. "You got that chicken foot in your bowl. But don't tell me that's got you all scared off booyah forever. It's all parta the fun of booyah, right? You never know what you're gonna get."

He lowered himself onto the couch, just for a few minutes. "Yah, but in some places a chicken foot's a terrible curse."

"Not in Wisconsin it ain't. More like a Cracker Jack prize."

He obviously didn't consider it a joking matter. "I get that chicken foot an two days later I get in the accident."

"That was then?"

He nodded. She knew better than to argue with him, silently filing it away along with all his other quirks. "Well, you can get a couple brats or somethin'. Or one o' their Dew Drop burgers. You like them, right? How's that?"

"Sounds like a plan, then." His voice was tired. Only as he sat there on the sagging couch did it occur to him his whole body was tired. Even his brain felt tired. It had been a hell of a day. Hell of a couple weeks. He couldn't believe those damn protesters were still out there when he headed for his truck that night. Sometimes he wondered about these folks.

"Let 'em stay out there, freeze to death, they're gonna act that way."

LeAnn was putting on her boots. "What's that, hon?"

He looked up, for a moment not realizing where he was or that he'd said anything aloud.

"Oh," he told her with a shake of the head. "Nothing really. I'll tell you about it over beers."

✠

"Yah?"

"Mr. Lindstrom?"

"Yaaah?"

"Hi, Mr. Lindstrom. This is Deputy Vandenberg from the Kausheenah County Sheriff's Department, and I'm afraid I need to ask you a difficult question."

"Aw, jeeze."

"Yeah, I'm very sorry about this, but it's part of a current investigation."

"Don't have the money to be donatin' nothin' to nothin'."

"No, Mr. Lindstrom, I'm not asking you for money. This is about Lars."

"Lars? . . . Yah, Lars, he died some four years ago. You're lookin' for him you can try over to Cravenswood. The mausoleum there. Guard'll point him out."

"Yes, yes, I know that, Mr. Lindstrom . . . I was wondering if you could tell me, when you were dealing with the Unterhumm Funeral Home—"

"Unterhumm? That's the guy got shot, right?"

"Yes, he is, but—"

"This have somethin' to do with that? 'Cause I heard they got that kid an' his ma. That preacher lady."

"Well, Mr. Lindstrom, yes, that's true, but this is another part of that investigation, see? We're just looking into some stuff."

"Oh. Well, then."

"So when you were dealing with the funeral home, did you give them the okay to sell Lars's femurs to the University of Wyoming Medical School?"

"His what, now, to who?"

"His thigh bones, I think? To the University of Wyoming."

"Oh, hell no. Why'd we do a thing like that? That's crazy talk. My boy was buried whole."

"Okay, Mr. Lindstrom. Thanks very much. This is a big help to us. So thanks for your time, and again I'm real sorry—"

"Only thing is, though, we didn't take Lars to Unterhumm's. That's over in Beaver Rapids, right? Nah, we went to Burke an' Sons, over by us here."

✠

When the station door flew open and an excited young hunter charged in, it took Leona a moment to register the face. Behind him on the sidewalk, the protesters were still marching and chanting, and their numbers were growing. There must've been a good twenty, twenty-five out there by now.

Sgt. Ziegler was dressed in camouflage gear, an orange hunter's vest, and an equally orange cap. A paper license, the numbers printed in black, was taped to his chest. He was carrying a hefty burlap sack over his shoulder like some backwoods Saint Nick, the bottom soaked in drying blood.

"Jeepers, Zee," Leona said when it all finally came together. "Took me a sec, there, eh? Don't think I ever seen you out of uniform before. But what the heck's that smell?" Her nose wrinkled as she reluctantly sniffed.

"Yeah?" Ziegler's smile looked almost painful. "Buck lure! Just got back from the woods and had to show youse guys. Been out there every year with my dad an' brother since I was nine and never bagged a thing, eh? Look, you gotta see." He swung the bag around and dropped it on her desk.

Noticing the hubbub and the unmistakable odor of buck lure, Ellsworth wandered over to find out firsthand what kind of stupid shit Ziegler'd gotten himself into this time. "Kinda small, ain't it?" he asked as he approached, nodding toward the mystery trophy. Leona was staring in some horror at the bloody sack the little moron had just dumped across her schedules, messages, and paperwork. "What, you bag a deer fetus, or what?"

"Naw," Ziegler said. "Better! Look!" As still more officers collected around Leona's desk, Ziegler tugged open the top of the sack. "I had to break off the arrow like that to get it to fit in the bag. But pretty good shot, eh? Gotta admit that."

As Ziegler swelled with unashamed pride, Ellsworth peered into the bag. Inside was the twisted and bloodied body of a bald eagle, a broken arrow neatly piercing its throat.

"C'mon, look," Ziegler encouraged the others. "Just hadda show you guys before I took it home and cleaned it."

"Ah, Ziegler?" Ellsworth said, moving back to let the others take a peek for themselves. "Uh, yah, see, three things come to mind here. Christ, where to start?" He slipped his hands in his pockets. "Okay, first of all, it's deer season. You were supposed to be hunting *deers* out there, not birds. Second, even if it was bird season, killing a bald eagle, I think, is a federal offense. Even if it ain't federal, it's still illegal, there. Symbol of the nation an' what have you. But the biggest thing of all, see, is that bow season ended over a damn week ago. Numbnuts. If you were a civilian, you'd be looking at three years right now, minimum."

As Ziegler's smile collapsed, the tears began welling up in his eyes and the blood rose to his face. Finally, unable to take the strain, he broke into sobs. "I'm sorry," he squeaked out before turning and running from the station, leaving the eagle carcass behind on Leona's desk.

✠

"Ah, hello Sheriff Koznowski. Thanks for getting back to me."

"Oh. You betcha, Sergeant Susparagus. Woulda been sooner, but we just brought in a couple suspects in a double homicide case yesterday . . . dunno if you maybe heard about it. Sure it's not much for you big city boys, but it's big news up here so things've been a little crazy." He paused in consideration. "'Sergeant Susparagus'—that's a toughie, eh? So now what can I do for you? Hey, an' how's the weather down in your neck of the woods?"

"Clear and too cold for November, that's for damn sure." Sgt. Frank Susparagus of the Eagle Bluff Police Department cleared his throat. He despised empty, banal chitchat about the weather but knew what was expected of him. "Yeah, well, Sheriff, just checking something out here. We had a young man from up around by you come down here a couple days ago to file some very serious charges against a priest at a local parish, Saint Barnabas."

"Oh yah? By serious, you mean it's one a those?"

"If by 'one of those' you mean sexual abuse, then yes."

"Aw, jeeze, hey?" Koznowski said as his stomach tightened. "Can I ask you who it was, then?" He heard a brief shuffle of papers on the other end of the line.

"His name's Daniel Bubich, age twenty-three, lives out on—"

"Oh, sure," Koznowski interrupted, "Danny. That's Jocelyn Bubich's boy. Thought I saw him at the station here a week or so back, but it was pretty nutty so I wasn't sure if it was him or not. Never found out what he wanted."

"Yeah," Sgt. Susparagus said. "That's what I'm curious about. See, there are two things about his story that leave me scratching my head."

"Oh yah?"

"Yeah. First, he says the alleged molestation took place ten years ago. Between ten and twelve years ago to be exact, and he says it went on for a while."

"Hooboy," Koznowski said. "That's some bad news, eh? Y'know, you read about it in the papers an' such in New York an' Chicago, but never around here. An' Danny Bubich too? Kinda makes you feel sick. Didn't even know he was Catholic."

"See," Sgt. Susparagus went on, ignoring him, "that the alleged incidents took place so long ago has me worried."

"Yah, I can see why."

"But the bigger issue for us down here is Mr. Bubich says he was molested by a Father Kinnealey, and we don't have a Father Kinnealey down here. Not at Saint Barnabas, not anywhere."

"Well, that's sure a corker, eh?" Koznowski offered.

"We checked, and the Bubiches lived here at the time of the alleged assaults. Church records also confirm he was indeed an altar boy at Saint Barnabas, and he can name all the other priests who were there at the time. But they have no record of a Father Kinnealey . . . So I was wondering if you have a Kinnealey up by you? Maybe he's just confused about the name. Case of this nature, that's something you don't want to get wrong."

Koznowski shook his head. "'Fraid I can't help you there, Sarge. We got Saint Timothy's up here, and I can tell you for sure they never had a Kinnealey. 'Bout as close as they came was a Father Cochran, but he passed on oh, nine, ten years ago."

Sgt. Susparagus sighed. "All right. Figured it was worth a shot. Given all this, though, if I can ask you another question? We need to take every possibility into account before proceeding with this."

"Yah, shoot."

"How much do you know about Daniel Bubich? I mean, does he have a history of making up stories, filing false reports, anything like that? Any trouble with your department or mental issues you're aware of?"

"Danny?" The question took him by surprise. "Aw, hell no. Wouldn't even know he's around. Helps his mom out on the farm ever since he lost his dad, keeps to himself most ways. At least in, y'know, in terms of anything that might bring him to our attention."

"Yeah, okay Sheriff, gotcha. Many thanks for your help. Guess I'll go ask a few more questions at Saint Barnabas. Maybe there's something they forgot."

"Okay there then, Sergeant. Sorry I couldn'ta been more help today. But keep me posted, you find out anything."

"Will do. And you do the same. In the meantime have a Happy Thanksgiving."

"Thanks . . . giving?" Koznowski asked.

"Heyas?"

"Ah . . . hello? Is this Charles O'Bannon?"

"Oh, you betcha."

"Hello, Mr. O'Bannon. This is Deputy Deliah Vandenberg of the Kausheenah County Sheriff's Department, and—"

"Hey, you gotta be shittin' me. Delish?"

"Deputy Deliah Vandenberg, yes, and I—"

"Hey, don'cha remember Chuck O'Bannon? I'm hurt, eh? We was in fourth grade together. Mrs. Sweeney's class before she went all nuts?"

"Oh . . . um . . . yeah, of course. Hiya, Chuck. Ah . . . how's it, y'know, going?"

"Can't complain too much, I suppose. I mean, what the hell good would it do anyway, right? Been outa work for a couple years now, an' there's only so much disability'll cover when you're dealin' with four kids. So's I mostly just wheel 'round the trailer here, watch the tube till the wife gets home from the mill over to Jefferson . . . Hey, but look at you, in the Sheriff's Department over there like that. Never woulda figured, eh? So why you callin' here? You arrangin' a class reunion or somethin'?"

"Oh, ah, not exactly, Chuck. No. Y'see, I'm kinda workin' on this investigation here . . . and Genevieve's name came up."

"Ma? Oh, that's kinda crazy, eh? Ma ain't robbed no bank or nothin', did she? Sure hope not, given as she died, y'know, a few years back. It was real bad news."

"I'm real sorry to hear that."

"Yah, the cancers just ate her up. Then she had a stroke an' fell outa the hospital bed an' broke her hip."

"Oh my God. That's terrible, Chuck, I'm sorry. But that's what I'm calling you about."

"Yah? You investigatin' that shitty hospital? Ask me, them people should be in jail."

"No, no, this is something else. Now—"

"Hey, you said Vandenberg? Same last name you had in school, right? Unless you married some guy named Vandenberg, but that don't seem too likely, eh? You an' Ronnie Jacobs ever get married?"

"Who?"

"Aw, you gotta remember Ronnie Jacobs. From our class? You two were quite the thing."

"That was fourth grade, Chuck. No, I never married him."

"So, what, you never got married?"

"No. I, ah, I never married. Now c'mon, if I could ask you—"

"Oh yah? That's too bad. Some lucky guy missed out, gotta say. But hey, y'know, just to toss it out there . . . like I says my wife's at the mill most days an' the kids're off in school, so it's just, y'know, me here all day an I always gotta couple cold ones in the fridge if ever maybe—"

"*Chuck* . . . did you give the Unterhumm Funeral Home the go-ahead to sell your mother's body to the United States Army?"

✠

A light snow was falling and the day's high temperature wasn't expected to climb much above thirty, but it didn't seem to bother anyone. The sidewalks of the Beaver Rapids commercial strip were lined with hundreds of locals, as it was every year for the Thanksgiving Day parade. All the kids had been nudged forward to the curb, not only to get a better view but to have a fighting chance in the mad, sometimes brutal scramble that ensued whenever any candy was tossed their way.

The only empty space left along the half-mile-long parade route was the circular vacuum some twenty feet in diameter surrounding Sheriff Koznowski. No one spoke to him, no one dared come close for fear of what the others would say, and he didn't give a good goddamn about any of it. They were gonna be stupid that way, let 'em. It meant no one would block his view. He stood motionless and stoic, arms folded, just another citizen watching the parade, if a little less enthusiastically. He had his men out there at six that morning setting up barricades and positioning themselves on rooftops as per the mayor's instructions. Now all they had to do was wait for the terrorist sniper or nuclear volley, and when either arrived (as the mayor was convinced they would) his team would be ready.

At least half of the cheering adults up and down the parade route seemed to be carrying that week's *Chronicle,* whose banner headline howled "Sheriff Gambles Away Our Future." Koznowski hadn't read the story, but LeAnn had. She told him he could probably sue Mockery for libel but he'd never been the litigious type. No, he had other ideas. And if Betty just happened to accidentally show up for Thanksgiving dinner, he might try them out on her.

The Blue Devils marching band heralded the beginning of the parade as ever, the almost rhythmic thumping of the bass drums announcing their approach from way down on Knox Street as the rest of the band bleated out a tinny, unbalanced oompah transcription of "I'm Easy."

Given there wasn't much else by way of other bands or floats or giant balloons, it was the goal of the parade organizers to stretch things out as long as possible to give the crowd its money's worth. It was another two minutes after the Blue Devils passed down the street and away before one of the local alfalfa farmers grumbled by on a new model John Deere tractor, pausing every ten yards or so to rev the engine to a roar, blasting a thick plume of oily black smoke into the air. Koznowski thought it a little odd the crowd would be so wildly entertained by the tractor. It was after all the same damn tractor they saw every year doing the same damn thing, but the people on the sidewalks were hooting and hollering like he'd never heard before. Maybe it was the simple comfort of the familiar. It wasn't until the tractor paused in front of him and the driver waved that he saw the hand-painted FREE E.Z. placard hanging off the side. Koznowski made a mental note to give that guy a ticket for something.

Five minutes after the editorial tractor was thankfully down the road and out of view, the town's only convertible slowly cruised past, and again the crowd whistled and applauded with an unnecessary fervor. It was less, he figured, for the appearance of that year's Beaver Princess perched atop the backseat, or even for the handfuls of candy she was hurling into the gutters, than it was for the IMPEACH KOZNOWSKI sign on the passenger door.

As the convertible rolled past, the Beaver Princess seemed to choose something special from the tub of candy in the backseat. Taking careful aim, she tossed the single piece of candy in his direction. It skittered and rattled across the damp asphalt, bouncing off the toe of his left boot. He looked down and saw the Dum-Dum sucker at his feet. He did not bend to pick it up.

A boy of about six, seeing his perfect opportunity, darted from the safety of the mob into the void surrounding Koznowski to make a grab for the sucker. He'd almost made it, too, when his panicked mother, fearing what kind of soul-damning curse might be brought down on the whole family should he get too close to that wicked and awful sheriff, dashed after him and snatched him roughly by the arm, dragging him back to the sidewalk while shooting Koznowski a malignant look.

XI

The melted Velveeta dripped out of his microwaved roast beef sandwich and plopped unceremoniously onto his tie. This had happened so often over the years strangers might simply accept the tie as a carefully conceived design hand-painted by an Italian modernist. He set the sandwich down and reached for a napkin, haphazardly swabbing the orange goo away. "Y'know," he said as he mopped. "Like catapults and such."

"Catapults?" Deputy Vandenberg was more than a little incredulous. A bank of cold fluorescent tubes lit a cramped afterthought they jokingly called a breakroom, which boasted a leaking sink, a bar fridge, an unwashed coffeepot, a microwave, and four folding chairs around the Formica-topped card table where Koznowski and Vandenberg were seated. It wasn't terribly comfortable in there and was in desperate need of a scrubbing, but it was still better than eating at your desk or driving a few miles to a fast food joint.

"Well, maybe, y'know, maybe not catapults so much anymore, but other things. Landmines and new guns and what have you, to see what kinda damage they can do to real bodies."

"They actually do that?"

"Think so, yah. Read something about it in the papers once. You tried calling the army base and asking them straight?"

"Yeah, sure thing, but I got stonewalled. If that's what they're really doing, who would sell his own ma to get blown up like that? That's just creepy."

Koznowski thought about it. "Maybe he didn't like his ma much but didn't wanna admit what he done to her? Seems a little extreme, but who knows?"

Vandenberg nodded. "Could be. He's kinda the creepy type. But still. She has a gravestone out at Cravenswood. Why spend all that money?"

Koznowski shrugged. "Don't ask me about people. Never can tell what kinda crap they'll do. Hey, you tried any those other places? The hospitals and so?"

She nodded. "All they said is they receive all their medical specimens from reputable, licensed dealers. Claim they never herd of Unterhumm."

"Well that is a sticky wicket then, ain't it? From the looks a things, Unterhumm might've been up to some sneaky business on the black market, eh?" He half-smiled, strangely pleased with himself for finding a legitimate reason to use a line like that.

"In Wisconsin? Seems pretty far-fetched, you ask me."

"You got a better explanation? Question is, how to prove it either way. And what do we do now that Unterhumm's dead? Could be one for the federal boys. They were selling across state lines, selling bodies to the U.S. government . . ." He finished the last bite of the sandwich, crumpled up his napkins, and crammed them into the brown paper bag as he pushed himself back from the table and emitted a quiet belch. "But that's your job for today, there, Deputy. Figure out what the hell we do now."

"Thanks a lot there, Chief," Vandenberg mumbled into her own sandwich as he left the room.

When he reached his desk he was still wondering how Unterhumm's black market operation might be connected to Pollex Christi. It made some sense, he guessed, but how in the hell would they find out about it? And how the hell long does it take to run some damned ballistics tests? He could probably do them himself in his own damn backyard, have an answer in five minutes. His phone rang and without thinking he picked it up.

"Well, Sheriff, I hope you're happy with all that money you won, because . . ." the voice on the other end began, and Koznowski reminded himself to never, ever pick up the phone. He also reminded himself to fire Leona.

"This is you ain't it, Mockery? 'Cause you're digging yourself a hole you can't cash, son."

Maybe it was a good thing Mockery wasn't listening too closely. "So lemme get a statement from you, Sheriff. Now that you cost us the game, our chance to go to State, and your chances for winning another reelection next year, how much longer do you plan on holding E.Z. on those trumped-up charges while the real killer's still walking the streets?"

His second impulse was to hang up, but he knew if he did this asshole would blow it up in the paper. Instead he tried to remain outwardly calm, diplomatic, and most importantly unfazed by that fucking gambling story. "We're still awaiting the, y'know, lab tests on the firearm found in Mr. Boefinck's room. Once we have that, well then, we'll decide how to proceed." Yah, that sounded pretty good, he hadda say.

Then he hung up the phone before Mockery could make some snide remark.

Fifteen seconds later the phone rang again. He scowled across the room at Leona. She was holding the receiver to one ear, pointing at her temple with her free hand. If this turned out to be Mockery again, he thought, swear to God he was gonna put Millie on the front desk.

The voice on the other end was muffled. "Good day, Sheriff Koznowski." It was a hiss, quiet and urgent, almost as if it was trying to sound menacing but not quite cutting it. Unfortunately it was so quiet and so muffled Koznowski couldn't understand a word it was saying beneath all the general background clamor around him in the station.

"Wait, *what*?" He shouted into the phone. "I can't hear you. You sick or something? Got a cold? . . . If this is you, Mockery, I'm gonna haul your butt in for making harassing phone calls. I'm gonna get a new receptionist too." He again glared at Leona's back.

There was silence on the other end, leading Koznowski to believe it really was Mockery.

"All right, Sheriff," said a voice that was most definitely not a newspaperman's. "We'll play it your way."

"Jeeze," the sheriff said, relieved. "I couldn't hear you back there, all whispery like that. Thought you had a cold or something. And who the hell is this anyway?"

"Shut up and listen. Certain inquiries from your office are causing some discomfort among people you do not wish to make uncomfortable. Our customers are getting nervous, and some are growing hesitant to deal with us. They're going to other suppliers and we're losing money."

"What the hell are you talking about? Deke, if this is you you're gonna get such a smack."

"I told you to listen." There was something vaguely familiar about the voice tickling at the back of Koznowski's brain. He was sure he'd heard it before, and not that long ago. "Okay," it went on. "So you figured out there's an underground market for medical specimens, so what? It's just supply and demand, same as it's been since the early nineteenth century."

"Oh!" Koznowski said a bit too loudly. "*That's* what you're talking about, eh? Jeeze, I thought you was talking about the Boefincks. Yah, okay, that clears things up." In clearing things up, he could at last also place the voice, which was starting to drive him a little batty. "This is Burke, ain't it? Um, Harry Burke, right? Yah, one a my deputies mentioned you the other day. Been meaning to talk to you again. How's it goin', there? How's the weather over in Plainfield?"

"Oh, Jesus Christ," Burke groaned. "Just shut up, wouldja? Shit." He'd come too far at this point to back off. He couldn't leave it there. "Look, Sheriff, the other day you were asking about ASS MEAT, what we really did. I told you that you didn't want to know. Well, now maybe I think you should. Because if I'm going down they're going with me."

"If it's selling body parts illegally, yah, I know that already. In fact. my deputy an' I was just talking about it at lunch not ten minutes ago, and here you just confirmed it without anyone even asking. Just called up and did it. Man, Vandenberg'll get a tickle outa this, eh?"

"*No!*" Burke yelled into the phone. "Well, I mean yes, but that's not all. That's just the start of it. You wanna know what the members were really up to? You might want to pay a visit to kindly ole Doc Unterhumm's subbasement."

"Subbasement?" Koznowski was in no mood for any more nonsense with this case. "Oh, for Pete's sake now. What the heck is this, some kinda monster movie? That's just dumb."

"Just pay a visit to the subbasement. It might help your murder investigation."

Before he could remind Burke they had their killers in a cell downstairs, the mortician hung up. "Jeremy H. Christmas," Koznowski muttered. If this was the kind of crazy place Kausheenah County was turning into, maybe he didn't want another term after all. This shit's just nuts.

"So you're saying you saw Bigfoot?" Sgt. Hogstune asked the bearded hunter sitting beside his desk a few yards from Koznowski's. "That it?"

"No," the hunter corrected. "I'm sayin' I saw an old naked guy out there by the edge of the river under the Wolf Bridge. Big white guy, not Bigfoot. Christ almighty, think I can't tell the difference?"

Yes, well, like I was saying, Koznowski thought. He slid open his desk drawer a few inches and felt around for his pill bottle. What the heck was it he was gonna do before the phone started ringing? Didn't matter. Christ, it was only quarter after twelve. He just wanted to get home that night. He could use a drink, and LeAnn, he knew, had one of her turkey casserole's going. Koznowski always liked the casserole better than the damn Thanksgiving turkey anyway. He stood from his desk and went looking for Vandenberg to let her know she was headed back to Unterhumm's yet again. But this time at least she'd have a few other officers with her. No telling what sorta wacky hijinx that undertaker's got up his sleeve.

Ellsworth approached the cell and rapped lightly on the bars with his nightstick. "Hey Tammy Faye, your lawyer's here."

As she'd been doing several hours a day since her arrival, Rev. Boefinck stood in the middle of the cell, head back and arms outstretched, rocking from foot to foot as she received the unfiltered word of the Lord and demonstrated her persecution to anyone who passed by. Upon Ellsworth's announcement, the Lord directed his attention elsewhere and her arms dropped to her sides.

The deputy unlocked the cell with a clank and jangle and slid the door open.

"Ding dong all," chirped Jerry Kerlin, the slim blond public defender, as he bounded into the cell. He carried a black leather briefcase, his open trenchcoat covering an impeccable tan Armani suit. "Update time."

The woman remained in the center of the cell, glowering at him with the same venomous distaste she generally reserved for Koznowski. "Buggerer," she spat through tight lips.

"Yes, you just be that way," Kerlin replied, accustomed to this from her by now. "But I'm here to see E.Z., so why don't you just go do whatever it is you do over there someplace?" He nodded toward a far corner of the cell before taking a seat on a cot uncomfortably close to Ezekiel. After adjusting his coat, he laid the briefcase across his lap. "So how you holding in there, E.Z.?" He patted the boy on the knee, letting his hand linger a few shades too long.

"Fine," Ezekiel said. The lawyer skeeved the hell out of him. He didn't like the whole touchy-feely thing. He didn't like the lisp or the singsong voice or the whole fey way he had of carrying himself, but it was still a welcome distraction from his mother.

Kerlin unsnapped the briefcase latches and flipped it open. "Now," he said, "I have some good news and some bad news. Bad news first. They're pushing for two first-degree murder charges and two counts of conspiracy to commit murder against you, E.Z., and two counts of conspiracy against your lovely mom, there, and a few counts of being an accessory. In your case, if they charge you as an adult, it means we're looking at twenty-five to life without parole up in Waupun. That's what they want, anyway." He paused and offered the clearly terrified teen a sympathetic look. "But we'll see what we can do about that."

"Filthy concubine of Lucifer," came a voice from the other side of the cell, where Rev. Boefinck had taken a seat on her own cot.

Kerlin glanced at her briefly and stuck out his tongue before focusing once again on the boy. "The good news, though," he said, "is they haven't formally filed charges yet. Part of that tells me there's still some question whether you'll be charged as a minor or as an adult. The more important thing is it tells me they don't have the evidence to make the charges stick. In any case if formal charges aren't filed in the next seventy-two hours, they have to let you go. How's that sound, eh?" He squeezed Ezekiel's knee again, giving him a reassuring leer, and Ezekiel let him.

"So!" Kerlin barked suddenly as he grasped both sides of his briefcase. "Let's start figuring out how we're gonna get you out of here before that, shall we?"

✠

By the next morning Koznowski decided he really didn't care much for turkey casserole. Although he'd never say anything to LeAnn, he hoped to God he wouldn't have to put up with it too many more nights. His stomach was a mess as it was. He swallowed another acid belch as he steered the truck toward the station.

Maybe it wasn't the casserole that was riding him. Maybe it had more to do with Betty, who was now stopping by like clockwork every single goddamn night just as they were sitting down, as if the cow was expected. No such thing as a free lunch my ass—try telling that to Betty. Ate and yapped and never lifted a damn finger, unless it was to her mouth with a gob of whipped cream.

It had reached the point where Koznowski's stomach started clenching up at the very thought or mention of supper, because it was a reminder the chip in Betty's head was gonna sound the alarm, and there she'd be on his doorstep again. Fucking tornado on its way and she'd still show up looking for meat loaf. That was something else he couldn't mention to LeAnn, who for some godforsaken reason seemed to enjoy Betty's company even though she was perfectly aware of how he felt. Spend a long damn day tracking murderers and such, then come home to that every night? One of these days he was gonna break her fork arm. Either that or find out where that chip was and rip it out with his teeth. Way his drinking'd been going, some night soon he might just get enough vodka in him to do it too.

"Ah, hell with it," he said. He turned the wheel, pulled into the parking lot, and headed for his spot. At least the protesters were gone. He hoped it was because they'd come to their senses. More likely it just got too cold for them. He checked his watch. Seven forty-five. He knew then it had nothing to do with common sense or even the early December chill. It was just too soon yet. Come ten or so, they'd be back demanding Boefinck be released in time for some, hell, dodgeball tournament or some crap like that. He shut down the four-by-four, walked around to the front doors, and headed inside. Along the way he noted that someone would need to get out there and salt down the sidewalk. Last thing they needed was one of these mental defectives slipping and breaking a wrist. He'd send Ziegler out there with the bag of rock salt. Nimrod might slip and break a wrist, too, but at least he wouldn't sue over it or run to Mockery screaming police brutality.

A warm breeze slipped past him as he pushed the door open. "Heya, Leona," he said. "Any, y'know, excitement? That's real nice, by the way."

At the moment, Leona was hanging candy canes and marble-sized ornaments off a two-foot-tall plastic tree sitting atop her desk. She was also wearing a handmade red and green sweater, one of several she would be wearing until January third. Leona took her holidays awful seriously. "Oh heya, Chief. Wanna candy cane?" She held one out to him. "Might help that tummy ache."

He froze for a moment. "Shows that much, eh, or you just gone all psychic all of a sudden? No, thanks . . . So anything going on I should know about?"

She hooked the candy cane over a stiff lower branch. "Oh, 'bout same as usual, I'd say. You got another message from Eagle Bluff PD. Put it on your desk."

"Okay, super. Thanks." As she maneuvered around the tree to check for empty spots he noticed something. "You limping there, Leona?"

She stopped decorating for a moment. "Oh, yah? You never noticed that?"

"Guess I don't see you walking around much."

"Yah, been pretty busy at the desk here." She unwrapped a candy cane and stuck an end in her mouth. "God I been like this for months now. Walkin' like you, Deke said."

"Yah, that Deke's a card."

"Anyway, this past summer I went to Summerfest with a couple girl-friends? We do it every summer."

Koznowski was already regretting having shown any concern for his receptionist's well-being.

"So one night I was doin' a buncha Jäger shots, eh? Guess that mighta had something to do with it. See, Megadeth wasn't coming on for another hour—"

"Megadeth."

"Yah, that's who I was really there to see. So anyways, yah, they weren't coming on for an hour. Guess we'd all had a few, so we got it in our heads to go over to this tent and get toe rings from this hippie there."

"Toe rings." He would never ask Leona a personal question again. His stomach couldn't take it.

"Yah." She pulled the candy cane from her mouth with a slurp, examined it, then replaced it. "Guess something musta gone wrong with mine, 'cause ever since then my foot's been givin' the peace sign an' I been walkin' like you. Serves me right for gettin' a toe ring from a hippie."

"Yah," Koznowski said slowly and cautiously, needing to bring this story to an end. "You're, ah, always fulla surprises, there, Leona. So any word how the Boefincks are holding up?" He began unzipping his coat.

"Ah," the receptionist said. "Ellsworth says that lady's preachin' at anyone who waltzes by, but no one can tell what the heck she's sayin'. He didn't say 'heck,' though."

"Yah . . . yah, that's Ellsworth. That lawyer Kerlin been by?"

"Oh, don'cha know it. Twice yesterday, an' he should be here again any minute now." She glanced at the wall clock.

"Yah, super. Wonder if he's asked the kid to run off to Mexico with him yet?" Koznowski slipped out of his coat and limped for his desk. "Iffen you can gimme a heads-up, I think I'd rather avoid him."

"Will do, there, Chief." She turned her focus back to beautifying the plastic tree, grabbing another handful of candy canes out of a nearby box.

Funny, with just the mention of Kerlin's name, his stomach started churning again. He should get the lawyer and Betty together, preferably on a leaky boat in the middle of Lake Superior.

"Oh," he shouted over his shoulder. "Just so's you know, a call from the FBI might be coming in, and if it does, do wha'cha can to find me or Deputy Vandenberg, eh?"

Leona froze in mid-dangle. "FBI? Why in dickens would they be callin' us. Denny Blodgett break out?"

"Nah, not that I know, anyway. But Deputy Vandenberg put a call in there yesterday, y'know. Figured this black market thing might be something they oughta know about."

"Black market?"

"Body parts, yah. Selling off bits of corpses an' so."

"Huh?" Leona could feel the Christmas spirit speedily departing her body. "Jeeze," she said quietly. "We really are turnin' all Milwaukee, here." She wasn't sure how much she liked that idea anymore.

"I don't get this shit at all," Deputy Keller said as he and Vandenberg crept downstairs into the shadowy bowels of the Unterhumm Funeral Home in search of a subbasement. Both trained flashlights on the path ahead, and Keller had his gun at the ready. "Now I know why you wouldn't tell me where the hell we were goin'. If you had I woulda said no fuckin' way, dude. I mean, ain't you or the chief been to the movies lately? And why the fuck am I leadin' the way, here? It's because you know Freddy'll grab me first, right?"

"That was the plan, yeah. I wanted you out of the way, so Freddy and I cut a deal when I was here working upstairs." Vandenberg rolled her eyes behind him. These whiny kids today. "We're here, dipstick, because these guys here were selling body parts illegally, without telling the families or anything. One of 'em turns state's and says we'll find a murder clue or something down here, so we go take a look."

When they reached the bottom of the stairs, they once again found themselves in the corridor leading to Unterhumm's prep room. This time, save for the weak beams of their flashlights, they were in complete darkness. Keller turned to Vandenberg.

"Turns state's? What're you now, Judge Wapner? You need to see a few more movies, there. Go screwing around in a funeral home for any reason, you're gonna get hacked up. All there is to it."

"May be right about that, you don't shut the hell up. Get the lights over there, why don'cha? Be useful . . . Might as well a sent Ziegler with me."

"Yah, but why'd we have to come here at midnight?"

"It's three thirty. You see the light switches?" She swung the flashlight beam in a circle on the wall in front of him to make it clear.

Keller flipped on the hallway lights. "I ever tell you 'bout the time Ziegler got lost in the bathroom?"

"Yah, you did."

"Been in there a thousand times, right? But then this one time—"

"*Yeah,* Deke, for chrissakes, I know that one. Now c'mon and focus here."

For a moment he did, but then the silence and the sound of their echoed footsteps bouncing off the cold walls started to inch in around him. "Yah, the lights don't help," he said. "You ever see that *Phantasm*? That place was bright, too, then this silver ball with spinning metal knives comes flyin' down the hall—"

"Just please shut up, Deke," Vandenberg pleaded. "And for godsakes holster your weapon. Nothing down here to use it on."

He reluctantly slipped it back into his belt. "So this place give you the creeps when you was here before?"

They unlatched the door, stepped into Unterhumm's empty prep room, and Vandenberg slapped the light switches on the wall. The banks of fluorescents flickered on overhead, revealing the central embalming table and the leather chain hoist still dangling from the low ceiling.

"Little, sure," Vandenberg admitted. "But I didn't see any zombies or ghosts. And I sure didn't whine about it every fuckin' step of the way."

"Yah, but you ever come down here?"

All the bodies had long since been transferred, the bloodstains mopped up, and the cryptic message scrubbed off the wall. Squire had even come by to see if there was any vital abandoned equipment he could salvage, given no one else was using it. Any instruments or chemicals or notes that might give him some clue to Unterhumm's magic. Still, under the cold lights, there was something sinister about the silent room. Trays of polished tools lay on the counters, and the table dominating the center of the room looked as if it were waiting. That was all. Just waiting.

"Shit," Keller said. "I don't even wanna know what any of this was used for. Looks like a torture chamber." The hoist gave him a few ideas, but for once he opted to keep them to himself.

"Yeah, I'll give you that," Vandenberg agreed. "I know how some of this stuff's used, here, and you really don't wanna know. Just try to put it out of your mind and be looking for some other door."

"Do we know it's in here?"

"No, but it's as good a place as any to start, yah?"

"What about that one over there?" He pointed at the black door on the far wall. They both stopped.

"Oh. Well I guess that was pretty easy, weren't it? How the fuck did we miss that when we were all here?"

"Because we're dumb, I guess."

As they stepped around the embalming table and cautiously approached the door in the back corner of the room, Keller poised a ready hand near his service revolver, just in case. Unconsciously, Vandenberg did the same.

"What're you trying to tell me, here? That don't make no sense."

On the other end of the line Sgt. Frank Susparagus took a deep, patient breath. He couldn't tell if Sheriff Koznowski was feigning disbelief or was merely a half-wit. "Okay." He tried to explain again, more slowly. "According to our records, there were several complaints concerning inappropriate sexual contact with minors filed against one Father Kinnealey of Saint Barnabas Parish in the late seventies and early eighties, but the church has no record of him. Nothing ever happened with any of the claims, but the local paper here ran a small item about Father Kinnealey being transferred in 1982."

"Yah, yah, yah," Koznowski said. "So the Bubich kid mighta been telling the truth then is what you're saying. I get that much. It's that other part that don't make no sense to me."

"I'm saying that, according to the paper, Kinnealey transferred up to Saint Timothy's by you."

"See now? That makes no sense, 'cause we ain't ever had a Father Kinnealey at Saint Tim's. Heck, we ain't had a new priest at Saint Tim's in over twenty, almost thirty years now. Just old Father Molloy. 'Cept for Father Avalone. Father Tim they call him. Father Tim of Saint Tim's."

"And when did Father Tim of Saint Tim's start there?"

Koznowski thought back, trying to recall what Avalone had told him. "Oh, guess that woulda been right around '80, '81 or so. But I can check."

Sgt. Susparagus sighed, concluding the sheriff wasn't feigning anything—he really was a half-wit. "Sheriff, has it ever occurred to you Father Kinnealey might've changed his name?"

"Oh," Koznowski said as the possibility finally became clear. "Aw, jeeze."

✠

"*Ho-lee shit,*" Deputies Keller and Vandenberg whispered simultaneously.

The cramped, airless subbasement was lit, in its way, by several electric candles mounted on the rough stone walls, their glowing artificial flames quivering red. In the middle of the room sat an embalming table identical to the one in Unterhumm's prep room above, except instead of stainless steel it appeared to have been carved from polished black marble. A bloodred silk cloth had been carefully draped across the top. A black metal tray carrying medical instruments sat atop the table, holding the silk in place. The instruments resembled those Keller and Vandenberg had seen upstairs but were somehow different.

On the stone wall at the head of the embalming table hung a red and black tapestry. Maybe "banner" would be a better word for it. In the center, a flaming skull was balanced over a crossed trocar and syringe, the image resting against a pentagram and flanked by garlands of lilies. Bordering the banner was a series of symbols almost like letters but from no alphabet either of them recognized.

Across the top were the letters M E A T, and near the bottom, in an archaic German script, the slogan "We Shall Not Heed the Worms."

"Somethin' about this really ain't right," Vandenberg said.

"Yah, like where do you suppose they got that made, eh?" Keller asked, staring in awe at the banner. "It's pretty fucking cool, gotta admit, eh? I mean, if I still had my band?"

"Shut up, Deke. Guess I'll have to tell the chief it really was 'heed the worms' after all."

✠

Koznowski dreaded what he was about to do. He dreaded not only what he might find, but also what he wouldn't. More than anything, he hated giving the job to Sgt. Ziegler, knowing what kind of a hash he'd probably make of the whole thing. But he supposed it was better than letting Ziegler sit at his desk all day playing with rubber bands, which is what he'd been doing since he arrived that morning. Those rubber bands sure kept him happy.

"Ziegler," he said as he approached the desk. "Got an assignment for you." Even as it came out of his mouth, he couldn't believe what he was saying, but there was little choice. Ellsworth was guarding the suspects, Vandenberg and Keller were at the undertaker's, a few of his people were still out hunting, and everyone else was actually doing his or her job.

Ziegler had at least four rubber bands of different widths tangled between his two hands and wrapped around his fingers. His hands slowly came together and dropped to the desktop as he looked up. "Oh yah, Chief?" He began peeling the rubber bands from his fingers (inadvertently shooting one across the office in the process) and eagerly stood. "Ready and willing, sir."

"Ah . . . right." Koznowski looked him up and down. He wasn't going to suggest he shine his shoes or tuck in his shirt. There was no point. "I wan'chata go through the complaint records downstairs there, from January of nineteen eighty-two to the present, see, an' I wan'chata pull any complaints filed against Saint Timothy's. You got it? Real simple, eh? Even wrote it down for you, here." He handed him a piece of paper. "Show this to Jackie. She'll help you."

Ziegler nodded enthusiastically as he took the paper and scanned the instructions. "Oh, you betcha, Chief." Koznowski felt his face go slack at the hopelessness of it all. He just prayed Ziegler never opted to breed, and so long as he lived with his mom it wasn't likely. "I'm especially interested in any complaints against Father Avalone but, y'know, just pull 'em all." He figured the broader he made it, the better. No need to go into sordid details.

"Father Tim?" Ziegler asked, a little shocked. "He ran the youth group when I was there. Coached the basketball an' softball teams too."

"Yah, still does. You know him then?"

"Me? Oh, yah, you betcha. Father Tim showed up last year I was an altar boy. An' I was on the softball team later. Played left field two summers running. He was real good."

"Uh-huh." *Maybe that explains it.* "So lemme ask ya there, Ziegler. That Father Tim, he like to ... y'know ... hang around the locker room a lot?"

"Oh sure. He was just like one of us. But he was the coach, y'know? I mean, if he didn't hang around the locker room he sure wouldn't be a good coach. Kept us kids in line."

"Yah, okay." Poor guileless lad. He decided to hold his follow-up question until some later date. "Yah. So why don't you run off now, go find me them files, eh?"

Ziegler nodded and took a few steps, then stopped and turned. "Hey, why're you after Father Tim, anyways? He didn't do nothin' wrong, did he?"

This was starting to feel like more of a mistake than he originally imagined. "I'm not after him. This is for the police department down in Eagle Bluff. They just wanna, y'know, clear something up. Case of mistaken identity, that kinda thing."

"Aw, gotcha. Okeydoke." He saluted sharply. "I'm on the case, Chief. Letcha know when I'm done."

As his deputy turned to scamper off to the file room, Koznowski stopped him. "Yah, hold on there, Sergeant Ziegler. I think I changed my mind. Why don'cha go down to the holding cell instead, relieve Ellsworth. Tell him just what I told you."

"About the locker room?"

Koznowski closed his eyes briefly. His stomach burned. He should've gone straight to Ellsworth and let Ziegler play with his rubber bands. "No, Sergeant. About the files. Tell him to go look for the files I told you to look for. Give him those instructions, there."

"But if he—"

Koznowski raised a hand, knowing exactly what Ziegler was about to say. "No. Please don't. When he goes to look through the files, you stay at the desk by the holding cell and keep an eye on the suspects, okay? Then when he comes back, or someone comes along to relieve you, you come back to your desk and fill out . . . well just fill out any reports that need filling out. You got it? Ellsworth goes to look for the files and you guard the suspects."

"Gotcha, Chief." He saluted again and headed toward the door.

"Yah there, Ziegler?" Koznowski called after him. "Please don't go letting anybody outa the cage this time?"

"You betcha, Chief! You got me straight on that now."

"Good, yah." Koznowski watched the sergeant go, just to make sure he got through the doorway without hurting himself.

XII

The development and refinement of the reagent continues, but alas what might be called "true success"—Glorious Success—continues to elude my grasping fingers. Each minuscule advance follows upon a dozenfold failures. Yet I can smell it. It is here, in this room. In me. It smells of Edelweiss and the mists of Valhalla.

My so-called colleagues seem at once amused and fretful over the recent advances. The hue seems to be of particular concern to them, with Drs. Makurji and Dobbs suggesting perhaps blue would be preferable to black. Or a more pleasant yellow. The *hue*! What fools I have become associated with, arguing like petulant children over pinks and greens, while the astounding possibility lay before them, unnoticed and unappreciated. Should the opportunity arise, I see no reason why they should taste the sweet nectar of the reagent—*my* reagent—in their veins. But they remain necessary for the present, oblivious, misdirected mongoloids though they may be. My beloved J.M. would never tolerate the yapping insolence of such venal dogs. Ah, but dearest J.M., times do sadly change and unholy alliances must sometimes be forged and maintained for the sake of an orderly silence. Somewhat orderly, and somewhat silent, in any case.

My attempts to explain that the hue was immaterial, was of absolutely no effect or concern—a mere natural chemical accident—only led them to redouble their insistence it be altered. West, who knows nothing at all, insists not only it be green, but that it *glow* as well! What a tiny mind he has, never once considering the chemical alteration to the base such a nicety would entail. I so want to smack him one of these days. Slap him across that pretty mouth always dribbling on about pretty things. Glowing green. Such useless idiocy. I explain to him neither life nor death are "pretty." They are messy and ugly, but at least with life we can clean up the mess until the next one arises. But does he listen? My patience grows thin. They think I am mad.

Yes, mad! I hear their whispers. They ignore the art and the magic, but my singular success has convinced me the long struggle will be a fruitful one for us all. My beloved Master J.M. would be delirious with joy. Again he would dance the polka as he did on only those rare occasions when he was most pleased with his students. One day I will overtake him. One day I, too, will dance the polka.

28 May 1986

Some have accused me of diabolism, of performing acts of voudou. For this reason and this reason alone, I have suggested the inclusion of the holy man as a distraction. I tell them he is present to provide ethical and moral guidance. A vigilant beacon ever on guard against this supposed deviltry of which my colleagues accuse me. Alleged men of science speaking of devils! It is absurd and pathetic, yet they believe me, as they are fools.

The holy man understands, or attempts to. The others—esp. Squire—tremble and squirm in his presence, which I take to be nothing but petty prepubescent jealousy. I have no time for such schoolyard nothings. The research is foremost. The serum. My chemical excitant. They quiver like hairless rats following last month's failure and my bold insistence we move onward. I explain the Dornburg man was the wrong subject. A wholly unworthy vessel. He was too large, his cellular structure too dense, the cells themselves choking on one another and gas. To only further complicate matters he was an imbecile. J.M. give me guidance.

27 August 1986

Many before me (even Dr. Niemann and his pioneering work in electrobiology) have tried, but failed to capture that profane secret of which God was so famously jealous. If it was in my hands to resurrect him, I would graciously refuse. Yes, graciously! Ha! It is too late now anyway. The worms have been feeding well on the Lord of the sheep. And despite our chosen banner, our rallying cry, this time I shall do the opposite.

    Ha!

20 April 1987

A day of celebration and contemplation and a rekindling of the flame scorching the path toward the peace that follows the final victorious battle.

8 December 1987

I had it for an instant, this final elusive dream of men and gods. It was in my hand. The subject proved it to them all! They saw—they saw and they knew. Until that blind bumbling fool Burke spilled his soda pop drink and used the nearest thing at hand—my papers—to wipe up and blot out the very future of our species. How many months or years has it been now? I must look back, but *no*! I will not. It is only forward that matters. Forward to Glorious Success. To this day I know it was no simple incompetent accident. He was as jealous as God, and for this I will never forgive him. He tries to destroy me, but never will. I hate him so. I am again so very close, and so must keep a careful watch upon him. He is less bumbler now than schemer, a veritable Cassius out to destroy my life's work. Well, Dr. Burke, we shall see who is destroyed first. If it is you, I pray you do not hold your breath for the new life.

12 January 1988

If "life," as the heathen have come to call it over the centuries, is nothing more than a collection (indeed a complex one!) of mechanical and chemical processes, as my own research into these matters has forced me to conclude, then it is most certainly possible, under the proper conditions, to restore and sustain—to literally revitalize—this state of "living" indefinitely, albeit with occasional but necessary pauses along its ceaseless journey. Just as a traveler must pause and rest while wandering happily in the Alps, so must we. The key is to capture and reformulate that residue so long sought. When all other larger organ failure has occurred, that residue left behind *is* life itself, but at that moment life in repose. How simple it all is, yet so apparently impossible for my so-called colleagues to comprehend. I begin to think I made a tragic mistake in judgment with the formation of this cabal. I once believed their youthful enthusiasms would offer me new perspectives and buoyancy along the quest, but instead they offer only bland stupidity and blinking cow eyes. They are as pockets full of stones as I attempt to swim across the deepest of rivers. O Great J.M., again I wonder in awe at your achievement considering your assistants (and subjects!).

8 February 1988

Makurji suggests we plastinate the subjects in order to preserve them until the rejuvenation process can take place. Such idiocy. I suggest he instead go to the department store, purchase several clothing mannequins, and attempt to restore *them* whenever he is ready. Then when he fails, he can put the mannequins in the caskets and present them to the heathen. He is a cretin. What is the point, I ask you, of plastinating these subjects before rejuvenation? They cannot move or breathe, as they will be solid plastic. IMBECILE! Dobbs then suggests the secret is in the blood, and has begun his own research. He too is a fool, but at least he is thinking. Foolishly and archaically, but thinking.

25 May 1988

It is clear to me now, though I will never admit it to the others, that my singular Glorious Success was the result of an accident. One unforeseen but critical contaminant or miscalibration in the formulation of the chemical excitant. My own figures are perfect and always have been—but for just that single instance there was something else, the hand of God. Or perhaps it was instead another of this dead God's cruel jokes? Alas, such is so often the way of science. Still the search goes on. I will find it or perish in my efforts.

Also, Burke has unexpectedly and suddenly expressed doubts about our funding. After all these years (during which he has profited quite handsomely) he finds himself suffering from pangs of "conscience." Not only is he an idiot—he is a coward as well. I told him as much. His great-great-great-grandfather would spit on him in contempt.

30 August 1988

Squire, citing the work of Dr. Beaumont, suggested that, should the technique be perfected, the rejuvenated subjects be put to work in the sugarcane fields. When I reminded the simpleton there were no sugarcane fields in this part of central Wisconsin, he relented, suggesting instead perhaps they could work in paper mills or the dairy processing plants. While hardly ideal, it is an idea worth considering.

2 November 1988

At its heart, embalming is a technique of disinfecting and chemically treating a corpse in order to facilitate preservation. To delay decomposition and restore outward appearance to acceptably human levels until the time of burial. Our job is to create the illusion of life. But *why*, I ask, *why* do we stop at simple appearances and illusions? Appearance is the play of children. Yet we stop there only because we live in a world of appearances. Of screens and mirrors and images and lies spouted by small men. Does life itself not matter? Does it end on the surface of the mirror? Is this why I am forced to work in this hole beneath the ground hidden from view?

13 November 1988

Partial success. Elderly woman. Three days expired. Heart fibrillated for 95 seconds, twitch in right index finger. Flutter of eyelids. I will repeat the procedure tomorrow a.m. with larger dosage. Hesitant optimism. Report anon.

Across the bottom and up and down the margins of each page, arcane mathematical and chemical equations had been scribbled with the same hand that wrote the entries. In some cases entire pages were filled with equations, graphs, dashed-off sketches of unfathomable molecular compounds.

Koznowski closed the dense leather-bound book and stared at the black cover. He'd been skipping around, reading random entries. By the time he stopped he'd read only about half the journal, but that was enough.

"Now I gotta deal with zombies too?" he wondered aloud. "What the fuck?"

"What's that, hon?" LeAnn called from the kitchen after turning down the radio. Koznowski had been reading silently in the living room for the last hour.

"Nothing, mama," he called over his shoulder. "Guess I gotta deal with zombies now, is all."

"Oh. Okay, then. I'll bringya some coffee cake in a sec." The volume on the radio returned to its original shuddery pitch as Ed Ames sang "Who Will Answer?"

Nothing in that book made the slightest damn bit of sense to him. Very little about this case made any sense to him anymore.

Vandenberg and Keller found Unterhumm's journal in a locked side compartment of the examination table, or altar, or whatever the hell it was down there in the funeral home's subbasement. They also found two small, unlabeled jars filled with a black liquid and a coffee cup filled with blood-stained surgical instruments. They called into the station and requested

Orville Jenkins be sent over with his camera, just so no one could accuse them of making any of this shit up.

Upon their return to the station, they delivered the black liquid and the cupful of bloody scalpels and probes to Randy up in the small lab on the third floor to be analyzed. The book they delivered to the sheriff. And now the sheriff was, in a word, bewildered. What kind of town had Beaver Rapids become since he was a boy? People thought things were going to hell in a handbasket when a few Hmongs and Mexicans showed up. They had no idea. What the hell would they do if they ever caught wind of the sort of crap their friendly neighborhood undertakers were up to? It'd probably give Pollex Christi a big boost, that's for damn sure. But that was the least of his worries.

Standing in the middle of the recently mopped holding cell, Rev. Boefinck rocked from side to side, palms upturned, stomping her feet in that other-worldly holy rhythm of hers. Eyes closed behind her glasses, she screeched a wordless hymn at the top of her voice. She had been singing (and chanting, and mumbling prayers, and sermonizing in her God voice about the evils of embalming) for six hours straight. The day was less than half over.

If her goal was to win converts, she had been only partially successful. Those few overnighters who'd found themselves locked up with her usually left the next day vowing they would stop drinking, driving recklessly, and beating their wives. The radical changes in attitude had nothing to do with having come to salvation during their encounters with Pollex Christi Ministries and God's son in the flesh. They simply wanted to get as far away as possible from that crazy bitch, and would do whatever it took (even if it meant being stone cold sober for the rest of their days upon this mortal coil) to keep it that way. None, upon questioning, would admit to having any particular feelings this way or that concerning the moral ramifications of embalming. Still, her efforts at reform, accidental as they may have been, had Sheriff Koznowski considering making Rev. Boefinck a permanent fixture in the holding cell.

On an uncomfortable iron cot in the corner of the cell, Ezekiel, who did not have the blessed privilege of being released from his mother's presence, not then, not ever, lay with a pillow over his face. When she started doing this at home, he could escape by using a team practice, a school or civic or

Scout meeting, or simple training as an excuse to get out of the house and far, far away. There was always something. Even during services, while he was obligated to remain in her presence, he at least did so with the knowledge it would all be over in a couple hours. This cell, however, this inescapability, was unbearable. How many days had it been? He'd lost count. It was all a blur, one long, loud, maddening blur. If asked at that moment, he would've confessed to any goddamn thing they wanted. That faggot lawyer told him not to, but he just didn't care anymore. A few years in the state pen up in Waupun sounded like a vacation in Barbados compared to this. Hell, he'd even come to look forward to that lawyer's visits, even if the queer kept making passes at him and squeezing his leg. At least while he was there his mom shut the hell up.

Her voice rose to a shrill, piercing howl even the pillow—even a dozen pillows—couldn't muffle.

A second later, the flat, hard pillow struck Rev. Boefinck squarely on the side of the head, knocking her eyeglasses askew.

"Jesus *Christ*, Mom! Can't you shut up—just shut the fuck up—even for one fucking second? God!"

There was an abrupt dead silence in the cell, apart from the quickly fading echo of Ezekiel's hoarse voice bouncing through the white bars and down the hall.

Sgt. Clem Edwards, the officer on duty at the time, didn't notice any of this as he had his Walkman turned up to full volume in order to drown out the chanting. He didn't look up from that month's issue of *Bowhunter* magazine until the beating was well under way.

✠

When Father Avalone once again invited Koznowski into his office and offered him a seat, it seemed the priest was in an unusually gregarious mood for a man who'd been accused of repeatedly raping a twelve-year-old boy.

"As I told you on the phone," Father Avalone said, taking a seat behind his imposing desk and crossing his legs, "I drove down to Eagle Bluff yesterday and met with the officer there about this whole business. I just wanted to get it cleared up as quickly as possible."

"I'm taking it as you're sitting here now you were, ah, able to do that, then?"

"Well, yes, of course. I mean, I feel awful for the Bubich boy. I'm not saying nothing happened to him, only that I wasn't the one responsible." He paused, reflecting for a moment out the window. He was again dressed in jeans, sneakers, and a sweatshirt. "See, Sheriff, I've studied quite a bit of psychology. It's a standard part of our training for the priesthood. So I know how easy it is—can be, anyway—for a sharp psychologist to plant a memory in a young and impressionable mind. So many people in recent years—not just priests, but teachers, parents, babysitters, anybody—have been falsely accused of doing terrible things to children."

"Yah, I read about some a that." Koznowski was quietly growing impatient.

"Again," the priest continued, "I'm not saying that's what happened here. Something terrible might have been done to the boy. But it was so long ago, there's no way to prove it one way or another. In some cases, well, people have momentary lapses in judgment. They make mistakes."

"Yah, sure, but the boy was twelve, there, padre. An' he says it went on for years. That's more than a momentary lapse in judgment, there. That's, ah, wha'cha might call a repeated lapse in judgment. Which I guess is more than a lapse."

"Again, Sheriff, our memories of childhood can be so distorted and exaggerated. For instance, I think back on my own childhood. I grew up just outside Madison, and everything that took place between the ages of seven, say, and fifteen took place—in my recollection, I mean—when I was nine."

"Yah, I'm not real sure a your point there, but uh-huh." It was more than a little disturbing that throughout this whole discussion the priest wouldn't stop smiling. "So anyways, there, you're saying you weren't Father Kinnealey at Saint Barnabas."

For just a blink, the smile dropped a hair and the eyes hesitated. "Well…yes. Yes I was. So then you ask why did I change it? The name, I mean? As I explained to Officer Susparagus—and I admit this freely—I made some mistakes of my own. There was a drinking issue. No one was ever hurt, but let's say I wasn't always as…reliable as I might have been. When the diocese transferred me up here, they suggested a change of name might help prevent any untoward and frankly unnecessary rumors from following me. They would just get in the way of the important work at hand. With Christ's help, I've since gone through counseling provided by the diocese, and everything's fine now."

Koznowski was now both impatient and puzzled. "So that's why Saint Barnabas destroyed all records of ever having a Father Kinnealey? 'Cause you were a drunk? Jeeze, that's the case, a lotta churches gonna be destroying a lotta records." His eyes wandered over to the well-stocked liquor cabinet in the corner. "Hey, an' didn't you tell me you were out to the Dew Drop with Unterhumm?"

The priest smirked. "I never said I was a *teetotaler*, for godsakes, just that I had the problem under control. Remember, it's part of a priest's job to drink wine in remembrance of Our Lord's sacrifice and the cleansing of our sins. That's every Mass. Sometimes we offer four Masses a day. By the end of the day, believe me, another couple with a friend are no big deal."

Koznowski shifted in his seat. "Guess that explains the liquor cabinet you got there, too, eh? But I ain't here to talk about a guy's drinking problem." He leaned over and opened the satchel he'd parked against the side of his chair. "Though I guess it might help explain these two complaints here." Father Avalone's eyebrows rose in curiosity, but he said nothing. "Now," Koznowski studied the page he'd pulled from the bag. "Back in April of '85, Alma Ramirez says here her son Carlos came home one day with alcohol on his breath. She asks him where he got it, an' he says he and the other kids from Saint Timothy's soccer team were over to your house, here, an' that you gave it to 'em."

The priest closed his eyes. The smile was gone.

"She says here she thought he musta been lying, so she smacked him a good one. When he stuck to his story anyway she started wondering. He also told her you gave the kids access to . . . ah, how to put this? Some dirty magazines." He lowered the paper to his lap. "It seems the matter was never pursued."

Avalone waited until the sheriff was finished and began speaking before opening his eyes. "Sheriff, hm. Where to begin with that? Well, I don't know if you know Ms. Ramirez. She's a . . . she's a very devout woman, and a very strict woman. And while there's nothing wrong with that—sometimes I think we could use more women like her—I'm in a different position. It's part of my job, you see, to draw young people into the church, not push them away with a bunch of 'thou shalt nots.'"

"So then you're saying you did this here. Because the other complaint says pretty much the same thing. That was from a little over a year ago. Last October. Basketball team this time. Again, nothing was pursued."

"Was that Ms. Ramirez as well?"

"Mrs. Hogaartsen."

"Right." He nodded, looking the sheriff in the eye. "And those are the only two?"

"Yah, only two on file. You expecting more'n that? Don't know why nobody from my office approached you before now."

Father Avalone leaned back in his chair, seemingly very relaxed about the whole thing. "Well maybe your people spoke with Mrs. Ramirez and Mrs. Hogaartsen after I did. And I'll try to explain to you what I did to them. Explained to them, I mean."

"Yah, I figured."

The priest sat up and leaned forward, still looking Koznowski in the eye. "These are different times, Sheriff. A lot different from when you and I were these boys' age. We need to hold these kids close to God by whatever means are at our disposal. Sometimes it means taking the occasional unorthodox approach. I need to understand who they are, to speak their language. If I can't communicate with them, I've lost them."

"By giving 'em booze and smut? These are minors, Father. As in contributing to the delinquency of." He was starting to think he should've arrested the Boefincks on day one and not even bothered with the rest of it. Then he remembered this whole business was about the only thing he was juggling at the moment not directly connected to the Unterhumm murders.

"Sheriff, now, listen. A couple times a year I have the kids over to my place for a little party. My house is right out here behind the rectory." He gestured with his thumb to the wall behind him. "It's one of the few chances we have to get together and do something social that's not a practice or a Bible study, you understand? We can relax and have fun and it gives me a chance to get to know them as people."

"An' get a little snockered, apparently."

Much to Koznowski's surprise, Father Avalone smiled at that. "Now, Sheriff, I let those who want one have one beer each. For godsakes, we're in Wisconsin. You know well as I do most kids are drinking with their parents' consent by the time they're twelve. And if letting them have a little beer makes it easier for them to see me as a real person and not just an authority figure in a white collar, then it helps my cause. And helps the kids, too, for that matter."

It almost made sense. "So what about the porn?"

The priest's eyes dropped to his desktop as he thought about it. "It wasn't anything too rough."

"What's that mean, no S and M?" Koznowski was starting to have his doubts about the priest's smooth talk. "Jeepers creepers, there, padre. You realize I could bring you in right there."

The priest's eyebrows shot up again and he raised his hands defensively. "Now, Sheriff, I'll have you know all those boys still come to Mass at least once a week. Most are still involved with the youth group—"

"W'hell yah, sure," Koznowski blurted with a rough chortle. "Free beer an' porn? Who the hell wouldn't? Kinda wish you were around when I was a kid, eh?"

Ignoring him, Father Avalone continued trying to make his point. "And I know for a fact you haven't picked up any of those boys for any criminal offenses."

"How're you so sure about that?"

"Because," the priest said assuredly, "if you had, a lot of them would've called me before they called their own parents. Believe it or not, there are a lot of unhappy families in Beaver Rapids, a lot of dysfunctional homes. That I've been able to keep these kids in church is nothing short of a miracle. Without the church, a lot of these kids wouldn't have anything at all."

Koznowski took a deep breath as he again considered the paper in his hands before slowly sliding it into his bag. "Guess that answers that, eh?" He saw the priest relax. "But that's not the real reason I came here, anyways." He reached into his bag again and extracted Unterhumm's diary.

✠

Well that was a waste, Koznowski thought as he climbed back into the truck. Without ever mentioning a word about where it had been found, he'd handed the journal to Avalone, who looked at it as if he'd never seen a book before. Then the more he read, the more disturbed the entries seemed to make him. He denied any knowledge of any attempts on Klaus's or anyone's part to resurrect the dead. He thought the diary might have been nothing more than a record, a product, of Klaus's fantasy life. "He loved horror novels," the priest said. "Especially the classics, like *Frankenstein.* Maybe he was trying to write his own? That's how it reads to me."

What's more, the priest admitted to knowing nothing about science—nothing at all—so it was never something Klaus and he discussed. They mostly debated social issues. "We disagreed on virtually everything under the sun, but I loved him like a brother," he'd said. He never mentioned a thing (and Koznowski didn't ask) about any kind of weird altar room in the subbasement, claiming instead that when he attended ASS MEAT meetings they usually took place in the small mortuary chapel or one of the presentation rooms, as those were the only two areas large enough to seat all the members comfortably. Finally, when asked about the squabbles and infighting and assorted animosities recounted in the diary, Father Avalone dismissed them as samples of Klaus blowing off steam (or establishing conflict within his novel). Yes, there were professional differences regarding tools and techniques, he admitted, but nothing anyone got that upset over.

Koznowski seriously doubted it would be worth asking Father Avalone about Unterhumm's involvement in the black market sale of body parts. He wouldn't know anything. You'd think, though, if Unterhumm was bringing in as much money as those files seemed to indicate, he might've lived in a nicer place.

Pulling out of the church driveway, the sheriff snapped on the police radio. Instead of the sharp crackle of officers' voices, the first thing he heard through the static were the thick distorted strains of what sounded like "Here Comes Santa Claus." Woman sure did love her holidays. He shook his head and called Leona to let her know he was on his way back to the station. It took some shouting, but he finally caught her attention during one of the breaks between stanzas.

"Heya, super," she yelled back over the music.

"Anything going on there?" he hollered. "And turn that music down, for godsakes, eh?"

"Here Comes Santa Claus" vanished before he heard her again. "Let's see, couple folks are worried about Fink Anderson. Say his shack's still out there on the lake, but they ain't seen him in a few days."

Koznowski rolled his eyes. "Well, if he ain't caused a ruckus no place, I'm sure he's just sleeping it off somewhere. That's it? Nothing from the FBI yet?"

"Naw, uh-uh," she said. "Not a peep, there. But when you get here, you're s'pposeda head right up to the lab. Randy's got them test results for you."

Koznowski thanked her, dropped the handset to the floor, flipped on the siren and hit the gas as, over the radio, the volume once again came up and Tex Johnson and His Six Shooters broke into "Wait for the Wagon."

XIII

Still wearing his coat and out of breath, a limping Koznowski burst through the door to the tiny lab. "*Randy!*" he bellowed.

The diminutive, nearsighted man in the lab coat jumped and screamed and spun, clutching a glass beaker to his chest with both hands. "Holy cow, why doesn't anybody knock anymore? Are we all that far gone? *Jesus*, Len."

"Yah, sorry," Koznowski said as he moved deeper into the lab. "Just hadda run that damn gauntlet down there. You wouldn't believe the things some a them people called me. One lady whacked me with her sign. Told 'em I'd have all the proof I needed in five minutes. So gimme some good news there, eh?"

What passed for the Kausheenah County Sheriff's Department forensic lab was not much bigger than the break room downstairs, and was about as tidy. The shelves were crammed with beakers and test tubes and burners. Beneath a spice rack full of chemicals sat a microscope that would've been considered an embarassing relic in most any American high school twenty years earlier. Over in the corner was a stained white refrigerator where blood and urine samples were stored and it was hoped remained fresh until Randy could get around to them. The only place to sit was a single wooden bar stool, upon which Randy perched ten, sometimes twelve hours a day, mostly running drug and alcohol tests. The things this Unterhumm case had thrown his way made about as much sense to him as the case itself made to Koznowski.

"Good news?" Randy, who'd been told more times than he cared to count he bore an uncanny resemblance to Wally Cox, thought about the request. "Well, ah . . . Packers might still make the playoffs. That's always good news. Plus it's almost Christmas. Peace on earth and goodwill and so forth." He noticed he was still holding the beaker and gently placed it on the scarred black countertop beside him.

Koznowski was in no mood for Packer updates or cheap holiday platitudes. He'd been waiting too long for this. "You know what the hell I mean, here. Don't be a big dummy."

The lab tech knew this meeting was coming, dreaded it, and put it off as long as he possibly could. Now that it was here his stomach was telling him it was going to be even worse than he imagined, likely as a result of ducking it for over a week. He shook his head sadly. "I think you're gonna have to let the kid go, Len. For now, anyway, until you get more evidence."

The sheriff couldn't believe what he was hearing. There was no way. "Don't tell me that, Randy. We got too much riding, and this here's the key."

"Come with me a sec," Randy said. He walked the sheriff around his stool and down a narrow makeshift aisle to a bench where Ezekiel Boefinck's shotgun lay beside a tray of test tubes and a beaker half filled with a yellow liquid. "See, this isn't the gun you're after. Not the one that killed Unterhumm and Mudge. They were shot with a twelve-gauge. This here's a thirty-thirty. And this one hasn't been sawed off, like the weapon that killed Unterhumm. You can tell from the blast radius and the entry pattern left on the bodies."

"Really?" Koznowski asked. "You were able to tell all that with, y'know, certainty, then?" He felt as if he'd been repeatedly kicked in the guts.

With a quick, embarrassed shrug Randy shook his head again. "No. Not really." He paused as he began to blush fiercely. "Hell, I dunno. Maybe? Christ, Len, I'm sorry. I'm a chemist. I don't know anything about firearms. I don't even know what 'thirty-thirty' refers to. Just heard it on TV and thought it sounded cool. I'm real sorry."

The sheriff was about to reach into his holster and teach the little twerp a few things about firearms.

"But the real kicker is, and this I can tell you for certain because I'm a chemist, is that this weapon here"—he gestured at the shotgun—"has not been fired in a very, very long time. If ever."

Koznowski stared at the gun as his body melted into the floor. So where did that leave him? He had nothing at all now, save for a web of bizarre tendrils he couldn't comprehend spiraling out from an empty core. He was starting to understand why it was people shot up post offices.

"Ah, horseshit," he told Randy. "Can I at least hold him on weapons charges?"

"All registered, all legal."

The sheriff scowled, then brightened. "Hey, everybody thinks he's Jesus. Howzabout criminal impersonation?"

"You're the legal expert here. I'm just a chemist, but . . . no."

"Even with the confession?"

Distracting himself with a clipboard holding a list of the blood and urine tests he was expected to run the next day, Randy said, "Len, you ran it past the judge already. It's not a confession if he says he didn't do it. He said he was going to kill Unterhumm but didn't. If you could charge people for thinking about killing someone, we'd all be locked up. Your mom would be locked up. You got nothing here, Len. I'm sorry."

"But it's just too damn weird, the same night an' all." Something swirled in Koznowski's head and a wave of warm nausea swept upward through him. Thinking for a moment he might faint, he leaned his hands on the bench to try and take some of the strain off his legs and back. "You're not bein' real helpful here, Randy."

"Well," Randy offered, trying to be helpful, "on the bright side at least all those protesters'll go home finally."

After inhaling several times through his nose while fighting off the urge to slam the little weasel's smartass head against the wall a few times, Koznowski righted himself. "Well, before that swishy lawyer sues me for something, suppose I'd better go start getting the release papers in order. And filling out an application for the Grease Pit. Maybe I should call first, make sure they're hiring, eh?" He removed his hat and wiped the sweat from his forehead. "What a day, huh? Oh, and been meaning to ask you, there. Any luck with them chemicals or whatever Vandenberg and Keller found at the funeral home?"

Randy looked both shocked and disgusted with the question. "You fuckin' kidding me?"

"Don't matter anyway, I suppose. Not at this point. Yah, thanks, there, Randy." Figuring he felt well enough to walk, Koznowski replaced his hat and headed for the door.

"Oh," Randy called after him. "One thing I've been meaning to tell you."

Koznowski stopped and turned. There was nothing hopeful or expectant in his face.

"That writing on the wall at the murder scene?"

"Uh-huh?"

"I was wrong that first day when I said it was Unterhumm's blood. I think it was Unterhumm's, but it wasn't blood." He looked embarrassed, as if he now regretted bringing any of this up. "How to put this delicately? It was, um, feces."

Koznowski stared at him, his face impassive. "Well, guess that makes sense, don't it? Much as anything else."

✠

LeAnn dropped herself onto the couch beside him and handed him a newly opened beer. "Oh, hon," she said. "Wha'cha gonna do, ya think?"

"Aw, same as ever, I s'pose," he told her after taking a sip. "Something dumb. Maybe I'll just enjoy the season and hope everyone forgets them two men been killed."

"Heard on the news today," LeAnn said quietly, "they're plannin' big parades for that Boefinck boy an' his mom. Prar du Morte an' Beaver Rapids both."

Koznowski showed no reaction and did not look at her. "Yah, well. Means the mayor'll probably call me tomorrow, ask about security."

For a moment they both stared silently out the picture window over the yard and toward the street. The sky was as black as the damp asphalt, and the snow glowed an electric blue under the moon and the streetlights. Across the way the strings of red and blue and yellow lights outlining the neighbors' windows blinked too cheerily for his taste. He'd opted out of the outdoor decorations bullshit this year, and was glad he did. Waste of time. And for what? So the neighbors have another reason to feel superior. Well, hell with 'em all and the whole thing.

"I'm up a tree without a paddle here," he said half to LeAnn and half to himself. He took a long draw from the can, then continued staring out the window. "I dunno what the hell anything means anymore. Just don't understand it at all."

"Oh, hon," she slipped a soft, heavy arm around his shoulders. "It ain't just you. World's always been a crazy place. You think about it, I betcha peep into anyone's windows around here, you'd see a buncha stuff didn't make no sense, eh? An' so. Heck, I see stuff in the papers every day I don't get at all. These kids with their blue hair or whatever."

He smiled sadly and leaned into her. "Yah, probably. Oh, we're getting old here, hon. World's speedin' on ahead." He turned his head slightly. "So you tell that fat, loudmouth mooch we's going out tonight?"

LeAnn nodded and lightly patted his shoulder.

An hour later after helping her wash the dishes, he opened another beer, popped two more pills, and moved back to the living room. He snapped on a table lamp, set down the beer, grabbed his satchel, and lowered himself slowly into his easy chair. Trying to tune out the blinking lights across the street and the distant metallic carols coming from the portable radio in the kitchen, he fished around in his bag and pulled out Unterhumm's diary. From the dozen or more entries he'd read, he couldn't imagine much of anyone being too sorry that Unterhumm was dead. Except that J.M., whoever that was. He didn't seem like a very likable fellow. That kid was another story, though. What mattered was someone had killed the guy. Mudge too. Mudge, wherever he was now, was like an afterthought in all this. Koznowski had the sense whoever had killed Unterhumm was after Unterhumm, not Mudge. But Mudge was there, so he had to die. Even killing him was an afterthought, poor unlucky bastard. Now they couldn't even deliver a body back to his folks.

Given the mortician seemed to deal with so few people, and liked even fewer, narrowing down the pool of possible suspects shouldn't've been that hard. According to the diary, he didn't seem to like any of those other morticians one bit, and Koznowski could only assume the feeling was mutual, in spite of what they'd all told him. He didn't for a second buy that whole "novel" idea Father Avalone tried to hand him either. Especially considering none of them went to the damn funeral.

He paused. *I'm trying to track down the guy who killed Dr. Frankenstein, here.* If what was in the diary was real, anyway. Even if those parts were a fantasy, like the priest said, there might be a hint in there somewhere.

He'd read only a couple of the ranting, semicoherent entries when he noticed the last few pages of the book kept trying to open seemingly of their own volition. He grabbed the pages more tightly but could still sense something. Finally giving in, he let the diary fall open where it would. It was near the very end.

Koznowski leaned closer, then reached in a finger and ran it down the crease. He felt the ragged edges of the missing pages cutting into his fingertip. Somebody had ripped at least two pages out, looked like. It might have been Unterhumm himself, upset with some nutty calculations that didn't work. Or maybe it was someone else, trying to dispose of a little evidence.

He checked the entries to either side. To the left was November fifth, and to the right was the thirteenth, the final entry, jotted down hastily, the night before his murder and moments after his final success. That didn't tell him a whole lot. Unterhumm didn't make daily entries. Sometimes it was twice a week, sometimes he could go two months without adding anything. All he could do here was narrow it down to a little over a week. Considering what was recorded on the last page, what if it was the formula? The one that seemed to work this time? That's the way he generally handled things through the rest of the diary—jot down a formula on one page, then the results on the pages that followed. What if someone was after that formula?

"Super, now all I gotta do is wait for some mortician to start reanimating the dead. When he does, I got my killer. Yah, gonna call Mockery with that one tomorrow, eh?"

"What's that, dear?" LeAnn stuck her head in from the kitchen.

"Jeeze, did I say that aloud? I'm sorry. Yah, it's nothing. Never mind."

"Okeydoke." She vanished back into the kitchen.

He closed the book. He had enough to worry about right in front of his nose without adding mad scientists and zombies to the mix. It was a little melodramatic anyway, like something he'd seen on *Eerie Street* a long time back.

Why in the hell did no one think to have the diary dusted for prints? Oh, he just didn't have a very good sheriff's office, is all.

✠

Dwight was vacuuming the office wildly and randomly, slamming the Hoover into chairs and walls and giggling to himself when Dr. Squire opened the door, stepping into the room with Sheriff Koznowski in tow. "It was simple blackmail," Dr. Squire shouted to be heard over the machine. Dwight quickly snapped off the vacuum cleaner. "We just got sucked into it."

Dwight cackled wildly and both the sheriff and the mortician stopped and stared. Dwight stared back, still grinning, a pale hand half-covering his mouth. "Yes," he lisped. "Sorry."

Squire turned to Koznowski. "You must forgive him. He's part of a program," he explained before returning to his assistant. "Dwight, now, thanks very much for cleaning up that mess on the floor downstairs. Let's try to keep it clean, okay? But as I remember, you still have a lot of work to do in the prep room, so perhaps you should get started down there."

"Oh yes, yes!" Dwight exclaimed, clapping his hands as he charged from the office, leaving the vacuum cleaner behind in his excitement. As Squire closed the door, they could hear Dwight's voice echoing outside. "*Downstairs! Downstairs! Downstairs!*"

"Yes," Squire sighed. "He's . . . special. But I keep him busy, keep him cleaned and fed. He's actually quite helpful around here, though I try to keep him away from the customers."

"Yah, had a brother like that," Koznowski offered with no further explanation while taking a seat and removing his hat. "But back to this group of Unterhumm's."

Dr. Squire seemed much more relaxed than he had at their first few meetings. Perhaps because the immediate stress of the situation had faded, or perhaps he felt he no longer had to hide anything given the others had already opened their big yaps. "Well, as I told you, it started like any other group of specialized professionals. But after a few meetings Unterhumm began pushing us into these shadowy deals with assorted institutions. Even before we got started with any of it he told us if we didn't play ball he'd spread the word we were doing it anyway. Even had some forged invoices made up to prove his point." He paused, plucking the novelty skull off his desktop and dropping it into a drawer with a hollow klunk. "He was a very unstable man, Klaus was. So as you can imagine, rumors like that, even false ones, could put us out of business."

"Yah, now," Koznowski said. "They weren't just rumors, were they, there? Not for long, anyways. You really did start selling off parts of people like they was, I dunno, chickens or whatever, without permission."

"Before you start in on me for that, let me explain how Klaus laid it out. There's a serious shortage out there of medical specimens for teaching, research, transplants, whatever. Don't think so? Just try to get a kidney transplant. People are lined up, they're dying, waiting for transplants that never come. So as illegal and unethical as it was, we would simply be filling a need. Supply and demand. And to be honest I didn't have a single family member notice a femur was missing, say, or a brain. Across the industry, the practice is more widespread than people may care to think."

"Yah, y'know," Koznowski said, "I'm not really the one you're gonna have to be explaining all this to."

"And we'll have to deal with that, I guess. It's why I'm talking to you now. Just so someone knows what the story was. See, he started this whole business—the tissue sales—to fund his experiments. Oh he claimed we were all involved, that we'd all get credit, but they were his and his alone."

"Wait, you're shittin' me," Koznowski said. "So he really was doing that then? It wasn't just him writing a, y'know, a nutty story?" Personally, Koznowski would have much preferred the latter.

Squire nodded with a sneer of disbelief. "It was no fantasy. It was real. Yeah, he was trying to reanimate the dead. He had charts and graphs made up. Had that banner made up. He even had us wearing robes, did anyone mention that?"

"Robes?"

"Black hooded robes. Like in some damn horror movie. He was fucking insane."

Koznowski jotted something in his notebook and thought about that one for a second. "So I'm taking it, there, you didn't like him much."

Dr. Squire cleared his throat. "As I mentioned first time we spoke, he was a despicable man. A brilliant mortician, but a despicable man. Have you found his Mengele scrapbook yet?"

Koznowski frowned. "Found his what, now?"

"Well it's around there someplace. Fat leather book with a swastika on the cover. It'll turn up."

"Yah, okay," Koznowski said, making a note of it. "So you all hated him, is what you're saying."

Understanding the situation and the sheriff's point, Squire chose his words carefully. "Well . . . we weren't best buddies, no."

"Did you kill him?"

Squire glared at the sheriff, who glared back, trying to read his face. Then Squire relaxed, almost smiling. "You implied that once before, Sheriff, and the answer is still no."

"Worth a shot, eh? Gotta admit that 'heed the worms' business is a mighty big clue."

"No, I have enough business as it is without—" Suddenly both of Squire's hands flew into the air and slapped down on the desk. "Oh! And that's the other thing. In that diary of his, does he ever explain exactly why he was trying to bring the deceased back to life?"

"Well," Koznowski said, "from what I can reckon so far, he just wanted to, y'know, be God, which I guess seems simple enough."

Squire shook his head. "No. I mean, yeah, but that was just a side note. He already thought he was God. Second only to Josef Mengele, of course. No, this was purely an economic issue."

Koznowski leaned back in the upholstered chair and folded his hands across his belly. "Economic," was all he said. He didn't know if he could take much more. Sitting here talking seriously about resurrecting corpses was bad enough.

Squire was looking nervous again. "You're gonna help me out here, aren't you? When the FBI shows up, I mean? Tell them I cooperated with your investigation?"

Koznowski coughed a dry cough and averted his eyes. "Oh, you betcha."

"All right, then." The mortician paused. When he spoke, he spoke hesitantly. "I know this all sounds insane, and it is. Like something out of an old horror movie. Yeah, and I guess the robes and the hidden room don't help things much. But Klaus . . . Klaus was developing a formula. He kept the details a secret from all of us. All we knew was it was a modified version of our standard embalming fluid. He combined that with a compound known as Methylene Blue and something he called a chemical excitant. He said it was the residue of life."

The sheriff, who had started to take some notes, stopped and looked up. "I'm really trying to follow you here, Doc," he said calmly. "Remember, I ain't no scientist."

Squire pressed his lips together. "Don't worry," he assured the sheriff, "this isn't really science. Just think of it as a horror story . . . Do you mind if I smoke?"

"Bad for you, they say."

"Yeah, I know, but we all gotta go sometime." He was already opening a desk drawer. He retrieved the skull and set it atop his desk, screwed off the top, and placed the skullcap upside down in front of him. He then reached inside the skull and plucked out a pack of cigarettes and a lighter. He slid a cigarette from the pack and lit up. He blew the first lungful out his nostrils before continuing. "Klaus said that after the body died a residue remained. Somewhere. Something that still contained the fundamental chemical basis of life. Got me so far? So by combining that with the embalming solution, making a few minor adjustments in the molecular structure, he felt he could create a chemical reagent—a drug, really—to restore life to the deceased." He studied the sheriff's face the same way he studied Dwight's several times a day to make sure he understood what he was being told. "I'm trying to keep this simple."

"Yah, following you there so far, Doc. So could it work, you think? This drug of his I mean."

Squire snorted more smoke and tapped the ash into the skullcap. "Absolutely not. And for a million and one reasons. Like I said, the man was insane. It was all just craziness, and not in the good way either."

"All right then, good," Koznowski said. "So long as it wouldn't work. All I wanted to know. But I'm still wondering why this was a business matter. There was some stuff in the diary, there, about putting these . . . guess you'd call 'em zombies for lack of a better term, eh? Putting 'em to work in the mills. So you're saying he wanted to create an army of zombie slaves, that it? Seems the usual route, you watch the movies."

Dr. Squire shook his head, eyes downcast, drawing quickly on the cigarette as if he hoped the sheriff wouldn't notice. "No . . . well I think Makurji suggested that, but he was joking. No, I told you Klaus was insane."

"Several times."

"Okay then. See, his idea was much stupider than that."

"Really." The smoke was slowly filling the office around them, hanging in the air and clouding the light. Koznowski hoped the next bereaved family who showed up in that office wasn't there to bury someone who'd died of lung cancer.

Squire nodded. "He was after repeat business."

"All right." Koznowski's brain was starting to hurt. Through the window, he noticed it was starting to snow lightly.

"See . . ." Squire ground out the cigarette in the skullcap. "If a mortician could bring loved ones back to life—for a hefty fee, of course—it wouldn't make any sense to bring them back and leave them that way forever, right?" He forced a weak laugh. "It'd put us all out of business before too long. Not to mention the effect on the world's population."

Koznowski shifted in his seat. None of this was making the slightest bit of sense to him. This was Boris Karloff territory, not something people ever really thought about. Not in Kausheenah, anyway. "Guess so," he offered.

"So the effects—this restored life—had to be temporary." He reached for another cigarette. "It sounds insane, I know. I can't believe I'm telling you this. But you see Klaus presented it as a way to double or triple our income. More than that, even. Someone passes away and they're brought to us. If the family feels they need more time with the loved one to say all the things they meant to say, we restore them to life, send them home, they live another six months, a year, then die again. And we get paid for our services each time they come around, for either a funeral or a resurrection. Klaus had a whole fee scale worked out." He took another long drag. "Theoretically, it could go on forever." He was quiet for a long time, letting the implications sink in and awaiting the sheriff's reaction.

Koznowski stared back at him. "That's, ah . . . jeepers."

"Told you. It was all about profits."

Koznowski was going to need another pill when he got back to the truck. "So, kooky as it is, there, can you think of anyone who'd wanna kill him on accounta it?"

Squire's gaze was level. "Not one of the morticians, no. We wanted no part of it but were trying to get out in our own way, not by killing the son of a bitch."

"So you're saying you got a code of conduct." He leaned his head on his fist and smirked just a little.

"Well, yes, of course, but it mostly involves billing."

"Nothing about conducting unholy experiments on the deceased or selling off hunks of folks' bodies without telling the families?"

"Please, Sheriff, I'm trying to explain the situation to you."

"Yah, okay there. You'll deal with all that later. Still, though, back when I asked iffen one a you coulda killed him you said it wasn't a mortician. You implying something with that?"

Squire shrugged slightly but didn't hesitate. "Just that Klaus and Father Avalone were very close." He considered the cigarette in his hand, then ground it out.

"I know all that already, but you seem to be saying something else, here."

"I mean Father Avalone was much closer to him than any of us were. Real close. If any one of us might know anything, it's him."

Koznowski sighed. "Talked to him couple times now. He seems to know a lot less than you do."

Dr. Squire scratched the corner of his mouth. "Well, remember there, Sheriff, I lied to you too." He picked up the pack of cigarettes, tapped it, then shook out another. "Have you tried talking to him when he's not home?"

The sheriff squinted at him in confusion. "Well, what the hell good—" he began, then stopped. "Oh, I get it now."

Dr. Squire nodded.

"Okay, then. Maybe we'll give it a try." He began to gather his things together. "Well, thanks for your time there, Doctor Squire. Been real wha'cha call enlightening. Keep it in mind when the J. Edgars roll into town. They asked me to remind you not to, y'know, leave town or nothin'."

"I still got a business to run," Squire said like a man defeated. "For the moment, anyway."

"Yah, super." Koznowski pushed himself up and shook the mortician's hand. "Oh, one more thing." He slipped his arms through the sleeves of his coat and bounced it up around his shoulders. "You know if Kirby Mudge's parents ever found their boy's body? Hate to think the airline rerouted it to Denver or something, eh?"

Squire didn't join in the sheriff's laughter. He didn't even smile. His eyes dropped to the floor. "Ah . . . no. Not that I'm aware of, no."

"For all the shenanigans around here, none of you got any idea where it mighta gone then?" Koznowski watched the mortician, who said nothing, merely shrugged and shook his head. "Ah-hah . . . Okay then, there . . . Sure I'll be seeing you again real soon once them feds get here."

Squire looked up, both shame and fear in his eyes. He wasn't nervous, he wasn't cocky anymore, but scared. "If . . ." he said quietly, forcing each word out. "If you talk to them—his parents, I mean—you might want to tell them to try Texas A and M Medical School."

"Really."

"It's, ah, worth a shot, yeah. But they better hurry."

Koznowski dropped his hat on his head and reached for the doorknob. "Thanks, Doc, I'll give them a jingle soon as I get back to the station." He opened the door and stepped into the hushed, carpeted showroom. Before pulling the door shut he leaned back in. "Oh. And you do realize you're officially out of business as of this moment, right?"

"I kind of figured as much, yeah," Dr. Squire replied.

✠

"Unbelievable," Koznowski breathed aloud to himself during the drive back to the station. The snow he'd noticed through Squire's window never grew to more than a minor dusting, but now it blew dry off the fields and across the gray two-lane ahead of him like light sea foam, or ghosts.

Folks in town thought things had gotten as bad as they could get when a few Mexicans started shopping at the hardware store. They had no fucking clue. Things like this just weren't supposed to happen in Wisconsin. Not in Kausheenah County, anyway.

Sure, but if not here, where? Anywhere, really, he guessed. Anywhere but here. There'd been that Ed Gein case over in Plainfield, some forty-five miles away. But that was thirty years ago. He'd heard that Gein had died over at Mendota a couple years back. Now he's seeing kids wearing Ed Gein T-shirts. Made no sense.

Maybe LeAnn was right, though. You peek in anyone's window, Lord knows what you might find these days. Hell, necrophilia was still legal in this state. Guess that says something right there.

The radio was silent. He'd taken to snapping it off and leaving it that way, checking in with Leona only when necessary. He'd continue to do this until she stopped broadcasting those godforsaken Christmas carols all day long, which probably wouldn't happen for another week at least. Maybe two.

He shook his head again and frowned. It was a ridiculous, crazy world, and one he just didn't understand. Sometimes in quiet moments, moments he never shared with anyone, he started wondering if he even belonged here anymore. Crazy goddamned place.

XIV

The sun had been out earlier that morning, but by one that afternoon the wind had picked up, dropping the temperature down into the teens and dragging the heavy, low cloud cover along with it.

Father Avalone revealed nothing beyond calm, gentle surprise when he opened the door. His small wood-frame bungalow was located some twenty yards from the church rectory on the grounds of St. Timothy's. St. Tim's boasted the largest congregation in the county with a wide and sprawling complex of buildings, but the church itself was hardly an elaborate architectural wonder—a white stucco structure with a fake stone facade, a steeple that stretched eighty feet into the winter sky, a bell tower in back, and some prefab stained-glass windows depicting long-forgotten saints in psychedelic designs that were unmistakable artifacts of the early seventies. The attached rectory, added some ten years later, was more like a modern office building, a three-story cube built of smoked glass and polished steel. The violent contrast between the two was something no one seemed to notice. Or, if they did, it didn't seem worthy of comment.

The junior priest's bungalow was much less ornate than either. "Hello there, Sheriff," he said with a smile that tried to be warm. Then, looking around the front porch, "Officers."

"Hiya there, padre," Koznowski said. "Real sorry to, y'know, bother you at home like this without calling first."

"Oh, it's no bother at all," the priest said. "Priests are like cops, we're always on duty."

"Oh, yah," Koznowski said. "I bet that's true, eh?"

Father Avalone looked around at the four of them, waiting for someone to explain what the hell was going on. "Is, uh . . . is there a problem?"

In response, Koznowski offered him an exaggerated frown and a reassuring shake of the head. "Oh, no. No trouble at all. Just wondering if we might step inside for a sec? Wind's getting kinda bitter out here, don'cha know." As if to back up his claim, deputies Keller, Vandenberg, and Ellsworth kept their hands in their pockets and their shoulders hunched. "This'll just take a minute. Again, yah, I'm sorry if this is a bad time. I know you must be real busy, what with Christmas an' all."

In spite of his confusion, the priest stepped back and let them inside. "No trouble at all. I have a three o'clock Mass, then youth group and practice after that, but I have some time. Is this about Klaus?"

In contrast to his lavish and comfortable office in the rectory, Avalone's tiny home was spare, leaning toward bleak. From the looks of things, he had less room than he might have in a standard trailer home. Visitors stepping through the front door found themselves in a living room furnished with mismatched secondhand furniture—a couch, two chairs, a coffee table. Through a doorway Koznowski saw the dreary kitchen, and he presumed the closed door to the left led to the bedroom. Either that or the bathroom. The only visible decoration was a six-inch-tall wooden crucifix on the wall above the couch.

Father Avalone picked up the half-full highball glass from the coffee table. "Just a little pick-me-up," he said with an embarrassed smile. "I know you're all on duty, so I won't offer you one. I'd be happy to make some tea, though, if you like."

"Yah, no, thanks," Koznowski said as he looked around the room casually. "We're all fine. Just had some lunch, there."

"So . . ." the priest asked, "what can I do for you folks today? Does this have something to do with the investigation?"

"Mind if I sat, here?" Koznowski asked, already lowering himself onto the spartan couch with a slow groan. "This weather, it really messes with my legs."

Father Avalone looked to Ellsworth, Keller, and Vandenberg. Of the three, he knew only Ellsworth. "I'm afraid I don't have enough chairs for all of you, but if a couple of you cared to squeeze in on the couch . . . ?"

"Kind of you, there, padre. Won't be necessary," Koznowski told him, reaching into his inside coat pocket and removing a piece of paper, which remained folded. "I got a search warrant, here, but it's really no big deal. Nothin' to, y'know, worry about or nothin'. I was just wondering if the officers here might take a look around the place, so long as they promise to put everything back where they found it?"

Father Avalone's eyes darted from the sheriff to the deputies. "What's this all about? Is this about those beers?"

"Oh, no, no, no," Koznowski assured him. "Nothin' like that. This here's just a standard part of the homicide investigation. We gotta go do this with everyone connected with the deceased, there."

"But, ah . . ."

The sheriff waved a hand. "Yah, it's fine, really." He patted the couch beside him. "Tell ya what. You let them do their jobs, and you sit down here with me, finish your drink, there, and I'll tell you all about it, eh?"

Once more Avalone looked to the other officers for an answer that wasn't coming, then reluctantly he took a seat.

"Yah, this won't take but a minute. It's not like I'm expecting to find anything. Believe me, yours is just the next name down on the list. We gotta long couple days ahead of us, so there goes Christmas. All but, anyways, eh?" Koznowski turned to Deke, Deliah, and Ellsworth. "Okay then, you guys know the procedure well enough by now. But be sure an' be super careful and don't make a mess. Remember you're dealin' with a man of God here." He tipped his head toward Avalone, who was nervously sipping his drink. "An' we need all the help we can get, eh? Let's just do this thing and get outa his hair so's he can get ready for mess. Mass."

Avalone turned to Koznowski. "I've never heard of such a thing before, except with suspects."

The sheriff shook his head. "Aw, no. I remember you telling me you tried to get into the academy there once, well, so here's a free lesson. This here's a regular part a most any homicide investigation. They don't put it on the cop shows, though, on accounta it's real boring."

"I see." Avalone took another drink, and Koznowski leaned back, relaxed.

"So since you had to let that boy go," Avalone ventured, "how's the investigation coming?"

"Well, given as it's ongoing, as they say, there's really nothing I'm at liberty to discuss with the public."

"But Sheriff," Avalone pressed, "I'm not the public." Either the chitchat or the booze was loosening him up a bit, and he edged in closer to Koznowski. "Klaus was my best friend. Plus I'm a priest, remember? In spite of how I'm dressed. It's our job to keep secrets."

Vandenberg had gone into the bedroom, leaving the door open only a crack behind her. Keller was out of sight in the kitchen, moving pots and pans, opening and closing the refrigerator and oven doors, all very carefully. Ellsworth headed into the basement.

"Sure, I understand that," Koznowski said. "But I really can't say nothin', 'cept when I hadda let Boefinck go we lost our prime suspect. Some of us still got our suspicions, there." He sighed and considered the floor, then looked earnestly at Avalone. "But lemme ask you. Were there any secrets you were keeping for Dr. Unterhumm? Y'know? Something he mighta shared with you might help us find whoever killed him and Kirby Mudge? We could really use you're help here, Father."

The priest rattled what was left of his ice cubes, then set his drink on the table. "You know, Sheriff, ever since this happened I've been thinking and thinking, trying to remember anything that might help. But I really can't think of anything else. I've prayed to God every day for enlightenment but nothing. Nothing I haven't told you already."

Koznowski leaned an inch closer to the priest and slapped him lightly on the forearm. "Yah, gotta say you been a real big help to us as is, and I appreciate it. That's why I feel so bad being here like this today, eh?" His eyes darted to the bedroom door then back to the priest. "But like I says, it's protocol." He leaned back again. "But hey, while I gotcha here. You ain't happened to remember where that 'heed the worms' business mighta come from, have you? Still sounds like the Bible to me, y'know?"

Father Avalone shook his head. "No, I really can't help you on that one, Sheriff. Except I never encountered it in all my scriptural training." He reached for his drink. "And that's the kind of thing you'd remember, right?" He coughed out a mirthless laugh.

"Yah, that may be the other unsolved mystery here, eh? Until we catch the killer, that is."

Both men were silent for a moment, listening to the officers shuffling quietly around the house. Koznowski looked at his watch. "I'm real sorry, there, padre. These guys'll be done here in just a shake. Promise."

"I appreciate your courtesy, Sheriff. I know you're only doing what you need to do." He looked at his own watch. "Speaking of which, I'll be needing to start preparing for Mass soon. You wouldn't believe how long it takes to get into uniform."

"Yah, I can imagine. All those robes and collars an' such."

They heard Ellsworth's heavy steps tromping up from the basement. "All clear down there," he announced to Keller as he stepped into the kitchen. "Yah, here, too," Keller responded. The two of them entered the living room just as the bedroom door opened and Vandenberg emerged. "All clear in there, Chief," she told Koznowski, who looked from one to the other. Nobody was carrying a sawed-off shotgun. Nobody was holding any evidence bags.

"Okay then," Koznowski said, clapping his hands and pushing himself up from the couch. "That's it." He turned to the priest and held out his hand. "And Father, with our apologies for the, y'know, the inconvenience an' such here. I hope you and Jesus both can forgive us an' so."

"It's perfectly all right, Sheriff." He took Koznowski's hand and stood.

As they headed for the door with Father Avalone following, drink in hand, Koznowski said over his shoulder, "And padre, you find my people here made a mess anywheres, you call me, eh? I'll personally make sure the guilty party comes back an' fixes it. They're real good with carpets too."

Vandenberg opened the door and stepped out into the solid afternoon chill.

"Oh, I'm perfectly certain that won't be necessary, Sheriff. They're good people." He clapped Koznowski on the shoulder. "And may the Lord be with you and guide you for the rest of your investigation."

"Yah, thanks, Father. Little guidance'd come in useful 'round about now, eh?"

Father Avalone closed the door behind them and the four officers followed their own footprints back through the snow toward the parking lot, saying nothing. Only after they were all in the truck did Koznowski allow his palpable disappointment to seep out.

"Well, fuck-all is all I gotta say," he said twisting in the driver's seat as best he could to face his deputies. "Sumbitch lied to me about heed the worms, which is something, I s'pose, but you didn't find a goddamn thing in there? You telling me not a one a youse three deputies knows what a goddamn shotgun looks like?"

"Somebody might've tipped him off we were coming, Chief," Ellsworth suggested. "Who knows? Maybe it was Squire."

"Maybe God tipped him off," the always helpful Deputy Keller offered. No one seemed to be listening. "One interesting thing I found. There's nothin' in the fridge but beer. There ain't a scrap of food in the whole kitchen. Just booze."

"Sounds like my place, "Ellsworth mumbled.

"C'mon, just hush, now," Koznowski said, gripping the steering wheel but not starting the engine. "Can't believe we didn't find that weapon." He wasn't talking to his deputies so much any more as he was berating his own failures. "There I was sitting and talking to him like a sucker, an' he's laughing at me all the while. Yah, bet somebody tipped him, and he cleaned the damn place out completely, there." He was quickly growing more upset than any of them had ever seen him. "Now where the fuck do we go? We got *nothin'*." He slapped the steering wheel hard with the palm of his right hand.

"Oh I dunno, Chief," said Vandenberg, who hadn't spoken a word since leaving the house. "He might've tried to clean the place out but he didn't quite get everything." She reached into her jacket pocket and removed an evidence bag. Inside the clear plastic bag was a bundle of snapshots and a business envelope. "And guess where I found it?"

"Sock drawer," Keller and Ellsworth answered in unison from the backseat.

She handed the bag to the sheriff. "It's always the sock drawer. I left the dirty magazines there. Don't think they were his, anyway."

Koznowski stared at the bag in wonder, then smiled. "Deputy, I'd give you a kiss, but I know that's all wha'cha call your harassment an' such, so I'll just buy you a Coke instead."

In the parking lot around them, elderly women were beginning to arrive at St. Timothy's hoping to say a few novenas and Hail Marys before Father Avalone's three o'clock Mass.

Sitting at his desk, flipping through the snapshots of the young boys—many of whom he recognized—Koznowski felt a deep and growing sickness spreading throughout his body. It wasn't just for what had happened to the boys. He was also dreading how he was going to break the ugly news to the parents. He was never any good at things like that (not that he'd had to do it much). This sure as hell wasn't his county anymore. These things didn't happen. Maybe he'd send Vandenberg to talk to the parents instead. Hell, maybe he'd go ahead and make her sheriff while he was at it.

He stacked the photos together and replaced them in the evidence bag. He removed the envelope and opened the flap.

"Heya Chief, ya hear?"

Koznowski looked up expressionless to see Sgt. Ziegler beaming in front of him. "Hear what, Ziegler? I'm a little busy, here."

"About E.Z. Boefinck?"

Koznowski stared at him silently. "He the new pope?"

"Naw, he tripped in the first heat a the four-forty at that state invitational thing. Shattered his right knee. They hadda rush him to the hospital for emergency surgery."

"Well, so much for Jesus, eh?" Koznowski said.

"Man, tell me about it, eh? That was his event too. They're sayin' he'll probably never run again."

"Yah, welcome to the club. Maybe when he gets outa the hospital they'll make him president." Koznowski returned his attention to the white envelope, half surprised Ziegler wasn't in tears over the news.

"You think so?"

Koznowski looked up only briefly. "Please go do something else, eh? Just . . . anything. But thanks for the news, that's kinda funny." Inside the envelope were two sheets of paper that seemed familiar, somehow. As he unfolded them he noticed one edge of each was ragged, as if torn from a book. Flipping them over, he immediately recognized Unterhumm's handwriting—a dense and heavy script with hints of a nineteenth-century flourish.

12 November 1988

The holy man was once more in confessional mode. He has weakened again with his young charges. He says "again," though I have never known him to exert the slightest strength of will to resist. Weakness is to be expected in those of his calling. He has a character free of will. None! Neither with alcohol nor with children. At times I fear he is hopeless.

He then foolishly insisted I give him access to the formula. Idiot. He knows nothing of chemistry yet demands a formula more complex and subtle than any known to mankind. The formula of the gods. And for what purpose? He desires the power to raise the dead, and wishes to do so publicly. Well la-de-da, as J.M. would so often say to overreaching students. The holy man's goal is to reveal to the herd beasts he has the power of his own Christ. He implied as well he planned to arrange his own death and subsequent rejuvenation three days later so he might steal the Nazarene's flock as his own. His first appearance following his resurrection, the cretin tells me, would be at Lambeau Field before a crowd of seventy thousand dead-eyed believers. For this he insists of course he would require my assistance, promising me wealth and power in his new earthly kingdom in return. Should I refuse to assist in the realization of his asinine program, he swears (to a long dead god he is attempting to usurp) he will kill me. I fear he has lost his mind as he has lost all else. In response I informed him that should he persist in his ludicrous demands for a formula he could never understand, I would have no choice but to report his dalliances with the youth to the local law enforcement authorities, pathetic baboons though they are. He responded by sulking, like all cowards. I could smell his anger, but it was an anger without strength or courage. The anger of a pillow. Such fools. Of any hands—including Squire's—his shall never touch my formula, I vow by the strengthening spirit of J.M.

Koznowski flipped the page over but that seemed to be the entire entry. On the second sheet was what must have been the final incarnation of Unterhumm's formula. Koznowski couldn't make heads or tails of the damn thing, but what had happened at the funeral home on the night of the fourteenth was now finally starting to come together for him.

"Jeepers," he whispered. Avalone had even stopped by that morning, asking if he could give the last rites. He presided over the funeral of the man he'd murdered. Unterhumm was right—the priest really had lost his mind.

He carefully folded the two sheets and slipped them back into the envelope. "Keller! Vandenberg!" he barked across the station. "You too Ellsworth. Get your coats on there, we gotta head back out to Saint Tim's."

He replaced everything in the evidence bag and resealed it. He checked his weapon to make sure it was loaded (something nobody'd ever seen him do before), grabbed his coat and hat, then headed for the door. As he passed her desk Leona called after him.

He stopped and turned, impatient. She was on the phone.

Leona placed a hand over the receiver. "It's that Mrs. Pander," she whispered. "She says the bells over at Saint Tim's are ringing."

"Jeeze louise, these people," Koznowski said. "Bells ring every hour on the damn hour at Saint Tim's. Tell her she don't like 'em, she should move to Rhinelander, yah?"

"Naw, Chief, that's it. She's upset 'cause it's only twenty after four."

Koznowski shook his head. "We're headin' there anyways. Tell her we'll look into it, and meantime she should just calm the fuck down. Yah, tell her just that." Ignoring Leona's stunned expression, he shoved his way through the front doors.

Two minutes later, with the lights flashing and the siren screaming, the Sheriff's Department truck ripped through the thick late December darkness toward Beaver Rapids. The snow was starting to come down hard. Those earlier clouds should've told him as much. At least the wind had quieted down so if it got bad drifting wouldn't be much of an issue. Sorry there, but someone else was gonna have to deal with Gus tonight.

"Okay, there, so we got no murder weapon, we got no witnesses," Koznowski explained to his deputies while keeping his eyes open for slick patches on the two-lane ahead. "We got no direct physical evidence. But we got motive and circumstance. We also got a double handfulla pictures that'll put him away for a while even if we can't nail him for the Unterhumm murders. Take what you can get."

"What if the kids won't testify," Vandenberg asked from the passenger seat.

"Then I guess we just break their little legs is what we do," he snapped. He shook his head, wondering where the hell that one came from. "Yah, let's not worry about that now. Right now let's just figure out what the hell we're doing once we get there, eh? This might, y'know, turn into a hostage situation."

"With a priest?" Keller asked. "Cool."

"Hey Chief." Ellsworth's voice arose from the depths of the giggling in the backseat. "You ever, like, religious or anything?"

Koznowski stared hard at the dark road. They passed the giant chicken out in front of the chicken coop bar, and everyone looked. "Was once," he said quietly. "Long time ago when I was a kid, I guess. But there was this night. Don't remember how old I was." He began drifting back to that moment he both did and didn't want to remember (which would be a hell of a trick), but then caught himself. This was neither the time nor the audience. "Yah," he said. "No, this ain't exactly the place for it, Ellsworth." He pulled into the left lane and sped past two trucks stopped behind a Toyota that had slid off the road. "Let's just say I was, then I wasn't, and that was it. And no, it ain't what you're thinking, there, Keller."

In the backseat, Keller snorted.

"Yah, enough of that, muttonhead," Koznowski said. "Now let's figure out here what the hell our plan is when we get out there."

"Oh!" Ellsworth chirped. "Can we do the hostage plan first?"

By the time the Sheriff's Department truck howled into the parking lot of St. Timothy's, the officers had yet to organize a plan of action. The headlights caught a crowd of thirty or forty people—most of them either elderly parishioners or adolescents—gathered outside the church. A few carried umbrellas as feeble protection against the snow. Several of the young boys were dressed only in gym uniforms. One carried a basketball.

"Now just what the hell's all this, d'you suppose?" Koznowski hit the brakes and the truck slid to a stop nowhere near a parking place. He killed the engine but left the headlights on.

As the sheriff and the three deputies climbed from the truck, they noticed no one paid the slightest bit of attention to the siren or the flashing lights. The crowd stood silent and still with their backs to the officers, every face turned upward toward the church.

Walking toward the crowd while trying to follow the collective gaze, Koznowski's eyes moved first to the rooftop, then to the steeple.

"Oh my God," Vandenberg said, slapping at his arm and pointing.

"Holy shit," Keller added.

The bell tower, like the steeple, was illuminated by three harsh spotlights, glowing stark white against the silk black sky, the drifting snowflakes catching the light and flashing brightly for an instant and then continuing toward the ground.

"Oh, I do *not* get this shit at all," Koznowski said, his visible breath snapping away with each word. No one in the gathered crowd made a noise of any kind. The only sound Koznowski could hear apart from the snow underfoot was the wind high above him.

A rope attached to something inside the bell tower stretched taut through a window and down along the outside wall. At the end of the rope hung the limp body of Father Timothy Avalone, pants gathered around his ankles, gently rocking from side to side against the tower's pale stucco facade. Snow was beginning to collect in his dark hair and on the shoulders of his black uniform, and trails of blood ran down both naked thighs.

"Well that's a little melodramatic, don'cha think?" Vandenberg asked.

"Guess he went to change his socks after we left, eh?" Keller added, his weapon still drawn. "This mean we can kiss off that hostage situation, Chief?"

Koznowski stared at the priest's body, some forty feet above the ground. "Christ." There was sinking disappointment in his voice. He turned to Deputy Vandenberg and quietly said, "Deliah, go back to the truck, see how long it'll take 'em to get a ladder company out here so we can cut the bastard down. Tell Leona to round up as many officers as she can, get 'em out here. Everyone who ain't on patrol and ain't Ziegler. Yah, we need to search the whole darn place, and we'll prob'ly need a little crowd control, eh?" She nodded and vanished. "Yah, and Deke? Holster your damn weapon. For godsakes, you're liable to hurt yourself." He let his eyes drift down to the frozen pavement of the parking lot. He was silent for a moment. "We never got a confession out of him. We got nothin' here. We got shit is what we got."

"W'gee, Chief," Ellsworth said, taking a step closer and glancing up at the tower. "Guy goes an' hangs himself when he knew we was on to him. Ain't that confession enough?"

The sheriff looked back up toward the grotesquely spotlit corpse, dangling there like some sick joke of a Christmas ornament. "For some people it would be, maybe," he said, as the full implications of what was happening—what had happened—became more clear to him. "Yah, maybe even most . . . Just think I'da been able to rest a little easier if we'd had a chance to hear what he had to say."

"Oh, we still can, there, Chief," Ellsworth noted brightly. "'Cept now all we're gonna get outa him is *ding dong!*"

A few shocked and silent heads from the back of the crowd, their blood-less faces glowing in the truck's headlights, turned to stare. Koznowski was about to say something when he saw Father Molloy walking quickly toward him, his face stained with tears, the skirt of his robes wet and salt smeared. "Just go check out the house again," Koznowski told Keller. "See if you can find a note or something. Anything at all, eh? Ellsworth, you start seeing if you can convince any of these folks to go on home. Should have some help out here in a jiffy. I'm gonna ask Father here if we can kill the spotlights. No need to turn the whole damn thing into a . . . I dunno, a goddamn nightclub act."

"You betcha, Chief."

Koznowski had taken only a few steps toward the approaching elderly priest when he stopped and looked down at something. A single naked footprint in the densely packed snow.

"Father Molloy?" he asked, not looking up as the priest stopped beside him. "Have you seen anyone out here lately walking around barefoot?"

Father Molloy, still stunned mute by the image behind him, said nothing. With a single swipe of his heavy boot, Koznowski erased the frozen print. "Yah, crazy idea. Don't matter," he said. "C'mon, let's head back inside. Cold out here."